THE WITCH
SOME WITCH

The Witch Some Witch

Damning Her and Damning Me

Quleen O Queen

PARTRIDGE

ISBN: Hardcover   978-1-4828-8384-8
               Softcover   978-1-4828-8383-1
               eBook   978-1-4828-8382-4

Print information available on the last page.

To order additional copies of this book, contact
Partridge India
000 800 10062 62
orders.india@partridgepublishing.com

www.partridgepublishing.com/india

Contents

Acknowledgement

As ecstatic and trying the process of writing this novel has been, my parents and my brother Mustaq Singh Bijral have backed me throughout its making. High and lows. Ups and Downs. Ebbs and Flows. Father, with his humour and wisdom ensured I write patiently than in a rush while providing the necessary tools of great books, quotes and historic incidents. Mother, with her attention and insight, helped me focus and cherish the writing process when distractions almost broke my interest. And brother, with his sharp awareness and wit taught me how to express the apt aptly.

The novel also owes its making to the noble help of my peers and colleagues. To Richa Verma, columnist at The Logical Indian, for her tireless proofreading that underscored the spirit of the work, streamlined the flow of its thought and dotted the i's and crossed the t's. To Jasleen Kaur, for her critical study of the manuscript as an enthusiastic reader and analyzing the tone, theme and language of the work for better effect. To Simran Bhatia, for her attention to details and priceless suggestions. To Sana Mahajan, a good friend and a smart critic who has always offered me creative views to reach for a good piece of writing. To Bhasker Taneja, because of whom I was able to find the best proofreaders and great friends.

To the team of Partridge India Publishing who empowered a first-time novelist to tell a story to the world. From evaluating and checking the manuscript to making it happen and its marketing, I am indeed grateful to them. Special thanks to the members of the Partridge Publishing team -Pohar Baruah, Princess Mar, Stephen Espinosa, Christopher Socong, Mandy Andrews, and Pearl Jade.

Chapter 1

The Harp of Some Demon

It was a breezy night of the winters. There were grey clouds in the night sky and dark mist in the air. The fever in the wind was twisting the houses, the trees and the dogs into a fitful scream. A rumble of emptiness could be heard in the deserted buildings. While the tall towers lit with yellow light of warmth, the bottom dwelling rooms had a touch of grey death. The city bridge creaked with a stutter while the sea below it had its lips dried out. There were leaves, ash and white snowflakes falling on the fallen birds and squirrels on the ground. The legs of the birds would seem like a girl's hand coming out of the buried snow. While a squirrel's tail would appear like a monkey's claw. It was unsettling to see the unseen in places so unforgiving. In the dawn, the pigeons wouldn't chirrup as the night had frozen their warm blood. And during the night time, owls and bats wouldn't fly as the winds had become a solid rock of ice. Such were the winters. When the summers were a dance on burning coal, the winters had men and matters buried in frost. From the skin to the flesh, what was once pink had turned into a calming grey.

During one such winter, I was once out in the streets. Under the night sky of blemished stars, eclipsed moon and silver light, I was walking with a purpose. Towards a town which I needed to visit come snow or sun. Just then, I heard a woman's wail and it flushed my heart with a dreadful fright. Beep! Beep! Beep! In feverish panic, I followed it. To my horror the moaning but came from a broken chimney. Again, when I had crossed a mile, I heard a little boy's shriek and it murdered the calm in my nerves. Blighted by its innocent plea for help, I ran towards it as hurriedly as I could. On reaching the place, I was catatonic with self-reproach as the scream was nothing but the noise of a broken swing set. Twice I had been fooled that I felt so humiliated at my honest effort to rescue a chimney and a swing. I should have known when the streets are desolate like a dead sea, only useless things scream into the wind. So, in contempt of my actions, I began to stomp the ground beneath me. I even scolded myself, in case I wandered like a loafer to save things that didn't matter. In hours of beating myself over it, I then finally reached the town which was on my wish list. With a purpose I had come to visit it.

At its entrance, there was a tedious billboard covered with weeds, dense bushes and skeletal flowers. It had a map on it where the entire town was sketched like a vast space speckled with houses, shops, and guest cabins. Before I could've read more into it, a foolish squeal cut through the silence and mocked me for the third time. I did not stir even when it's crying shriek provoked me to act upon it. Not wishing to be deceived again, I did not heed it. Though it seethed the bottom of my heart, I did not care. But the scream wouldn't abate and kept badgering me with

1

its violent tremor. It was needy for help. Distressed. Tormented. Even lost to give up on the world. Pestered by its shameless neediness, I then had to follow it. Though I reluctantly walked towards the scream, I had no intention to help. Only to chastise the indecent screamer for its impertinence to mock me.

As I entered the town, I could see something was not right. Alarm then received me. On the ground, muddied with rain, I saw a girl of minor age. She was squirming prostrate in the wet soil. As she writhed and fidgeted, her armpits, mouth, and eyes got stuffed with smelly sludge. Her body danced almost manically as if to the harp of some demon. I had barely entered the town and was shocked to see something so strangely bizarre at its doorstep. I didn't look away or cringe at her but stayed with invested curiosity.

The girl was not in the nude. She had clothes on her body. Her hair was sewn in a nice little bow. Still, the look on her face was of intense humiliation. She was not in control of her body, but the girl was able to exhibit shame through her twitching face. Shame? She was ashamed even when fully covered, provided and protected by the misty darkness of the day. Why was she embarrassed then? It was such an emotion of hers that pandered to my curiosity. It drew me towards her like a child to a candy. Twisting, turning and scrubbing dirt into her mouth, she was a piece of art. Provoked, I strongly began to memorize her possession frame by frame. The swing of her arms up in the air and then down on the ground. The ballet in her pristine toes. The long swan neck curling the air into a twirl. I looked on and on while the girl went from fitful to catatonic in milliseconds of the time.

What ailed her though? A ghost? A man? A woman? Just then, far in the street, some boy of an intelligible face came running in our direction. He was a hound in his run. Out of breath, he was agitated and perspired with beads of cold sweat developing on his skin. On reaching the girl, the boy fell by her side as he was not able to leash his thrilling speed. Then picking himself up, he bent over and kissed the girl. On the cheek.

"Noor! I am here! Wake up!" The boy then screamed into the girl's distressed face. He didn't see me even when he had his black-rimmed specks on. As the girl's mellow skin trembled magically, the boy punched her with kind force to keep her awake. Then he yelled back at the empty hole he had come from.

"Granny! Christian! Noor is here! It's another one! Granny!"

It was with a curious instinct I wanted to dissect the girl. To know how deeply ashamed she was. What wounded her to feel it? How long would she keep at it? But the boy had most insolently interrupted us with his noisy presence. Even when the girl was in a terrible fit, she was silent. How civilized of her! But the boy with his grating voice had breached the serenity of the moment. He desperately kept calling out for someone to heed his hoot. Shouting in the wind. Spitting back and forth. Beating his chest so that someone could hear him. While the girl despite her noisy pain kept politely silent. Seconds into his rumpus, the boy then caught my presence standing before him. A stranger. A stranger with able hands. Though disturbed by my uncannily sinister presence, he nevertheless held out his hand for my help.

"Help me!" The boy cried out.

The despair of the moment had made him trust an odd bystander. He begged me with a pitiful clamour, but I did not listen. I did not want to listen to him as I fervently wanted to study the girl. In her spastic trance, the girl was breaking her bones most unnaturally. It was so abnormal that she seemed disenfranchised from reality. I curiously wanted to witness that unnatural thing of nature. Watch her undisturbed.

The boy, but didn't respect my needs and implored again, "Help me! Come on! Miss!"

Hearing him for the third time, I then woke up from my perverse curiosity and felt a migraine in my head. Anxiously then I rushed towards the girl and tried to feign my concern for the pitiful thing. I had to look concerned for her otherwise the boy wouldn't have trusted me. So I pretended to be distressed at the misery of the girl. While I perched myself opposite to the boy, I closely saw the girl's berserk contortions. Her entire body was shaking like the vibrating music of tins and tongs. Calmly I pushed down my hands on her body while the boy began to turn pale seeing the girl's wretched condition. It was certainly insulting of him to lose his spirits, so I scolded him for his indecent histrionics.

"Boy! Wake up! Hold her still!"

Driven by anguish, he quickly joined in and followed my movements even when skeptical as to the validity of my treatment. Vexed and confused, he shuddered, "Noor stay with me! Oh love! My sweet love!" Abhorring his tacky use of words, I grunted at him. "Hold her boy! Use both your arms! What's wrong with her?" Baffled myself, I had to ask.

"Don't know. No one knows!" He replied with a blank, sweat-ridden grimace.

While the girl ululated with a musical agony, I held my body stiff to not flow with it. The force of her fits was too strong to keep myself rigidly taut. The boy tried as well as he could, but I couldn't. So much so that my nerves began to move with her musical undulations. She would sway and I would sway a little. It was magical! Noor was her name, which the boy screamed into her face. I seemed to like the cadence of it. It was a unique name. Even the girl herself was unique. She was fitful in a way I had not seen before. It was almost divine. She cried out without a voice which was indeed a feat in itself. The girl had enchanted the moment into a mysterious turn of events. She was one of a kind.

As the boy and I reacted differently to her condition, at long last we heard footsteps running towards us. At which the boy's vigour spirited up and he shouted again.

"Granny! Come quick! She's having another one! I am here!"

What was that another one, that the boy said no one knew? A baby? The girl didn't look like she was expecting. Then what another one? I bent my eyes close to her and saw no bump in the girl's belly. I had thought at first perhaps the girl had gone to labour. It could have been good news but the girl was a bit minor to become a mother before she had become a woman. Still like an unforgiving riddle, it was inexplicable as to why the girl continued to moan, groan and whimper. While jabbing my hands on her stomach, legs and head to the nape, I noticed a slightly raised fever. Stomach wasn't beating oddly to suggest any infection or anything. Still, an uncanny rhythm kept playing inside of her. Then as my hands traversed towards her lower torso, I felt on her legs some cold melting metal. Dark was its colour while scentless its odour. But it made me cringe nonetheless. It felt like blood as it had me swoon in need for smelling salts. The girl was indeed bleeding. As a girl, I too used to bleed every month but it never caused me to shift the bones in my body. The girl's symptoms were certainly uncanny. Neither her blood nor her sweat could tell what ailed her.

"What are you doing? You a doctor? Are you…" The boy asked warily, as he could discern I was being more inquisitive than concerned for his friend. Realizing his incriminating suspicions, I curtly broke in. "Right now I am."

Taken aback at my strange demeanor, the boy became even more louder than before while screaming for help. He did not trust me anymore but also couldn't threaten me to leave. Broken by the sickness of his girl, he was too powerless to think right.

"Granny! Hurry! Find me in this halo damn mist!"

As I kept poking my fingers at the girl, the boy would protest and then succumb to his despair. The mist was so overpowering that whosoever was meant to find us, couldn't. It bought me plenty of time at the boy's peril. Besides, it was not my fault that the girl was in a twist. To top it, I also didn't wish to experiment on her as it was the boy who had begged for my help. After moments of disconcerted unease, he finally articulated his suspicion. "What are you doing? Who are you? Stop it!"

Outraged, even when he was in the right, I gave him a little thud on his shoulder and yelled back, "Move boy! I know what I am doing. Don't be so suspicious!" Deviously, I reassured him that his instinctual fear of me was exceedingly misplaced. Crushed because of my disturbing confidence, he backed off in a fright.

"Hold her legs together!" I commanded him again. Subdued, he responded by quickly doing as I said. "Hold her arms close to her body!" I ordered with conviction, and he obeyed. "Lift her head, check for any injury!" I shouted and without taking any offense he lifted the head. As we continued to have this fruitless conversation, he frantically kept on searching for any clue to the girl's misery.

"Now w-what?" He asked with a stutter as I had gone silent and obviously blank. "Let me think, will you!" I barked while his meekness began to grow into indignation.

I was a strange incongruous figure in the town. With a scarf on my head. A jacket above my sports bra, and shorts too low to care to wear underwear. I was indeed a rebellious oddity that in the month of winters I was practically summerish. Besides, I didn't have the time to change into something befitting the town. Though, even if I had, I still wouldn't have.

With time, the boy began to discern what I was. He certainly was agitated at witnessing what character of a girl I was. Noticing his doubts, I evaded his relentless stare. Then took off my pretty yet torn jacket and dropped it on Noor's bloodied legs.

"Why did you do this?" Skeptical, he questioned.

"She is freezing, can't you see!"I bawled at him.

Noor had a hard plait. I grabbed it to gag her tongue with it lest she bit herself red in the mouth too. I tried this and that trick, but the girl was adamant to debunk my half-baked treatments. How more could she twist and turn, I had wondered. Then soon, the girl began to give off a murky stench as her blood and sweat mixed with the mud. It was foul and it was fragrant. When I looked at her face, she had her eyes wide shut. Tears squeezed out of them. Her neck was awry. Hands clutched with nails piercing into the palms. Bosoms were beating as if the heart was trying to escape. Beep! Beep! Beep! And her bottom cheeks were madly pressing against the ground. I discerned all these minute details, as there was nothing fascinating left in her story. After long seconds, her moaning began to draw a yawn on my face. The more she trembled, the more I yawned. In her repetition of the same stunts, over and over again, I couldn't invest my curiosity into her. So soon I would tire of her, it was disappointing. Nevertheless, it gave me an opportunity to gaze at the surroundings and know a thing or two about the town. Nonchalantly and a bit discreetly, I then glanced behind the boy. There I observed a towering tree with roots covering the long lengths of the ground. To the right of the tree, I saw bushes of little interest. While more to the right, the street led to a hole at which the boy would scream the strange names of his kin.

"Granny! Halo! Pooh! Christian! I have found her!"

Circling again to the right, I saw a creepy fake hill which protruded out of the soil. Unsightly and bizarre, it stood tall as if to duel with the tree in its front. Then I caught something behind my back. With bated breath I saw a dark figure in the woods. It was chanting. The chant was ominous even when a plea for help. It echoed like a grim whisper so that no one could hear it. I was but able to. The chanter was cunningly hidden that my eyes bulged out to see who chanted in the woods.

"Halo! Halo my Halo! Save the girl!"

"Halo! Halo my Halo! Save the girl!"

It went on chanting like a forest fire in a hot summer night. The voice was dreamy as it crept inside my ears like a sad lullaby. Such was its menacing hold on my curiosity that I couldn't even move towards it but stay fixed in my posture. I certainly was bewitched by whatever the thing was in the woods. The mist wasn't helping and impaired by it, I could only hear the voice. Vague and desperate. I skewered my eyes at it, but it was stubborn to remain hidden and went on chanting the Maker's name in vain. Before I could figure out what or who it was, we got interrupted.

A mob menacingly approached the girl and attacked her with hands and prayers. They had come. The bearer of the strange names, the boy had called out to. It was a small party of varied ages from young to very old. Some of them blew air onto the girl to purge evil spirits possessing her. Some even smelt her. Among the crowd, there was one elderly lady whom the boy called Granny. The old lady, while scanning the girl up and down, asked somberly, "Lee I am here. What happened to her? Poor girl." Hearing the old woman, the boy, called Lee, stepped aside and relinquished his position so she could take it. I too stepped aside so the rest of the lot could do a better job than I did. It was but startling that none of them even noticed that I was standing in their midst. I didn't mind it even when it was insulting. After all, it was Noor who craved and deserved their attention and I was mature enough to let it go.

Granny seemed to notice the blood everywhere and detected which parts were spilt and which grew. She picked up the jacket, and then let it rest on her again. As she warmly pressed down on her, the rest went about discovering what caused the fits. Some looked underneath as they lifted her back. Some checked the ground nearby while the old lady surveyed the skin as if looking for any snake bite. After seconds of pointless surveillance, Granny declared with authority, "It's no good. We need to get her back to my house." Hearing her, Lee hesitated to move Noor lest she tore a muscle or fractured herself. But then had to agree as Granny was peremptory. He was helped by another boy, called Christian, as they cautiously picked up Noor and carried her towards Granny's house. It was difficult to pick her up as she was madly persistent in her unruly fits. The boys were not able to balance or firmly grip her. So it took time before they were able to carry Noor without letting her fall. Nevertheless they did while the rest of the gathering followed in grave silence. All of them were but oblivious to my screaming presence and the presence of my foreign looking jacket. It led me to assume perchance I had lost my opportunity to get introduced, but I knew I would get my cue.

As the crowd carried the girl, I snuggled in with them. To know the people in the town and memorize which breeze and which moons made it live. As no one was bothered to notice me, I didn't have to be discreet to tail them. Together we walked in some kind of a hearse whilst carrying the useless weight of the weak and the sickly. The jacket, my jacket was still on Noor's body and that became my reason to follow them. What if they asked why I was there and I would reply. "The jacket, a Good Samaritan's jacket. I helped your Noor". And thus I would cling to my humanitarian deed and it would bring me closer to their soft spots. I had the perfect alibi to rationalize why I stalked them.

Half-way towards Granny's place, Noor who was silent then began to mumble on about something. Her whisper was soft at first and even indistinct. Then it became rabid. She whispered in a violent way to get heard.

"Dead Winters! Sulphurous Summers! Night and Day!"

"What is she muttering?" Granny asked in a patient voice even when exhausted to mull over it. Noor was muttering something. She was mincing her words and I wished if she would just deign to be audible at least. It was already gnawing as her sickness was an enigma, and then we had to deal with her silent words. The boys were fatigued to carry her weight. The old woman was too old and time-worn to rack her mind over it. Even I became derisive of the girl's repugnant silence. Just then, she hit us. Suddenly her muttering escalated into an ominous tone. Her voice became more perceptible and even more portentous than the chanter in the woods. I regretted at wishing her to be clear. So soon I would regret it, the insanity of fortune. It alarmed me as I could not fail to unhear her words. The hostile words which she mouthed to intimidate me. Noor even in her inebriated state was certainly, most eloquently and without any speck of doubt crying hoarse about me!

"Winds are neighing! Girl changes into a worm! The Bridge heaves, while waters fall! The girl runs on her cycle while assailants chase! Buried deep to die and live again! She is among us! Among us! Among us!"

The girl went on babbling unreasonably, still what she was muttering about, it all pertained to me! I was a worm. I had come to the town when the winds were making noise. The Bridge, the assailants, the cycle. It was a memory of my life, which I had repressed deep in the depths of my mind. How then did she know about my memory? I was not being paranoid even when she was being witchy.

"What is she murmuring, Granny, what does it all mean?" Lee asked in panic, knowing fully well it was a futile attempt as no one knew. Clueless, the old lady inhaled gravely and then spoke in a dismal voice. "Her mutterings mean nothing. It will be over soon. It usually is. Poor girl." Granny assured her kin and they nodded grimly. I was certainly relieved as even though Noor's letters were scandalous, no one knew what she talked about. They conveniently believed Noor was a mad angel of the house and that there could be nothing lucid in her delirious incantations. It certainly comforted me. Lee but was beyond consolation.

"Noor, we are here! I am here. How can we ease her pain? Even if we can't stop it? How?" He spoke as strongly as he could. Lee's compassion was impressive although useless. Noor was making it harder for him to be pacified by anyone. She continued with her chanting and I, the only learned among them, knew the content and context of her ill forebodings.

"Too much mist in her lungs. The girl vomits. Off the Bridge, she jumps. A creature, a thing of nature. A worm! Her future weeps in blood. Hang her! Hang her! Bury her deep!"

"What does she mean? Is she trying to tell us something? What is it, Noor?" Lee, despite the vainness of his inquiries, nevertheless went on with it. And Noor went on narrating what was gibberish to her family. But to me it was psychic knowledge of what had happened and what was to come. I wrinkled my hands while heeding the girl's dominations. The rest of the party didn't care to discern the meaning of it. Only to ease the pain, or wait for it to pass.

That is all they could do, and that was all they did.

Besides, Noor was not coherent, so the crowd had to stop listening. Even when they gave up on her, I couldn't. It was magical to hear the girl speak of things beyond human philosophy. I didn't see her as a naïve little girl in pain, but a thing of dark magic. Though she cried like a girl. Whispered like a human. Danced like a little child. I curiously raised her as a divine thing beyond pain. Her own people had deserted her, but I stayed by her side for my own benefit. Intently, I listened to her haphazard words, as she continued to tell tales of things she couldn't have possibly known.

While she continued to mesmerize me, the group carrying her then came to a halt. Before us, appeared to be the house they were meaning to take her. It was Granny's house. A girl called Vicky, who was already inside opened the gate. On seeing Noor, she puckered her entire face in disgust. An emotion she craftily kept hidden from the rest. She was accompanied by another girl, who unlike her, was genuinely distressed. As we entered the gate, Lee and Christian carried Noor up the stairs into a room and put her as gently as they could onto a strange bed woven of threads. It was then left to the old woman to navigate the next course of action even when she too was convincingly lost. Picking up her spirits, she tried to take charge and inquired with urgency. "Where is Pooh?"

"I don't know Granny, shall I?" Lee responded, and before he had gotten up, a stoutly woman came barging in. I was standing at the door and she threw me away to reach after the girl, her daughter.

"Yes. Oh talk of her and…" Seeing her, Granny whispered to herself.

It was Pooh for Portia, Noor's mother. Panting all over, she was a monster in her stride. She swept past me while hitting me with her pointy elbow. I winced a little but kept it subdued. The moment Portia saw her daughter, she went from gasping to crying in shame. It was puzzling to see her more chagrined than hurt at her daughter's fit. Noor was covered head to toe, but the mother acted as if the girl was in the nude. As a good stranger, Noor's cracked bones and the beautiful blood glowing on her body didn't provoke me to shame her. Even the native gathering was not ashamed. We were not ashamed but the mother was. Noor was not molested which I could tell by no signs of it on her body. She was still in the pristine condition she was brought in. Yet the mother bit her tongue in disgrace as if Noor had mauled the honour of the family. She was ashamed of her daughter. What if it had been molestation? Then Portia would have discarded her?

"F-for how l-long, where d-did you f-find her?" The mother asked timidly, more out of discomfiture than concern. While Granny replied in a comforting voice, "Pooh, sit by my side. We know it will be over soon." The mother but refused to stay calm, "How l-long? How l-long?"

Granny then had to console the delirious mother of the delirious child. Deftly she did it without a visible hint of exasperation. Granny's peace of mind rested in the thought that no one outside the family would know of it. The mess that they were in. Oblivious of a meddling stranger, she was certainly calm. As for Portia, she was inhumanely vexed as everyone outside her family knew of it. Besides, it was her daughter and the mess was indelibly personal to her. Vulnerably closer to it had made her ashamed of it. And Granny who was farther from it, hence, was calm. The old lady again tried to appease the young mother.

"I don't know Pooh. I don't know. All will be well…" Granny was at ease as the criminality of the situation was contained within the room. Then she saw an alien and was definitely shocked.

"Who? Who are you? I don't believe it! What are you doing here?" She asked me contemptuously.

Granny saw me. Her eyes goggled out of her wrinkled sockets. She was nervous. Apprehensive. Guilt-ridden. Too shocked to maintain her graceful propriety. Vexed, she grunted at me again.

"Who? Who are you!"

Her derision pierced right through my heart. I felt hurt even when I was guilty. Such was her scorn. I touched my chest with my hand. Gave an innocent shrug. Then spoke with an innocent stutter. "I-I am Grace." I answered as cautiously and artlessly as I could. While the old lady became sterner, "Little lady? How did you get in? What are you doing in here?"

While faintly pointing my finger at the garish jacket as planned, I confessed. "A tourist. I-I saw the girl in pain and had to lend her my help". Stunned, Granny was at a loss of words. Even her tummy gurgled with ire. Seeing Granny's untimely pause, Lee quickly put in. "I had asked her Granny, but she was already there standing. I don't know what she was doing..."

Lee was malicious that despite my honest effort to save Noor, he backstabbed me with his defaming statement. It filled me with euphoric humiliation. The same feeling I had during the start of my journey. I cursed him. Lifted my invisible finger at him. That boy could be so vindictive, I was shocked. Before he could expose me any further, I interrupted him. "Yes, yes when I entered your town, I was drawn by the girl's screams. Or was it you, were you screaming? Lee is it? Uh, I don't remember, it is just so traumatic. Will she be all right?"

Lee let out a sneer while the old lady fell into an embarrassing fright. She was affronted as if I had seen her being indecent. It was fun to see them twist and turn. Even under the crushing burden of the day, they still tried to hold onto their formality.

"Yes she will be, of course. But I don't think you should be here. Besides it's late to welcome you, so the better half of it I shall reserve for tomorrow." She said formally, but was positively gnashing her teeth.

I simply nodded with a fractious smile. Observing the twist in my face, she asked the girl sitting by her side to see me off. "Halo, my child, have our guest find a room for tonight."

Certainly, I was taken aback at her sudden shutting me out. But expected it nevertheless. Granny was in an obvious haste to salvage what she could. The more she squirmed underneath her flamboyant grace, I got a little provoked to pester her even more. Besides she had slighted me in front of everyone. So I struck a conversation instead of leaving the room as instructed. I spoke, rather aimlessly. "Halo? It's a nice name. Isn't your deity also called Halo, if you don't mind my asking?" Certainly, it was an improper time to strike a banter. But I wanted to belittle the lot for evicting me so brusquely. Granny was stunned at my good sense of occasion, but replied nonetheless.

"How did you reckon it was our deity? Well, this girl here was named after Him. So we call her Halo. But little lady I don't think it is the right time to discuss names. Halo please take her out to the cabin." She spoke with added aversion.

Little lady? I felt insulted again. I had told her my name and yet she kept hitting my pride. It is true I should have left when the host had put up the sign. Stubborn and even megalomaniacal, I didn't and I couldn't allow the old woman to prick me where it hurt. She drove me mad. I wanted to wring her and prick her nerves. Incensed at her domineering stance, I yearned to break her. I would have but then Halo, the unrecognizable girl, nudged me. She didn't do it with an insult up in her sleeves but out of concern. In her eyes, as blank and dull as they were, it was clear. She wanted me gone not just to obey the old woman but to keep my own calm. Moved by her dull persistence, I let her escort me out. As I left with her, the gathering sitting around Noor watched with curious phobia, as to what manner and country of woman I was. They began to peel off the layers of my appearances to have a look at my hidden skeletons. They had the gumption to think they could read me, not knowing I was reading them. By some fantastic incident I had brought them together in one room. In a blink of an eye I had stripped them to see what hid under their grace of formality. The Grim Granny, Difficult Noor, Proud Portia, Dull Halo, Doting Lee, the Stand-up guy Christian and the Two-faced Vicky. I was made to leave, but I had captured enough moments to make a visual of the town. The town was too adamant to keep secrets secrets. Lies lies. Woods woods. It was their strength and curiously their weakness too.

Halo took me to a cottage which was not distant from Granny's house. There was nothing fancy about it. It was a plain worn-out cabin. It had a nice bed to repose on and felt like a nice bunker. But it certainly reeked of some drunkard who might have had lived in it. The brandy bottles weren't there in the open to signal such an allegation. But I found one under the bed which pricked my back through the skin. It hurt with a pinch of my blood leaking on the grey bed sheets. It would have left a scar whether I washed it or not so I let it be.

The town that I had come to was a rustic remnant of old towns. It was not an idyllic town per se, and not a tourist spot either to go summering. But the people, they were the art and craft of that rural yet not bucolic town. I was sweetly shocked when I got to peek what hid under their shiny veneer. The liars. The deceivers. The gentle folks. A beautiful lie is this mankind. The more the liars there were, the more I was orgasmic to memorize them for my personal records. That is what I did, record.

The township looked green, yellow and red when I looked at the flowers. The waters were blue, red and brown when I looked at the algae. While the mountains were beyond the pale when I looked at the fake hills. The trees seemed to be in a duel with the hills. Each trying to entomb the other. The ground was there to sit on and the roof was there to stare from. The houses of the old were painted in creamy white colours but with age, the natural growth of black had grown on the breaking wallpaper. Quaint still, it looked lovely and cozy without the doubt of oblivion brooding in. The houses of the young were tastefully mellow and bold. Whichever house I passed, it was lit-up like a lamp post. The streets were huge even when conveyance in the small town was either by foot, a cow-ridden wheel or a small powered truck. Woods were its beauty but barely anyone would enter it or think of camping inside the forest. Some fear, I could gather, had held them behind it. Could that fear be the chanter in the woods? That eerie chanter. Petite like red smoke. It was only with time to become clear. Lawns were pruned by constant work and play.

They dotted the town here and there. The streets and the houses had no walls to separate them from each other. A vestige of a gate would stand before the houses. Perhaps to keep the houses from growing into the streets.

The town was tri-partitioned into Zones. The Zone which I had entered belonged to the name of 'Black and White'. Adjoining to it like a Siamese twin stood the other Zone called 'Greys'. While the last corner of the triangle was titled 'Lights Off'. What unusual names, I had wondered.

Tantalizingly, hence, the few patches of the town fell unto my eyes from the first day to the few days to pass. Pinning my anxiety down, I waited for the inhabitants to unravel more and more about themselves. I only had to nudge, as people came on their own accord to mingle with an exotic girl from abroad. I was a sly stranger. A pesky outsider. But I was exotic. So I was wooed than having to woo and beg for an audience.

Halo, the girl after the deity, dropped me off at the unkempt cabin. She left with few words of formality to make a good first impression. To tell the truth, the girl wanted to stay and talk. But her pushy curiosity at what I was wearing, where I bought it, who I was and the meaning of my name disturbed me. I was supposed to be the reporter, and not her. So in implicit scorn, I shut her out. I wasn't too tired or exhausted to converse. Just a little disturbed when she tried to invade my privacies. So I had her leave before she could viciously pester me with her indelicate curiosity.

As she left, I tried to catch a wink. Though it was a sleepy night, I couldn't just sleep. The noisy banter of my heartbeat wouldn't let me rest in peace. It was violently loud that its noise cut through the pitch silence of the shack. Too proud, involuntary, and pampered, my heart kept me starkly awake while its beat kept beating. Beep! Beep! Beep!

Chapter 2

Something Foul in The Wind

Time flew by as I struggled and shuffled to find a little repose. But sleep was not for the likes of me. Looking out of the window, it was hard to tell whether it was dawn or dusk. Too much light like in a dawn. Too less a light like at dusk. So, it seemed appropriate to call it daynight. It was around this time, as I lay in the bed, an unforeseen invitation headed my way. Lightheaded and half-asleep, it took me a moment to realize who had sent it. It was the gracious old lady who had invited me to supper at her house. Unpredictable as it was, the supper was not however meant to welcome me. It was more of a clever ruse by which Granny wanted to present her people as normal folks than what I had seen the same day. It was also a strategic play at knowing who I was. For them to decode what anomaly I was. For me to see they were sane despite the magical aberrations of what had passed.

The shack as I had noticed earlier was not far from the old lady's house. Granny had quite tactically lodged me close to her lair. In case she felt like spying on my intentions. She was certainly sly. While entering her premises I patiently noticed how quaint her place was. It gave off a feeling of warmth which enlivened the unevenly cemented bricks. The house was a modest accommodation, even frail in colours. Yet in its charm, there was a tempting cordiality issuing from it. Two sets of lucarne were at equidistant places of the house. In the middle a balcony and on the gable there was an insignia which looked like footprints. Walls which were honeycombed surrounded the house from four directions till emerging into a keel at the entrance. The keel itself resembled folded hands as in welcoming the guests. She had a hammock in her garden. It was heavily stretched beyond its honour. To get out what more wear and tear one could get out of it. Certainly, it was a poorly handled business and no one seemed bothered about it. It had dust, mud, leaves, and even blow flies buzzing on it. Only someone like me would have folded it nicely. Given it the peace of body and mind at long last. The poor hanging bed, so undervalued indeed. It brought an odd melancholia…

As I entered the house, I saw Granny on the fourth stair. She saw me and scoffed a little. The old lady did not even hide her aversion and without greeting she went inside.

But, I didn't mind it. Instead, I perched myself in one of balconies of the residence. Standing there, I thought of staying put till all were assembled and had met each other. Halo had been by my side since the time she had brought the invitation. Overzealous girl, she was quite friendly in her conversations. In a name, I could discern the characters and histories of people. But her name was dryly unisex, how then I was to define her? Halo, a girl who flattered, and was always excited. Even unstable and highly effervescent. In her countenance there was a dull expression which however was concealed behind her predictable beauty. She would get sad when sad, and happy when happy, and it would be reflected on her. But to move another person to feel sad and happy with her, that would have been out of her reach. A rainbow looks good in the sky. But if it starts to occur on the ground, then in contrast with the lovely flowers, it would look dull. Such was the case with Halo. In the skies, Halo is the omnipotent Maker but on earth that girl was dull, ingratiating and curious.

"We are going to have a nice party, you will love it Grace". That is how the girl sold the invitation to me. She winked, and I accepted with equal grace, "Oh really, that is nice! I will come!"

Halo spoke quite effusively about the party. And yes we were going to have a party even when the time to have it seemed odd. Just few hours before, I had seen the lot of them prancing and dancing around blood. How could they then carry on sanely on their sanely roads? Where was their sense of occasion? Nevertheless, it was a clever deception indeed. Throwing a party when I had just witnessed the most horrifying fit. The sad screams. The wasted blood. The haplessness. Grief. Guilt. After all this, we were going to have a party. The town was fervent to debunk Noor's unspeakable possession. They were impatient to sweep the dirt under the bed. Besides this, the town went one more step further. They began calling that furious moment of time as the 'day of the puke'! It really had my nerves in a twist. Certainly, those people were prepared to take extreme measures by disarming the terror of that time. It was not a fit the girl had puked but a bag of vomit. Day of the puke indeed. How shrewd even when malicious. They didn't seem to bother about the girl except lacing her with false assurances. No one wanted to hear her side of the story. The girl was in a desperate panic. The colour in her cheeks was desecrated by a shock. I had her blood on my jacket which was truth. We all were there. But when it didn't happen, why bother indeed.

At Granny's house, from the balcony, I could see how the outskirts of the town had patches of woods covering its rim. Somewhere dense and someplace just bushes. The forest grew out of its will to bastion the town where it deemed fit. The official entrance to the town was via a street named the Brigand Street. The street itself forked into two more paths. The 11th Street and the Grey Street. Granny's house lay close to the entrance and opposite to the two streets. It had a post-mill standing clean and kempt which was right adjacent to Granny's house. The post-mill marked the street's end into a cul-de-sac. The post-mill was kept more like an antique to remember the past by, and nothing more.

At the balcony, as I conversed with Halo, Granny called us in. It was good to have Halo by my side. She seemed quite adroit in breaking the ice between complete strangers. Some people have that knack. As we walked down the stairs, Halo beamed with joy. She was looking forward to the prospect of introducing me to the others. As she escorted me to the verandah, I felt an itch run down my gullet. It was Portia and her daughter sitting before us. Demurely, as I walked towards them, they fashionably ignored me. Halo, then cut through the discomfiture and introduced me.

"She is Grace". So Halo began with spirited informality. "Grace this is Pooh, nickname for Portia, Aunt Portia. I began calling her Pooh, as it makes her look younger and the whole town calls her Pooh. Wouldn't you say Pooh?"

Portia smiled at Halo, rather with a full show of her teeth. And it seemed she was pretending to mean it. "H-Halo herself is a m-moniker. T-he deity after whom this girl was n-named, her full name being…"

Portia stuttered reminding me of a little lost cousin of mine. But her stuttering did not diminish that lovely smile of hers.

"Grace doesn't have to hear my real name, Pooh!" Halo interrupted her, and Portia while curling the locks of her hair, interrupted her back, "Why and-why not? Grace, she d-didn't tell you her r-real name?" Portia was more than cordial. She had jostled her elbow at me during the day of the puke, and at the get-together, she was courteous. It was certainly bothersome. I had seen her in shame, strong levels of it. She had crouched to hide her face from the others. And if the others had not been there, I was sure Portia would have slapped her daughter and pushed her out into the world. She was stammering the day of the puke, and I had thought perhaps it was the trauma of the moment shaking her resolve. But then hours later, when the trauma had lost its coal, she was stammering still. Guess, she was a habitual one.

Joining in the banter, I took a step towards Portia, and evinced "I guess not. Halo didn't… its news to me."

"M-may I d-disclose it t-then?" Portia stuttered with a smile, but didn't blush about it. She sat quite assertively belying the impression her stammer was giving off. And all the while, Halo was being very, how to put it mildly, obsequious towards Portia. As if she was trying her best to impress her. The way a worker would flatter the boss. And I could tell from their meaningless banter, Portia was putting on a show of joviality to respect the occasion. In Portia's act there was a deliberate affection to it. Yet there was no tinge of satire behind it. The interesting thing to see was that Portia didn't try to discourage Halo, or make her feel beneath her. If it were me, I would have gotten up with an excuse to go to the loo.

"How's the work at the shop, Pooh?" Halo babbled on, unaware of how she was monopolizing the conversation. Irked, the young mother nonetheless replied with a smile. "It's good. Noor helps me in the run." Noor looked at her mother, as her name got called, and butted in quite archly, "Yes I do, because I have nothing else to do." Noor had spoken in a manner of a retort. And Portia was a little taken aback. After all a stranger was in their midst. And Portia had manners.

She slighted her daughter's rudeness by avoiding it completely, and introduced her. "Ha! Grace, meet my daughter Noor. I think she is of your age."

Camel's neck on a tea pot. That was my first impression of hers when I had seen her before. Nevertheless, she looked quite charming sitting next to her mother. Dressed in pink. Eyes shadowed with black and grey hues. Lips glossed minimally. Cute sandals with straps. A pink handkerchief with red borders. Nails done with silver glitter. Hair tied into a bun. And most of all, she was not beating about the dirt like before. Rather, she was calm and composed, even when there was a faint sign of grief issuing from her tensed brows.

"Hello, is it Grace, right? Mother told me of how you helped. Um, your jacket I will return it soon." She spoke formally.

"Oh it's all right. I hope you are feeling better?" I bit my tongue after having asked that unseemly question. It certainly was improper asking her about how she felt, and reminding her how intimately close I was to her during the day of the puke. The girl was a normal girl. Yet she was making me very uncomfortable with her normalcy as I had seen her act abnormally. I could not understand why all of a sudden I was weighing what was proper and improper with respect to Noor and her condition? Did she remind me of my quirky childhood that I despised and yet subconsciously cared for her? Before she could reply, I had to interrupt her anxiety, her mother's chagrin and my own discomfiture, so I resumed talking after a split-second pause. "Your name is quite unique, what does it mean?" Noor looked at her mother, and replied uncouthly, "A meek girl, I presume, isn't that right mother?"

Startled at that apparently outrageous reply, Portia admonished her daughter. "Nonsense, Noor! Grace she is j-just always d-dramatic like that…" But the daughter gave out a grunt, and said, "Dramatic! It is the truth, you always say that to me."

I was a stranger, and Noor had decided to be intimate about her thoughts too. As if I had not seen enough of her. Perchance she thought I had seen her dance so there was no need to be formal with each other anymore.

On the day of the puke, Noor was in a frenetic trance unbecoming of her personality or health for that matter. And hours later, while sitting with her mother, she came across as despondent. Noor had put on a brave front to disallow any impression of hers to be taken as vulnerable. But I saw through it, and downright to its kernel, it was despondent. Being sad doesn't mean being a coward or a weakling. Noor was sad yet still came to the party to allay the shame of that day and for the sake of her mother's reputation. In a demoniacal trance of the underworld, she was exposed head to toe, and then she had to make a formal appearance. The girl had danced till blood spurted out of her, and yet she had to come to the party. The girl wasn't mewling over it and I saw her behave rather rebelliously against her mother. She indeed was being normally strong for herself. Granny was observing us since we came downstairs, and sensing the temperature rising among us, she called up Halo. And so dispersed us to resume the pretense of normalcy.

"Halo, come here. Sit by me. I have saved you a seat", she signaled at the spot that she had reserved for her.

"Granny. I knew you would." Halo smiled and left me standing by myself. So I took a seat where I could find and made no fuss about it.

During the day of the puke, Granny was less than cordial when she had terminated my stay as formally as one could to insult. And hours later, she invited me for supper. But my name she refused to utter in public lest it was taken as a recommendation letter. Like the rest, Granny knew me not. But unlike the rest, she was being more explicit in her aspersions about me. Since the time she saw me, it seemed she had me for a drug-addict. We had a tight rope between us but neither was she pulling nor did she want me to. Maybe she wanted me to walk it. A stalemate it was, and I had to work at it if the secrets of the town with its three Zones were to be surveyed. Granny had a clout in the town, and she seemed to have the only clout in that town. So I had to be in my best behavior to win her approval. Was I trying too hard that her rope just went higher and higher and droopier and droopier almost giving me vertigo with every raise? If she was endearingly nicknamed as Granny, then she would have to be sweet and charming too. Or was it the same with Portia being Pooh only to diffuse the seriousness? But Granny was sweet with others. I think she was not maliciously seeking to spite me. The old lady was being skeptic like an elder would be towards her daughter's choice of an eccentric boyfriend. And Halo was like her daughter. Her wearing me, a scantily clad outsider as a friend, was a concern for the old lady.

"Noor where are you off to? Noor?" Granny called her out as Noor made a move to leave. Without stopping, the girl responded. "I need some air, Granny. I'll be back." Granny didn't persist any further. "Sure, go ahead".

Noor was uncomfortable, as I could tell. In the fanatic mould I had seen her, she deserved to be left alone for a while. The same day she was forced to act normal because the occasion demanded it and no one was interested to handle it gently. I could understand her exasperation. The town had thrown a soup party to distract a guest. Lest ideas of untoward nature were guessed of them. They were doing it so perfectly. It seemed perhaps it wasn't the first time Noor's malady had been condoned off as nothing. Tired of its weight, and the burdening pretence, she couldn't for another second sit by her humiliated mother. So she left in haste, and I was relieved for her.

But when she had just reached for the door, Lee who also arrived then, interrupted her. Though he didn't demand any courteous hello from her, I wished if he would let her go. I was caring for the girl, even when I didn't want to. When she decided to leave the small party, I felt happy about it. What was with this vicarious thrill for her! This empathy for her, why was I concerned for the girl? Again and again! I wanted Noor to leave the gathering and go out for some air. Why was I so consumed by this narrative?

But I was glad nonetheless, when Lee decided to let Noor be on her own and walked in. Granny got up to meet Lee half-way. "Lee! What took you so long?" The boy wrinkled his nose, and replied coolly, "Hello Granny. I just got held up."

"Hmm I see you are busy with your pamphlet".

"Yes most of it is ready, just minor touches…"

He went on and on about some pamphlet he was coming up with. It wouldn't matter much, I thought, as only his side of the town would be listening to it.

"That is good. I pray it is not a satire like the last one. Something comical you should try too…for our sake. Halo, dear, help me in the kitchen. It's a treat I have prepared. Pooh, call Noor. She will love it!" As Pooh didn't seem to take up on that errand, Lee chivalrously stepped up to call Noor in. "I will go!" Granny didn't mind it, "Sure Lee you may, and hurry."

How solicitous of Lee to step up and look after Noor. The boy was a curious sort. Of all the people I would look at, Lee was the only one who stared back. Gazing till I caught him, and gazing again till I caught him again. I didn't feel uncomfortable but a little challenged to dissect him. In his gaze there was not a gawk. In his interest there was no lust. But a curiosity of any person towards an exotic thing of nature. Saying thus, he still didn't have the right to stare. Yet he did.

Lee was dissecting me to find a friend, and to find a piece for his pamphlet in the same old Galapagos Island. He was quite unlike most men who were always trying to literally dig themselves into my secrets. As much as I could bypass those dark circles hanging under his eyes, I could see Lee was a man who could be handsome if he worked out. Only his mind had the load of exercise to worry about. And naturally his nerves under the eyes had swollen to draw a lovely hue on his face. He slouched too which a lot of sitting desk work would do. Earlier, I had taken Lee to be a clerk than a writer. And he was a bit of both.

Lee called out to Noor from the door, but she insisted on staying put. Portia was infuriated at her, which her thumbs wringing each other could tell. Granny returned from the kitchen with Halo. Halo's tray which she tightly held in her hands was wider than Granny's. It moved me to see the smoke emanating from it in such a sensual fashion. Granny, on the other hand, held two trays. One which carried bowls and glasses while the other bore some other useless wooden crockery.

"A big meal and big hot soup is ready, so surfeit on. Noor! Get in here before its cold. Where has she gone now?" Granny asked while concealing her frustration at the girl.

Then, she began serving the soup in the slowest pace ever. It made me wring my own thumbs. Noor was smart to have waited outside. As Granny took her sweet time to pour the soup into each bowl. She would stir it and then pour it. It was such a time-consuming drudgery that the gathering also went quiet. I could hear the big clock tick tock, tick tock out of beat with the untapped water dripping down. That day, I again heard my heart ebbing up and down as blood gushed forth it. Beep! Beep! Beep! Ironically then, it was lulling me to sleep.

Then, with a thud, Noor barged in, and scowled at the gathering before her. "I am here, haven't left my body yet!"

Noor was back. I saw her. Her face and her bold statement. It was clear Noor hadn't just left to avoid the ramifications of that day, but to prepare an assault on the little assembly in the room. Nervous in her voice, she but hid it with a coarse bass added to it. Not knowing the details of her past, or the history of the town, I still felt for the girl. I had seen her writhe in pain, and then sit in the gathering feigning formality. Certainly I was then concerned and wished if she would show a little more confidence to hammer her careless kin.

She was cowardly in her voice. Even when in her stride towards her family she acted to be taken seriously. "No one is asking, so I will tell anyway."

Portia, who had enough of her daughter's impertinence, signaled it was time to leave. "Noor leave it. W-We are going home, now!" But, Noor was adamant to stay put. "Why mother, are you ashamed of me?"

"Noor, we are l-leaving!" Portia roared at her daughter.

Portia wasn't only mortified of her daughter, she had other fears. She was afraid, if Noor was not stopped, she would start believing herself as a puppet of the devil. I didn't suffer photographic seizures, but was made to believe I did, and it anyway happened. It was more a psychosomatic symptom which had latched onto me after my mother's passing. Even thinking of it made me dizzy and I would feel nauseated. Portia was hence afraid for her daughter. She was worried what if her Noor surrendered to her delusional delirium and enacted it worse than the last one. It was a valid concern. But her way of handling it was not.

"It was a blur! Yes a blur. At first I thought I was imagining things, but I-I saw it. I heard it. A blur in the woods. Someone was in the woods!" The girl declared with rickety vehemence. Granny, while hiding her exasperation, countered her as deceptively as she could. "How is that possible, sweet Noor?"

The formality of the moment had broken. Noor had tossed their lovely evening in a tailspin. The girl's experience of an untold blur had afflicted the room with unease. They all wanted to douse it, but Noor wanted a definite closure. She was not going to give in even when the day of puke had eked the color out of her cheeks.

Stubborn to let her voice be heard, Noor exposed the terrors of her mind. "I was thinking too much that I was not alert and thought my mind played a trick...But there was someone. You people hide your secrets in those woods. And I am to suffer for it!" She was no longer intimidated or coy. But some remnant of her fright was still holding her back. Nevertheless she tried hard to suppress her fears and shame the gathering.

Portia but was pushed beyond her filial tolerance. She wagged her finger as madly as she could, and thundered at her daughter, "Are you listening t-to her? She is m-mad! Listen g-girl, it is your pp-assion with signs, p-premonitions and p-possessions that chase you to m-madness! Now a b-blur! We are leaving, now!"

I listened as intently as I could. Noor believed she saw something. I believed as I saw it too. I was well and sharp in my senses to not mistake it. And Noor with her senses soaked in a draconian dance of a Witch's Sabbath still saw something. May be out of the tail end of her eye, but she saw it nonetheless. There was a blur. In the woods.

Hearing her mother's cruel castigation, Noor didn't relent, and talked back. "I have my signs mother and other repository I bought from hell. But there was someone in the woods...The woods! What lurks in there is a mala fide crime, and I suffer for it!"

Portia then gave up. And fell back in a thud to show her grievous annoyance at her daughter. But Granny was not giving up on Noor. She wanted to assail the girl to tell of what she saw.

"What, my child, tell me?" Granny asked with tender concern. Noor got a little pacified seeing at least the elder of the house was listening to her. She responded,

"Granny, I do not know yet. We need to find it together." But then Granny played a dirty game.

"I know why you would cook it up..." She said sternly.

Noor was devastated. Distraught of being called a liar. The girl did not expect Granny to accuse her like that. Granny of all the people. Disillusioned and shattered, Noor gasped, "Cook it up? Granny, I am not lying! Why would you say that?" To which, Granny replied with the same cold archness, "...So that we forget the day of the puke and many before it."

It was certain, even Granny had abandoned her. Naturally the girl started to pant and puff. Nevertheless, she still held her stand. And knew she had to bleed more rage to confront the hectoring old lady.

"That is harsh of you, Granny. I know what was in the woods, that blur. It was the witch, some witch! I can't sleep. When I do I picture a dreadful, shaggy, grotesquely bent witch after me! My legs are tight and restless with the pain I suffer in my sleep. I run Granny and there is no running away from it. The witch, some witch will eat me! It's dead. It is alive. It shrieks. It but never stops running and chasing the likes of me. What did I do? Nothing. Is that why it wants my soul?"

They heard her exclamations, but I heard something else besides it. I heard Lee. The boy was raving and ranting in his breath. He wanted to join Noor in her fight. He was furious. I was with one ear listening to the raising tumult of the room, and with the other I was intently hearing the rants Lee whispered into the wind. Noor was being harassed and that too by Granny. Lee respected Granny and he loved Noor. He had to balance his indignation for Noor with his respect for the old lady. But he was not going to stay silent for long.

Meanwhile, Granny approached the girl, and spoke in a voice of an echo to calm her. She was being mysteriously and sinisterly sly. What was she hiding, I had wondered.

"Noor, my love, there is no one in the woods. You must have heard a rustle of the leaves. These autumn leaves are dreadful at night. Any passing rat can cause imagination to flicker on and off. Any rat..."

She uttered the word rat again, and at that time her hand gestured somewhere in my direction. She was referring to me as a rat! It was a crude contraption of hers to distract the gathering into thinking perhaps I was responsible. It was certain then, that Granny was lying through her teeth. Rather, she was ardent about it. As she had called an innocent girl delusional even when the girl tried to prove she was sane.

"Granny tread softly, I am not insane!" Noor lambasted at the old lady while the old lady clubbed her arms around Noor, and softly consoled her. Was I moved by her warmth? I could have been. But behind that engaging warmth, I could see, the old woman was using it as a pretext to gag the little girl. Each remained silent in their embrace. The girl couldn't say anything and Granny didn't let her say anything. It was then Lee's cue.

"She saw the witch, some witch didn't she? That wouldn't be a start." Lee had it enough.

"The witch. Some witch. F-First Noor I-loses her mind, and n-now you enc-
courage my d-daughter!" Portia looked at him with pointed aversion.

But Lee had woken up. He ignored Portia point blank. And right when Noor had
started to lose sway, Lee took over the prosecution.

"Am I not right, Granny?" Lee spoke derisively.

"Lee? Now don't you start!" Granny didn't like it when the sensible boy
Lee took the delusional girl's side. But the boy was riled up. Not for his sake
but for the sake of Noor. Ever since the day I had seen him, it was certain he
was smitten. It was not a temporary infatuation as the boy cared for the girl in
earnest. He didn't care whether she knew or not. While attending to her as she
was fitfully unconscious, Lee was criminally fixed to not let go of her. Not even
for once, he had left her side. I found his love pathetic, even absurd as it was
too good to be true. Everyone else even the mother had only disappointment,
mockery and apathy for the girl. But Lee was hooked to his good side and
showed such levels of concern. It was beyond belief. Did Granny not know
about this? That Lee would, without doubt, stop her from badgering his love?
She foolishly expected the balance to tip in her favour, but the old lady and
her pride were wrong. Lee was furious, and he was not going to relent anytime
sooner.

"Granny, it is the witch, some witch. It has already started" Lee again spoke
irreverently.

"Zip it Lee! Hoax alarms of this kind I will not tolerate!" Granny reacted in anger.
Something I thought she was incapable of. Lee himself was shocked and as a result
toned down his voice. Lest he aggravated the old lady, who had enough of that
debate that too in front of a stranger.

Nevertheless, he was prepared to put her through the wringer. And spoke
cautiously yet fervently "Granny, those sightings out of thin air, and now this one?
Hoax? I do not think it is a hoax!"

"Sightings! What sightings Lee? Who else claims your theory besides you! Who
else is your partisan in this politics?" Granny tried to intimidate him, but he was
mulish to let go. One level after another, call it petty but I was thoroughly enjoying
the beating Lee and Granny were giving each other. Granny who had been terse
with me, when I saw her chagrined, it felt like poetic justice.

"Politics? Yes it is politics! The matter of the witch, some witch is a political lie.
Why has it not been settled, is all I ask!" Lee had a point and I assented with him by
letting out a puff of air. Granny again wished that I, a stranger wasn't in their midst.
Everyone was blistering with shame and turmoil, and strangely I was not. Like an
overt reporter with a covert sting camera, I was studying them quite imaginatively.
Besides, there was no reason for me to blister with shame as well. Did I abet their
problems, no! Should then I be blamed? No, not at all. Hence there was no need for
me to practice self-shame.

So I kept listening as Lee kept yelling. And all the while, Granny kept salvaging
what she could from the flotsam. The boy had taken up arms against the old lady

to speak for his beloved. To ensure the witch, some witch matter got settled once and for all.

"It is not the first time. Who is this darkly thing of magic, the witch, some witch?" he continued disconcertedly. "Why is she allowed to have its run, you know something, and you refuse to let us know!" Lee then paused to catch his breath, and then went on to aggressively lay down the crux of his torment. "There was a crime done in this town, and the witch, some witch is the consequence of it. Get rid of her! Confess and she will leave us! For the sake of Noor, do it!"

Granny, who had been browbeaten, slighted and exacerbated, still managed to maintain her poise, and returned Lee's accusation with a thoughtfully constructed answer. She rather played to the gallery by balancing her ire with an emotional appeal. She spoke, "Lee, my Lee what a fool you make of me, there is nothing insidious in our town, and nothing is supernatural about it. If there is something foul in the wind, I pray, I plead it not to hurt us…This town is ours and we are its own. There is nothing to confess, as we have done it no wrong…"

Moved by Granny's poignant sentiments, Lee got a little overwhelmed, and spoke kindly, "I know it Granny, there can never be. But there is one apparently, and we need…" He paused again, as if knowing he was falling for Granny's strategic diversion. And resumed his ire, "Granny, this town! It is going to the dogs, as apparently even the elders are…"

Granny rebuked him midway with a sharp rejoinder.

"Let me speak! You have milled in your mind such insipid horrors, that the sensitive members of my town are accepting it to be true! Enough! Enough already. This is how sedition once broke my town into three. Into three Zones, my HALO, anyone can make us cut each other's throat! Lee, Zones is a real issue, and the witch, some witch is a mere hallucination! How can you merge one with the other and blame my inaction on the witch, some witch as a herald of a crisis like the Zones! Then there is Noor's um delusions, if I provoke a talk about it, it will only make them real."

Indignant, and threatened, Lee attempted to apologize "Granny, I didn't mean…"

Granny, realizing his contrition, put her hand around his slouched shoulders, and said, "Oh Lee I cursed not you…" Lee who was still in distrust, plainly answered, more to vent his despair than fight her. "Cursed? Sounded more like I was accused…"

The old lady realized Lee would not bear any insults hurled at Noor. She also realized the boy would not stop till the matter was resolved for Noor's sake. So she started to pacify the girl in the hope that Lee stopped with his harangue. "Fine, fine", she spoke consolingly and continued, "Noor, I assure you if there is a ghost or the witch, some witch among us, I will not let it hurt you. Can you be strong for me, dear? Can you be?"

"Uh…" Noor didn't reply but only let out a gentle scorn.

"Peace lets all be…we have a guest here. Let's not make her uncomfortable."

Granny still didn't utter my name. At least she did not call me a rat. At seeing the turn of events, I was a tad bit frustrated at the old lady. The drama was much better than the soup party, and Granny had to kill it. It was frustrating.

There was collision in Granny's head. She was being attacked by the two kids who she thought would always remain kids. Noor, she declared was delusional. And Lee a warmonger! Such slanderous accusations didn't become her, but she nonetheless did it to have her way. Still, it was intriguing as to why Granny would go to such extreme lengths. The old lady was protecting something or someone dearest to her. As she was ready to throw her own into the cesspool. Who was the witch, some witch? What was the history of the Zones, they were talking about? From story to history, that daynight had opened up an itinerary of that town. It sure replenished my appetite for gathering tasteful scandals, gossips and unpleasant secrets.

Everyone had a stake in that room. We all were on a revolving stage. They were watching me hear their sessions, and I was watching them. Time was beginning to diminish our patience. But Lee just wanted to get it done with whether people were watching or reporting. As they locked horns, I curiously wondered how they would act later when I had seen them in their birthday dress. How can anyone?

Just when Lee geared up to launch another assault, a couple entered the room. "Are we late?"

They were the late arrivals of the party. I had seen them before, Vicky and Christian. Though they were together-together, they didn't look compatible. The boy was a serious fellow while the girl seemed to be a fake. Yet both held hands in hands like a couple.

Granny, glad to see a distraction, gushed as excitingly as she could, "Vicky, Christian! No you are not late. We were just starting. Lee will get more bowls from the kitchen. Lee?"

Lee wasn't the one to shape-shift his face when a distraction called. But in Granny's polite repetition of his name, he realized the old lady wanted him to let bygones be bygones. Too much was at stake for Granny. Noor was but oblivious of it.

"Why Vicky and Christian are family too, and there is nothing to hide here, Granny?" Noor charged at her. Belligerent but with a shaky resolve.

"Are we all a family here? Noor are you blind?" Granny discreetly urged Noor to really think over the question. After all I was there.

Noor realizing Granny's discomfort reluctantly agreed. I was not family, and Granny had to say it out loud to establish it. The couple was starkly in the dark at what had provoked Granny's pithy anger. Blank-faced with a disturbing flush of red in their cheeks, they were in distress to have entered at a wrong time.

Realizing Granny's signal, Christian didn't broach it. But Vicky was however anxious to hear some news.

"Wh-what, what is going on, Granny?" She asked the old lady with a glint in her eyes.

It wasn't concern that had piqued Vicky to ask around. But a silent yet vicious urge to hear some spicy bulletins. She was displaying a conniving interest in her family's plight. I looked at her and there was no love, affection or filial attachment perceptible in the girl. Rather she was parched of it. Christian, the boy by her side, however was not glad to be a party to her schemes. And was sure regretting to have arrived with her.

She pried again.

"Tell me, tell me what has happened, huh?"

The day of the puke came back to me. Vicky was strictly nosing around the scene and spying for some details to spice up her life. She showed no concern for Noor at all rather cringed at her. And when she pried again, I wished if the anger the old lady had reserved for Lee, she would throw some of it at the nosy girl. Granny certainly tried to, but the way she did it, it was so syrupy.

"Nothing my love, there is nothing happening here. You don't worry over it, all right dear. Everything is fine." Granny spoke to her with a sweet tooth.

What was I to make of it? Observing Granny's overly ardent love for that girl, I thought perhaps, Vicky was her daughter. Granny had, after all, leashed her self-righteous fury for the sake of the meddling girl.

"Okay, okay. If you say so…" Vicky with a tinge of insolence let it go.

"Good then, very good, Come on in, now, uh, Lee help me with the bowls…" Granny ignored Vicky's vicious attitude with a saccharine glow on her face. She was pleased to see things finally settling down. Finally some peace to cherish the delicacies she had prepared. No more to look back in anger. After all what was lost, she had regained it, or so she thought.

Christian, the boy of good looks, however wasn't in a mood to let go. But he was not disturbed by the perpetual sadness of Noor, or the burning red face of Lee. He was disturbed by some other occurrence. And pestered by it, he asked.

"Granny?"

He spoke with a strain in his voice. Granny must have thought – why was her family out of the blue tethered to the pole of the witch, some witch? But then she realized, Christian didn't mean the witch, some witch. He meant someone else.

"Yes Christian, what is it? You don't look happy to be here, what's the matter?" Granny was worried in her voice. The boy made an uneasy expression, and replied, "Someone else has come to your party, just like always sitting in your garden."

"Who?" she asked.

"The Elder…" he spoke with aversion.

Granny had suspected who it was even when she wished it was not true. Christian was also disturbed to sound his arrival. Not that a ghost had sunk its teeth in him, but he was huffing which I could tell by his rolled-up lips in disdain. If Lee and his lovely Noor had provoked Granny's fury, then the Elder was guilty of frustrating her patience.

"Vicky?" Granny asked as politely as she could.

"Yes, Granny." Vicky replied with an exaggerated confidence.

"Vicky did you umm invite him?" Granny was hesitant in her voice, and approached her question with heightened sensitivity. Vicky, did not like to be accused of as a liar. She rebutted her with shameless disregard.

"I met him the other day, but no I did not!" The girl was pungent in her curt reply. She was beginning to appear as a beloved spoilt child of Granny, and why the old lady couldn't see through it, it was beyond me.

"Of course my sweet, I know. How about you all get started, all of you. This might take some time. It's a reunion, isn't it?"

Chapter 3

He Would Find Me in His Bed

The Elder. Commanding, authoritative and sagacious. In a name I began to drawn him as a man of interest. A pious man with a mind to make decisions of welfare, mental peace and humanity. He had to be called the Elder because of his principles, ethics and decorum. An experienced old man. Yet there are times when names can be misnomers and official histories utterly false. Aware of these gnawing possibilities, I still kept my expectations high. After all, I was utterly curious to know who the Elder was. Could he be a chief? A very old man? The title of 'The' that had been accorded to him, was it out of respect? Or he did something to clinch it? Curious about that fellow, I wanted to rush outside to rest my glutton imagination. All except Vicky seemed to have a bone to pick with him. What had made him a beta-noire in the eyes of the entire gathering that only Vicky seemed to like him? Eager to seek the answers, it was then absolute that I saw him forthwith.

Carefully picking myself up, I approached the old lady. She was busy staring outside the window with Christian behind her. Walking past him, I nudged the woman to take my leave. Startled, she turned back, and wondered what I would want from her. Overlooking the doubt manifested in her face, I asked politely. "Granny. I think I should go now." I called her Granny. And she was positively pestered. I was forced to call her by that endearing nickname, as I didn't know her actual name. Besides, she had not been courteous enough to make introductions to begin with. Naturally then, a Granny it was. The old lady flustered under her conceited demeanour and gave out a shrilling response. "What!"

I awkwardly paused for a while. Did she not hear me then? She did hear, but was taken aback at my nerve to call her Granny. Tortured by her impertinence, I gulped back my dignity and asked her again. "Can I leave?" I was curt even when respectful in my voice.

"Good! You should by now. I will send you your share of the soup at the shack". She replied with a visible sneer and was happy to send me off. The old lady didn't even conceal her gladness and crudely bid me farewell. She wanted me gone so much that the woman didn't even care to pick up a decent mask while shooing me away. The worst part was, she did it in front of everyone. If she could take liberties to ridicule me, then the town would also imitate her insolence. Perchance it was her stratagem from the start. That the town did not take me for an innocuous stranger and that they stayed wary of me. Though I tried to hide the hurt she had inflicted, I genuinely wished to return the favour. Then again, I took pity on her for her old age. While walking out the door, I assured myself that the old woman would one day get her comeuppance.

As I reached for the door, I could see, Granny followed me in tow. As if she was making sure I didn't go back in.

"It's chilly. My feet don't seem to recall their speed." I spoke with deliberate innocence.

"Okay…" She still remained crude.

While walking down the stairs and exiting through the gate, I deliberately walked slowly. I had to take my time to read the Elder. It was certain Granny was not going to introduce me to him. So I had to discreetly make better of the situation and be circumspect about it. Even agreed to demean myself as jousting swords with the old woman would have cost me dearly. She, after all, was the town's highly regarded senior who happened to call the shots. And winning her approval was paramount. So, as she followed me from behind, I tactfully dragged my steps. In one of the green gardens of the old lady, I saw the Elder. He was anxiously waiting while chewing on the petals plucked from her garden. As we approached, he got up as urgently as his body could allow. Then I saw him from head to toe.

White everything, all of it, dressed to the nines with it. As if he was showing, rather self-righteously parading he was a forty year old virgin. His sandals had lost a strap or two and they were dirty like the tell tale dirt they had walked on. Whatever bare skin he exposed reeked of mushy sweat. And even without tanning his fair skin, being unkempt like his feet, had grown grey too. Strangely only his white robes were neat and clean. Hair was combed more than enough, when I saw his oily hairlines and multi-streaks. He looked slim from the back. But from front, one could see his huge sticking-out potbelly defying the limits of his spinal steel. Brows were sweaty. Lips but dry. Eyes shaped like the crescent moon and the nose as tiny as a baby's little finger.

We stepped out the door. And the Elder stood up as his potbelly swung right to left and back. Then he spoke.

"You could have called me from the terrace. Wh-Who is she?" He looked at me, and was stumped. Granny ignored him out rightly. Then while facing me with a fixed scorn, she inquired, "Little lady, you know the way back, right?"

"Of course." I nodded.

It certainly was insulting the way she rounded me off. Little Lady! But it was the Elder's despicable behaviour which was more loathsome. From the moment he had laid his eyes on me, he had gone quite jumpy. His lust scanned my endowments even when they were meticulously hidden. I guess it wouldn't have mattered. Hidden or not. Covered or not. He still would have ogled with his lascivious mind. The man believed it to be his right. As I found him disappointingly vile, I did not gesture my goodwill towards him. His face and tawdry manners didn't invite any decent hello to begin with. He still smirked as if after his business with Granny, he would find me in his bed.

The Elder was smitten for my skin. And I had such high hopes for him. Even thought he would be a sagacious man of immaculate wisdom and honour. Why would anyone call him the Elder? It was mockery of mockery. The man was repulsively lecherous and even the screaming presence of Granny did not shame him. I could see Granny was implicitly curt with him as if for my benefit. How paradoxical! In one frame, I was her worst intruder. And in another, she acted as my guardian shielding me from the Elder's dirty looks. Be that as it may, Granny did seem to cut me out of the conversation. It appeared more out of concern than insult. Such a change in her attitude made me rethink perhaps she was not what I had imagined. Then again, as my pride was still wounded because of her insolent behaviour, I remained mistrustful of her.

As I walked towards the gate, the Elder interrupted me again. Impervious to the sins of his vulgarity, he importuned, "Who are you? Who is she? What is her name, your new guest?" Granny quickly butted in. And affronted the man by changing the subject, "Why are you here, it is unexpected, and I don't like unexpected." He certainly felt snubbed, and did show it by aggressively wagging his eyes at my carriage. Granny noticed his stubbornness and then literally plunged herself between us to make him stop. It was then the Elder realized, he had no chance with me as long as the old lady was there. So he let it go.

Distracting him, Granny asked again, "Why are you here?"

"No Name then…well, I came to ask why one of the animals is inside your house? Why?" he asked bluntly. There was a heightened stench of impudence in his voice.

The old man had more than a passing grudge against someone in Granny's house. Such hate in that old age. I saw the creaks in his face, and it was certain, his hate had sped up his aging. The Elder looked old, but was not in his dotage. Was he called the Elder because of his age or could it be a representation of his leadership? It was uncertain.

"On my porch, in my Zone I will not have you insult anyone of us." Granny ordered him. She ordered him to tone down his venom.

"He is not yours! Not of any one of us! Those youngish copies are supposed to make our future, and they are on the verge of killing it. You know this, and I know this, and that's why I barred into three this town! Remember, Granny?" He was vindictive in his remonstration.

I had stepped outside the gate, and was past them. So I couldn't see anymore what manner of gesticulations they were throwing at each other. Granny had briskly escorted me out for reasons more to do with the lewdness of the Elder. But I wanted to stay and follow what topic of crossfire they were in. Hence, I dragged my feet and took baby steps while reluctantly retreating to the shack. I would discreetly pause in my retreat so as not to raise suspicions of eavesdropping while cleverly listening to the skirmish the two were in. Slow in my stride, it was still difficult to capture the entire story. Few words would escape my hearing. So I had to make up the missing portions of the argument. But once I knew the context, it was easy to figure out the plot of the story.

As the Elder finished with his tirade, Granny made a brusque retort. "Not here, not now." Granny was brief in her reply.

Her approach of stern taciturnity made me think. Was she suffering from a lack of words or was she unable to put up a valorous stand against him? Some could take it to mean that she was scared. As people tend to qualify a leader with the amount of words he spawns. When Granny remained ritually stuck to her brevity, even I felt contemptible of her meek offense. And as for the Elder, he kept hitting her with lofty words and ideals and continued with added rhetoric.

"Animals! And you would rather feed them, than cook them for meat. That is how they are! Animals! They are just like that. There is no love for heaven or dread of hell in them. Eat and mate. Just because in their genes, their masters tell them to. The real danger is from the carnivores. If they start to think, and dictate their genes to mutate at their will, there is evolution of their powerlessness to powerfulness. We all will die with them. I have taken an oath to rid this town of their bestiality! An oath, Granny!"

As if I was not impressed enough, the Elder threw in a monstrous parable. What was extraordinary about it? Not it's meaning, but the explosive force with which he uttered it. Compared to him, Granny had no tall tales to tell. She was dull and terse and unlike the Elder did not strike her hands and fist in the air. Who would give her a standing ovation? The audience only wants fireworks from their leaders even when it is all smoke. The Elder was imposing in his pandemonium. He spitted. He sweated. He bled his eyes red.

If Granny was silent, he was cantankerous.

If Granny was brief, he was melodramatic.

If Granny was poker-faced, his face was a whirlwind in the sea.

When the Elder had finished his parable, there was a riotous pause. Granny did not say anything to rebut his stirring speech. It seemed she had accepted her defeat. But then Granny spoke, though with the self-same meek brevity.

"If I hit you how will you respond Elder?" she spoke plainly.

"What?"Riddled, he asked. What tactic was she playing out, a parable for a parable? I slowed my steps to hear her well. Then she resumed with unmistakable drudgery. "If it's a surprise attack, you will shut your eyes, and cover your face with your wide hands. Right?"

Meanwhile, the Elder remained vociferously animated and replied with an exaggerated resolve. "Of course! Surprise if it is but then I will rise. I will rise! and I will!"

"I bet. And one day it wouldn't be a surprise, if I keep at it again and again. An ostrich would still dig its head underground but we wouldn't. Right?" She spoke with a tedious strain.

"It will, and we will not. And it will, but what is your point?" The Elder roared while Granny remained tired in her voice. Why was she tired? Perhaps she had done it before. And to have to do it again, there was a sense of despair in her voice. She tried nevertheless, hoping he might understand by some miracle. By some stroke of luck…

"You will learn to attack me. Fight back. Wouldn't you?" she asked with forced liveliness while the Elder responded with bursting thrill, "Of course! What's you point?"

Pausing for a while, she declared as calmly as she could. "That is what they are doing, Elder. You read one book on genes, and then with your tale, make harmful nonsense out of a harmless sense." Her voice was still calm, like she was singing a lullaby. But her succinct words, still succinct, carried a clamour for him to stop his nonsense.

Stunned and even indignant, he reacted, "You always do this, side with them. The sickening Lights Off. The young fools of this town. You have missed my point."

"You weren't making any…" She was curt.

"B-but…" The Elder paused, and it was a deafening pause. He wasn't in admittance of his defeat either. His face twitched in some parts humiliation and in some parts brazenness. He paused, as the Book of Knowledge that he had crammed, and that too only few pages of it, was over. He didn't know what more genes to throw in his parable.

"I leave you again. But the LO they are on my hit list. I will, I will!" he yammered with the self-same spiteful passion. A passion which had but lost the steam of reason. Or perhaps never had one to begin with.

"You will still return." Granny spoke in a patient voice. And the Elder continued, but then his voice lowered a decibel, "You still carry it with you, the rosary, you can't forget what happened." He was all of sudden calm. As if the sight of the rosary had pushed him to remember a grim memory. Even I had noticed a rosary on Granny's wrist which looked strangely mysterious. But then I had not thought too much on it.

The Elder wanted to confess the meaning of the rosary which goaded my curiosity, but then he let it go. Both turned sullen. More like guilt-ridden. Ashamed. Party to a crime. Granny then lowered her eyes while remembering what the rosary stood for and in a somber voice, she said. "I can't but I can forgive. Elder, we must not forget who in fact is to be blamed. Not them. Not the young…." She spoke while softly touching the rosary around her wrist.

The Elder stroke his head with his hands. As Granny kept on caressing the rosary, he began to breathe ever so pacifically. Both were hushed. A tumultuous memory had stung them into a sore silence. The rosary.

The conflict between Granny and the Elder, I would have written it off as a personal rivalry. But in days to come, I came to know it all had to do with a nasty incident. Something that had created the Zones, and something that had manifested the haunting existence of the witch, some witch. The Elder made a move to leave. Granny didn't stop him. In agreement with her, he then left. No one uttered any word. It was mutual disgrace. Something which only they knew. What was it that made them hang their heads in shame? Were those two even capable of such a crime? A crime that had left them frozen with self-reproach? If such innocent and old faces could, then certainly times were dire.

As the Elder went beyond sight, Christian who was hiding by the pillar, made himself known. He was hiding behind it all that long. Was he the animal, the Elder talked about? The boy was red in his face for having to hide in his own home. With pent-up anger in his voice, he approached the old lady. "Granny! He left."

"Yes, yes Christian. It was smart, smart of you to not show yourself. That would only have provoked him." Granny recognized it, but still maintained a tranquil face.

"For how long, how long to just stand back, and hide behind a pillar like some…" But he didn't want her to be calm. He wanted decisiveness. He didn't want his wounds to turn into a clot but to vanish altogether.

"You know why I wait." Granny again held on to her tactical pacification, and continued, "And you know abetting him is what he wants of you. Christian, my boy you are better than this, and… so many wondrous things you boys and girls have done, and, and that's why he is jealous of you, right?"

"You are right, yes, we are good there, and better. He wants us to bark, so he can rejoice in our tantrums. No we are good there, and there is no need to prove it to him, but Granny?" Christian reassured her that he understood, but he had a doubt.

"Yes, Christian?" She asked, clueless to what ailed him next.

"He knew I-I was here, he knew, Vicky must have told him…" he spoke timidly.

"She wouldn't! Never!" Granny put her foot down. Already she was regretting how she had assailed innocent Vicky with her doubts. She couldn't have Christian add to her mistakes. When it came to the girl, the old lady just couldn't see what was right before her eyes.

"Then how? You put too much trust in her." Christian, again, accused Granny of being blind. And the old lady got further riled up. She rather felt indignant to hear Vicky's name taken in vain. "Christian! She is like a daughter to me, and I wouldn't have you insult…"

Frustrated and even dismayed that Granny was not able to see through her, he raved again. "Daughter! And she is my friend. I only want you to admonish her, that's all. Why, why don't you see it?"

"She has done nothing wrong!" Granny was obstinate.

"You are blinded by this…" And he was obstinate.

The old lady was adamant not to heed the boy's suspicions. Even when a second ago she had applauded him for his wondrous things.

"No more. Let's go in. I will have to boil the soup again."

"Fine…"

Her voice lowered, and Christian let it slide for the soup was getting cold.

Chapter 4

Towards The Epicentre of Honour?

An hour or so had passed, since the grandiloquent soup party. Cooped up in the shack, I didn't want to sleep or stay awake. Jaded and worn-out, I yawned till my jaws broke and flies made bed in my mouth. Even eyes got watery. Cheeks pained a little and tummy began to growl with hunger. While touching myself, I hummed this and that stupid song to pass the time hanging over me like Damocles' sword. And just when sleep began to woo me, I heard some raucous crowd making its way to the Brigand Street. I looked outside the window, and saw one boy, whom I had not met, getting hugged by the assembled gathering. It was a snivelling event. It reminded me of how my mother would cry and say good-bye to father when he would go out of town. It was a nice feeling almost choked me to cling to my tears. Many of the faces in the crowd were recognizable. One in particular was Halo who kept peeking at the window, where I was standing. But it was not Halo who came to knock at my door.

"Grace you in there?"

The caller had scorn written all over its voice. I also repaid it with exacting curtness. "Hold on!"

"Fine." She said with immutable disdain.

It was Vicky. The girl had come with an interesting prospect.

The door wasn't bolted. Swishing it out, I stood on the third stair, and asked, "Vicky? What's up?" She didn't make a move to enter. While standing as firmly and as deignfully as she could, she replied, "The Elder asked me to call you." She spoke while pouting her lips in derision. What vexed her, I had thought, and then I knew my answer. The girl had come as an errand girl to deliver a message. To be used as a gofer, it definitely pricked her ego. She was discernibly disturbed in her face and even flared her nostrils at me.

"Why?" I naturally had to ask whether she liked it or not.

"I didn't ask." Curtly, she replied

She was being annoyingly offhanded. Though, I was used to people being a bit offhanded. But she was too much. If she was pestered to be made a lackey, then I wanted to pester her a little more.

"Why did you bring his message? You his cousin or something?" I asked knowing where to prick her nerve. Definitely irked, she spoke contemptuously, "He trusts only me, that's why. You coming?"

She was without doubt displeased when I put this question to her. But I was not done. I had seen her vile interest in Noor's ailment at the day of the puke. It bothered me. She was family, and thought it was her birthright to take vicious pleasure in

31

her cousin's malady. Needless to say, I wanted to annoy her. So I continued with my avenging taunts.

"Sure I will come, if he trusts you."

"The Elder trusts me! You have a problem?" She spoke with cemented disdain.

The Elder. Why was he calling me? It was not a difficult question to answer. I had seen his character lustfully desiring the company of a girl he had just met. The man was intent on an interaction. To befriend a stranger and make his nights glorious under the starry skies. It had me thinking as to what relationship did he have with Vicky then. Was she using him or he using her? Could love be a thing between them? Though I was not against age difference, but the girl could have done far better.

In an hour or two since we had met, the Elder had his errand girl sent me an invitation. And there she was on the doorstep carrying it on her molten face. She was infuriated as if I was in my mind longing to steal her Elder. She was sorely jealous. It had me giggle that she could think I would want to strike a chapter with that man. Nevertheless, Vicky took her time to realize that the question of it didn't even begin to begin with. The Elder wasn't a man to long for. Even his personality was in shambles like his cheeks and feet. Well not his dress, which was a fairest show. Then again, who was I to question his cheeks or feet, mine weren't stitched without seams either. But there was that matter of personality, and he didn't seem to care for one. The Elder had a fetid composition of character and he thought others were rotten. It disgusted me. I could see back then by Granny's garden, his pale eyes getting fiercer and brighter with red flush on his cheeks. So hot they almost parched his lips. And he had to lick them. Granny worsened it when she sent me off so tersely. That for him I became a forbidden guest he was not allowed to meet. He must have thought that I, a petite stranger, was marooned in the town. And would candidly accept just anyone's invitation. I certainly accepted his, for he wasn't anyone, he was a 'The'. And I needed to know why.

"Fine, when?" I asked. The girl hated that she had to be answerable to me. And replied rather condescendingly, "Now."

"Now?" I asked rather petulantly.

"Yes, now! We are seeing off Danny, my brother, to the city. You have time to dress up or whatever. I will be back in minutes." She made a move to leave at once, but I interrupted her again. "The city?"

"The city, yes for the last time!" Irate at my questioning she continued, "Uh, you see that road, where it leads, that is the Elder's zone. On second thought, you wouldn't need a chaperone. I will catch up with you. Wait for me at the border."

"There is a border?" I interrupted her while she made a hurried move to leave.

"Yes there is a border here! You done with the questions?" She sighed with frustration, and was positively incensed at my pesky inquisitiveness. So I plainly overlooked it, "Sure, sure."

As she left in haste before I could interrupt her again, I watched the mewling crowd bidding farewell to the boy heading towards the city. It was when they had their backs turned to the cabin, I slipped out. Most discreetly.

As she left the shack, I was somewhat delighted to have the road down below all to myself. The prospect of walking on stranger streets engaged my titillating curiosity. Besides it also reminded me of a jaunt I had once taken. That memorable jaunt was a strange journey in that it was sensitively unpredictable. Besides, when I was heading back home, it was then the whole trip had actually started. If only some sign in the sky or some premonition had warned me. It would have been nice. Sadly, such stuff works only for the beloved of the Maker. While for us, the house flies, there has never been a warning of what dangers are in store for us. Sadly.

There were two bridges in my life from whence I came. Heaving in the mist, long and cut out from the world. They were barren of lights. Nature's lights also couldn't pierce through it. One officer would be on duty on each extreme of it. If one would be alone on the Bridge, the officers were the only ones who would be around for company. Less traffic ensured what happened there stayed there. Besides they were the officers of law and who was going to suspect them. Calls didn't work except of nature; if one really had to go. During my outing, I had to cross them twice. Once while going towards my apparent destiny and second time while returning home.

At that time, I was wearing an artistically embroidered scarf which my friend, Rustam, had made for me. Rustam was a gentle girl unlike the most means girls I had come across during school years. What to talk about others, even I was a mean girl. During my growing months without a mother, I had developed this cynical, foul-mouthing and even depressingly cold attitude. At heart, I was still wounded of what had happened in my family. And perhaps to hide that weakness, I, for the sake of strong appearances, had put on such a vile mask. So underneath the nutty appearance, I was still a kind little princess of love, cuddling and miracles.

Rustam, but saw through my act and tried to connect with the real me. She wouldn't however see how much I was ashamed of myself, and even reproachful of my petty existence. The more she would claw me out, the more it kindled feelings of distress. When she wouldn't stop reaching after my heart, I then had to put a stop to her. One day then I impulsively insulted her while making crude jokes on her dressing sense. I did it in the school's canteen and made a laughing stock out of her. Hurt, even distressed, she walked away and we didn't speak for days at end. If by chance we happened to cross each other, she would intentionally look away. Strangely, the colder she became in her attitude, it hurt me more. It upset me so much that the venom of my shameless act began to gush forth self-pity, reproach and shame. I then had to put a stop to it else it would have broken me. Overwhelmed with regret, I then decided to make an apology as I was stupidly guileless inside. So, one day as she was sitting in the same canteen, I walked up to her and hesitantly apologised. The reluctance which was obvious in my shame, had her giggle a little. Nevertheless, she understood I meant it even when I couldn't express it so well. Rustam could see I was no bully but young to see that I was being one. What quality defined her sensibility that even when I did not deserve her forgiveness, she gave it?

Days later as our bond grew into mutual trust, Rustam knitted me a scarf more like a pashmina as a gift of reconciliation. It was a fusion of denim and khadi material and its mutant fabric smiled with vibrant colour and feel. I would occasionally use it to cover my head to breast as it was a little heavy to carry. But that day of the jaunt I wore it as the breeze was windy cold, and the scarf of Rustam worked just fine.

During the adventure, I had climbed tall mountains, ran on the deceiving sands, and swam abysmal streams. In each I had a close shave with slippery grass, quagmires, and sharp rocks underwater. Yet I was luckily safe and sound in all those formidable islands of nature. Nature had always been kind. When people would take out their frustrations on me, including my dad, I would then escape to nature. Snakes. Wasps. Beetles. None of these ever attacked me. Even when I went into the bushes at night. Or walked around places infested with hornets. There never was a cheetah which would size me up. Rains, hot days and moonless nights never threatened me to run for safety. Nature was always kind.

In the morning when I crossed the bridges, one of the officers had asked me of my quest. He was a friendly stranger. He even agreed to stay the night to ensure I reached back home safely. When I returned back from the mountains, the officer was still there as he had promised. The night had not gathered yet. But it was always dusk close to the bridges. Dark and misty.

I entered the first bridge and the officer waved his hands good-bye. A car towed by a truck whizzed by, and carrying my cycle by its lights, I reached the middle of it. Then I had to take out my cell to find my way through the rest of the bridge. Meanwhile it contorted as if its bones were writhing against the mist's wet flesh of the winter. It was sheer cold, so I had to peddle while stopping to warm my frozen hands, and rub my feet together. In this manner, hence I reached the other extreme of the first bridge. The officer in the picket at the other extreme asked me if I was warm enough in the freezing terrain. Caringly he looked left and then right to see if I had company other than the officers. I had none.

"Father I have crossed the first bridge. I am first so far. Okay you are close too. Good I must ride again!"

Some instinctual and subconscious fear cajoled me to lie. As I consciously didn't believe there was anything to fear in the crowd of those men. While acting so, I rode out to the other bridge. The officer, my eyes in the back somehow caught him, started playing with the lever of the Bridge. And it rattled again and again and again most moaningly. My cycle and I naturally lost balance and tripping on my knee I fell. As it was hard to ride and to keep my bike stable, so I walked it even as the uneven vibrations kept oscillating the heaving Bridge hanging in the mist. The officers ran to me. Four of them in all. I heard them panting.

First Officer: "Is your bike hurt? Fix it man. She needs to go home."

"I am calling my father. He is near. No need." I whimpered.

Second Officer: "We will fix it."

"Talk to my father. My bike is fine." I gasped.

Third Officer: "Give us the phone, we will talk to your father".

"No he will be here soon." I trembled.

Fourth Officer: "You can wait with us, till he comes, how about that!"

"No, th-there is no need…" I lost my voice.

They weren't listening to my persistent assurances, while one of them even started to loosen the nuts on the tire. They covered me from every direction to block any exits. While inside their circle I frantically looked for an opening. They were playing with me, the way I had played them. I wondered if they were admonishing me for my criminal lie. Was it so? There was one officer, the fifth element, among them who however did not play. He seemed to be the Head and had cunning in his eyes. Coldly as if tired of foreplay, he approached me and declared, "The network does not work on the Bridge, girl. Don't you know?"

I was frozen in my limbs. Terrified, I looked at him to figure out what make of a man he was. While he didn't even blink.

"It-it is-s working, m-my cell." I stuttered in absolute horror.

Flinging my arm to hand him the phone, I threw it away. They were left distracted while I ran to the other extreme end. Then they ganged up in arms, running together, turning and twisting while craving to chase me for the sheer pleasure of it. I felt their hands wipe past my neck, my hair, and the scarf almost got pulled. But I ran as fast as I could to the other direction. I was unaware of what I was in for, so I just feared for my life. As I frantically tried to escape, I thought to myself. It would be a clean death, if I jump off the Bridge. Than have any strangers circle me again. I hence jumped. I jumped without any second thought. The ground of soft grass, soft weeds and soft thorns shimmering with dancing dew touched my feet in a matter of seconds. And I didn't die or cripple from the fall. Nature's kindness didn't seem a blessing then. The officers jumped too, and I ran again into the far far neighboring sylvan parks underneath the bridges. And they followed me wherever I went. I had just provided them with a cold, misty and spacious bed. Running ahead, there seemed to be no end to the round garden. They knew there was no running far, and I was only giving them leverage by running so far into the dark.

Afraid of their large bodies drawing closer, I decided to return to the Bridge. Return to civilization. Civilization we hated so much that my people had built the bridges away from it. No lights, no homes in sight, I was drenched in fear. And it kept nagging me - why was I being chased? The gentlemen had waved first, and then they were meddling with my cycle. I was more scared because of their unreasonable behaviour and didn't even realize the stigma they would turn me into. I was little, my strides were little, and so I was stopped soon enough. The short one slobbered over my lips and I hit him in the nose with two direct punches. He sidelined himself to mend to his injury while the other officers stood awe-struck at my feat.

Then the Head shouted from the left.

The Head: "Pin her down, pin her down! The cat shown you the claws and you are wimping out!"

They were more in numbers, I was just good with alacrity. And as they shrunk for a second, I beat my heart to run back to the Bridge. Run aghast! Run aghast! From the end of my left eye, I saw the Head running to the left. I didn't bother to look back for the officers, and pounced back on the Bridge. Forward, forward I ran to the other extreme of the Bridge beyond which the road was lit with lights. All the while I heard them, shouting bizarre favours to each other.

First Officer: "Who will go first? I!"

They were enthusiastic about it.

Second Officer: "No you had your chance the last time. She died by the time it was mine. I can't duck a corpse again. It is a sin, and I want no more of it."

Third Officer: "It is not a sin. It's plain necrophilia, a disease."

Second Officer: "So what did I say? My turn. Pull out her gears. Fast do it now."

They knew I was outmanned and they could outrun me.

Fourth Officer: "Don't dirty the head scarf. I will need it."

Second Officer: "For a trophy?"

First Officer: "This one is with a temper. I will tame her first. I will."

The Head then jumped in front. If he had been one second late, I could have escaped. But he was on time. He surrounded me like a solitary mob, and pursued me back to the epicentre of shame where the officers were waiting to do things. As he hunted me, I saw his sickness bulging out of his pants, wet and cold. With a kick I wished and longed and ached to push his sickness in, but the officers wrapped me in a plastic sheet and dragged me to the abyss underneath the Bridge. There, the Head gave orders. The officers listened.

"Hey Grace, where are you lost?" Vicky called me from behind. She naturally expected that on hearing her call out, I would stop for her to catch up. But I was lost. I rather felt a modicum of gladness to see her come, as the aftermath of the Bridge, I didn't wish to remember. And Vicky's timing couldn't have been better. I turned back to approach her and saw a faint figurine of hers coming towards my direction. Though my legs began to follow her voice, my mind, struck by a dirty memory, was lost.

She called again. But to no answer.

"Hey you lost your mind!"

As she approached closer, I was grateful though that she had come. She took my silence, that too dumb silence as a cruel evasion of her. Affronted, she screamed into my face.

"I waved at you! Did you sleep?"

My mother had taken ill, when I was very young to know men than experience them. And she died even before she could tell me who was rancid and who was human. So I had to experience the rancidity than just know about it. I wanted to ask her, but I didn't know what to. Father didn't know how to. The first time I had experienced how some men can be like, that memory had always remained very pungent. The memory of the public hospital, where she was admitted when a growth in her womb had started to fester. She was anesthetized like the other patients to abolish pain. Their families were fatigued and most of them were fast asleep. While the ones who couldn't sleep were either leering or writing.

There were two men in the same room as my mother. It was a dormitory, as we were not rich enough to book a private room. The two men. Their wives were euthanized asleep of pain, just like my mother who was also eased of pain. I could hear her gentle snores making me feel at home. But it was no home. The two men. The younger one was decent enough to leer away when I would notice his indecent advances. But the older one, who was holding a baby, harboured such distasteful thoughts, I cringed. I couldn't make out what they implied, but certainly found them crawling on my skin.

The old man sometimes took a stroll outside the ward, and would boldly stare in my face. It was such a perpetual libidinous stare that I could only ignore it to make him stop. I tried to snub him by giving a frown but that only encouraged him. He rather felt I noticed him, and in my discomfiture he gratified his arousals. He was old and he was a pervert and the unnerving thing was, he was not ashamed. Was the thing about qualms and pangs news to him? That he preened his erect sickness unbeknownst to the qualms my mind was torching him with? The young man, his sightings even when I slighted, he would stop only to return. I would scold him as demoniacally as I could with my arresting brows and policing eyes, but he returned nevertheless.

"Grace? Hey! Girl! What the hell is wrong with you?"

My mother was not well. The wives were not well. They were ill and were brought to the hospital. The old man and the young man were there with them. All through the night they were hovering to take care of their sleeping wives and discreetly looking at me with sick euphoria. Neither was there an angel nor an officer to report to. Father was asleep fatigued of the daytime he had pulled in for his wife. I had taken the night shift to my peril, I didn't know.

To their wives who woke-up well rested the next morn, the men smiled with innocent eyes. Even when the night of carnality they had kept for a little stranger stranded in their midst. I wished to tell my mother the next morn, but I feared she might upset herself. Father I didn't, for some reason I feared what if he might slap me for it. I was also ashamed to tell on those men of how indecent they were. I was ashamed. Not because of cowardice but guilt like I had been bad and deserved to be leered at. Rather it was guilt that had forced me to keep it a secret. What if my parents scolded me if I told them? For something I did? What did I do?

Mother and wives were euthanized of pain. Men were erotized of lust. And I a youngling was nauseated. What did I do?

"Grace, you are drooling, wake up!"

At the hospital, I had a notebook and a pen. I would write on it to escape the leering eyes of the two men. If I had not been writing, then what could have I done in the hospital? I couldn't have left my mother for she needed my constant uninebriated watch. I also couldn't say anything to those men. As it would've brought unwanted attention and embarrassed me in front of my parents. Besides, they were my father's age. When I couldn't talk back to my dad, how could I retaliate against those men? So all I could do was write. Sink my face into my notebook, and hide. Avoid. Endure. Write. I thanked providence for reminding me to pick up a notebook on the way. It helped me write what they were doing, my own little ordeal. And it made me feel like a vigilante with a hammer. What a feeling it was that I could badger the men through my writings!

While writing, the leers even when they didn't stop shut down for me. They shut down for me when in epiphanies, I vented out the steam of shame burning my innards. Burning my harassed conscience. I reported the men in my reports and it gave me power that I could speak even when I couldn't.

The next morning, mother was discharged from the hospital. Doctors said it was just a cyst that had gotten her bed-ridden. A little pain that needed rest and medication. That is what we were told. And frankly we were relieved even when mother's body defied such a tenuous prognosis. Father hoped that perhaps the environment at home would cheer her up. But as hours passed into afternoon, right around 1.00, mother exhaled a severe whiff of air. I was sitting by her side. She exhaled. And did not inhale, at which I lost my breath.

Mom had left us and she left me in such a morbid display of death. Father still rushed her to the hospital. To bring her back. The same doctors who had played with her body explained to him how mother's blood pressure had shot through the roof. It was hypertension that had drastically and almost deceivingly made her condition worse. Besides, there was such a reverberation of pain inside her body that she had to let go. Further, they unanimously concurred that the cyst was in fact a cancerous growth. What was going on? Cyst. Pain. High Blood Pressure. What was it that took her? Father refused to believe the half-baked explanations the doctors tried to stab down his throat. He was inconsolably enraged! While I just blamed mother for leaving us behind. If she had the will to live, she could've lived. But she didn't want us, and so left us. She died willfully, and as a child I blamed her.

I blamed her again, and again. All through my living life. Only if she were alive and well. And we could've talked about the embarrassing issues that burnt my skin. The leering eyes. The blood every month. The iron-deficiency. The ways of the world. The ways of my body. The demands of the men. All these issues needed simple answers as they weren't so complicated. But father didn't care to take this responsibility. Was he embarrassed or just indifferent? The man drowned his sanity in alcohol, how was he to mend my troubles then?

Time hence past, and as years cemented years, I forgot about the public hospital. Other incidents of similar nature happened like getting groped in public buses, getting teased and whistled at, and those shameless pattings and kisses by strange relatives and senior well-wishers. What was all that? I would crouch in shame. Always felt guilty as if I was wrong. My contrition became so naturalized, that it felt deserving. I believed I deserved it. After all they were my senior relatives, how could they be wrong. My dad had dinner, tea, and drinks with them. If he was right, so were they. One incident after another, it kept happening, whatever it was. And all I could do was forget and move on. I could only forget to care less. And forget I did while unlearning the caution a girl needs to learn to become a woman.

The two bridges, then I had to cross someday…

"Wh-what! Are you having a fit! Grace! You will get me into trouble! Wake-up!" Vicky was right on top of me.

"Wh-what where were you? I am fine! Get off!" Convulsing, I pushed her away.

I had fallen on the road. It was a minor fit. Vicky had gotten suspicious, and wanted to pry me open. But I kept her at bay, as I didn't want her snooping around my past. It was good, though, she had come when she had. As the road was long and winding, I didn't want to go on resurrecting my memories or have them worm in my head. Some memories hurt more than the incidents they remind us about. If only I could erase them. I guess that is why I went on meeting complete strangers and out of reach towns. To replace my fulsome memories with the tall tales, scandals and secrets of others. Perhaps…

"Fine! Fine! No need to get rough." She spoke and pierced me with her meddlesome eyes. Meanwhile I wiped my drooling mouth, tried to find my feet, and gained my moorings as non-suspiciously as I could.

"You took your time…" I asked in a plain voice.

"I was held up. Granny has me garden with her, you know. But you sure you are fine, it's like you seen a ghost?" She remained wickedly curious to know what ailed me. I had to suppress my hyperventilation, to keep her off my past. And then sought to change the subject. "I am good, Vicky. Where does he live?"

Vicky tried to be cordial and was affecting it. In the state she had seen me, I knew she must be drawing inferences between Noor and me. Curiosity was making her cordial. She had suddenly toned down her derision at me, hoping I would confide in her my worst beginnings into adult life. The girl really believed that she was cunning enough to outfox anyone. In her attitude it was discernible how much she craved for any piece of tantalizing news. Was her life boring that she needed masala to thrive on? Or had the Elder deputized her to scavenge for virgin secrets? In any case, the girl was viciously desperate to snoop around my panty drawers.

"Elder? Oh we are not going to his house. At this hour, he would probably be in the castle. But forget about it. Tell me if anything is upsetting you. It will take a load off your chest." Slyly decoding my condition, she pried again.

"His, what now?" I digressed again.

"His place where he…you will see. Anyways, I just need you to know, you can tell me if you want anything, we can be friends, why not!" Persistent, she was not letting go.

But as I was still tormented by what had come over me, I had to divert my mind. And the word castle, along with the mystery shrouding it, became a good diversion from my terrors. I asked again.

"Castle, aye?"

"Yes". She said dryly, realizing I was not interested to take her offer.

A castle, a place of belonging for a king and a queen. The Elder had a castle, a place he called a castle to engender his name with power, royalty and righteous divine leadership. Vicky defined his castle with endearing salutation that beckoned a silly reaction on my face. She was positively entertained by my reaction. She thought that once I would see the castle up close I would be eating my own words and reiterating with her the blue-blooded heritage of the Elder.

"Like a castle, castle?" Piqued and even irked, I asked again.

"Like I said you will see." She remained proud and replied rather ostentatiously.

"How far exactly?"

"Across the border…"

The border she spoke of, it was a mere chalk line. And innocuous as it looked, it wasn't difficult to understand the trauma behind it. There always has been a tragic story behind the making of a frigid border. Some people had that need to create a skirmish, then a riot and finally a hateful war. It was when the war ended, that it became awkward to say hello to the other fellow when just a while ago each had tried to kill each other. The border then had to become a necessary wall among neighbours.

As we walked closer towards the Zone of the Greys, the surroundings began to diminish in their civil upkeep. The entire milieu beyond the border carried a dishevelled look. As if purposefully left to rot so as to differentiate the two lands of the same land. Sheets of plastic, and layers of untidy bricks plastered with uneven cement held the houses together. It was a mangled mockery of nature's adoration with shape and thought that goes before it. The nose of the house was its anus, the head not far away, and the cock or vagina where one's belly button is supposed to be. Colours were in lighter, stronger, bolder, weaker, sharper, duller shades of grey. I would have had peace with it, after all there was an order in the disorder. But the litter of dogs and humans alike had me reach for my nose.

"Vicky, that dog seems rabid. Walk behind me." I spoke cautiously.

"Oh he is mad just like that. Wouldn't bite." But she only evaded my concern.

"And that pack of five behind him?" I again tried to reason.

"They are fine. They know me." But the girl, as she declared, seemed to be in cahoots with the dogs. The dogs knew Vicky and wouldn't bite her despite their obnoxiously rabid natures. Some pack of five also knew me, and they were mad but they still bit.

"The rats too? You know them?" I spoke sardonically.

"Of course not!" She realized my satire and again puckered her lips in disgust. As we went deeper and deeper into the Zone, the area began to give off an alarming stench. Disgusted, I exclaimed at the situation, "It stinks here! Don't you smell it?"

Indignant with a fury, she replied crossly, "It's our town, mind your tongue!"

How much rudeness of hers was I to tolerate? Her logic to consider dirt, stench, and some loser the Elder as a king had me grab for sanity. But the way she was behaving, it was clear that the girl was afflicted with adulation. She seemed to worship the Elder just because he spitted lofty words and parables that rumbled through the wind. Inane as it was, I but kept my silence and repeated the tired words…

"Sure sure."

With a pleasant company, I was walking down to meet the Elder. And all through the way I strained my eyes to find something of interest. The road seemed dressed with coal a dozen times, going by the layers of the old that I could see. Like a tree and its xylem layers to mark its age. But why was the road made to enact a tree? I asked Vicky about it. Perhaps I wanted to humour myself with some incredible justifications she might throw at me. So I asked her about the recurrent macdemization of the roads, and she beamed with a full show of pride.

"It's a habit of our road builders to cover up the potholes with fresh additional layers of a new road." Vicky spoke as sagaciously as she could.

"How many times?" I asked to know more. "It is done half yearly every month." She again replied as if what she said carried profound meaning. She was certain it was the right way of doing things. So certain even when she had not seen the right way. The Elder was the right way for her, how could then she know who was in fact the right way.

"What's their frame of reference? Who is this Elder copying or is it his idea of fun!" I asked with a scorn. But she didn't seem to mind my contempt, and again quite astutely confessed how the Elder had the makings of a great man, "You can be rude, but I will tell you one thing. A time will come when our roads will outgrow our houses and may be we'll reach the moon this way...That is the Elder's dream!"

Did Vicky just quip, or was she really serious? Reach the moon while standing on the roads. Roads that had layers and layers put upon them to cover-up the gaping holes and lacunae! I didn't wish to prove her wrong. So I cared less whether she made friends with rabid dogs, the filth, the Elder or the town got overrun with trash. Still her confidence, I was disturbed by her confidence. Living a certain way, she had adjusted so much, that a better way seemed ridiculous to her. She was so used to the Elder's way of life, that Granny and her part of town disgusted her.

"I had nightmares when I first came here..." Then Vicky began to unravel her own past to me. The road indeed was long, and silence from either one of us was awkward. So she spoke, and I encouraged her to do so. Her voice was calming even when it carried nonsense.

"Nightmares, what kind?" I asked curiously and with gentle concern.

If she was forced to escort me to the Elder, Vicky thought she might as well enjoy it. She tried to chat, forced at times it appeared. She wanted to get something out of her system, and I wasn't the one to interrupt her with my ideas. So I listened and Vicky continued...

"Well, my brother had the most vivid ones. He dreamt once that a man bitten by a rabid dog scrams into his room to bite him. He then goes rabid himself and bites everyone to launch an epidemic. A break out! Dog-flu, he heard people calling it. But it was just a nightmare. My brother is already very nervous around dogs, and when he sees a shindy of them here, he flips. He is very sensitive."

"Has he gone to the city?"

"Yes, for job and all."

"He has friends there? In the city, it can get a little dangerous. Lots of dogs."

"No."

Vicky was a curious girl. She was curious about many affairs. But things she should have been curious about, I was dangling right infront of her. But she didn't take the bait. The city. I came from the city. Was anyone interested in my story, no. Did anyone bother to ask the lady of the city? No, not at all. The town sent their naïve little boy Danny to the city without listening to the city-bred girl in their midst. Naturally then, if no one asked, I didn't intervene. The town had disinherited me from their library, and it would've been boorishly unsolicited to entertain them. Besides, I was going to meet the Elder, and it was paramount I met him. Nothing else mattered for the moment.

The Elder's zone. I found most of it empty. May be people got tired of his yoke and deserted him. Though there were some left. Like few oasis in a desert, I saw old men sitting on their uneven porches. Sad and thoroughly dismal in their faces. They were wasted of age already, and the spirit of second childhood was also parched from them. I saw sadness in a weary woman. She was standing in a bow-legged posture, untying her tresses, and drying them in the cold wind. The wind lifted her hair, and struck her face. And they flowed. Much like a weather-vane hen on top of townish houses. With my eyes open, I saw that ordinary spectacle. In another house that we passed by, an old man with a stooped back was reaching after his underwear caught in the wire. It was annoying for him, and painful I suppose too, to seize it. And the wind wasn't making it any easier. The house adjacent to it had an old couple watching him and they were giggling.

Vicky saw how I was overwhelmed seeing the Zone's old men and women broken in spirit. She asked me in a patient strain, "They look vulnerable to you, don't they?" I looked at her, and then again gazed at the old people. They were without doubt, morose with pain. So I replied, "They are old, and sad..."

She but repudiated my claim, and uttered with force, "They are sad, no! They have been armed by the Elder." Vicky was assertive as she declared it.

"Armed? This lot? What for?" I asked with a tinge of satire. And she reacted as if eager to welcome the consequence, "A war is inevitable. The Zones will fight, and one will survive...The Elder."

"You mean the LO? Fight the LO?"

"The Lights Off has it coming. Those bratty kids, they will have to surrender. The Elder will leash them." Vicky proclaimed it with fervor.

The old fighting the new. The new fighting the old. The town fought when the old needed to rest and the young needed to grow. In the Zone of the Greys, I saw the frail, slouched and limping old men and women. Even when they had sticks and stones flanking their houses, the old certainly wished for peace. But tired and wearied to act, they had rather decided to sit and stare and brood over it. As if peace would just fall in their laps. They had heirs, their children to fall back on. But sadly the Elder had scandalized the kids as a shindy of brats that must be belittled and controlled. And so left alone, the old in that part of the town had all the time to chew the past and drudgingly prepare for war. Whose fault was it? The old people for jumping to conclusions? Or the kids for letting it happen? If only they had talked and bridged that yawning gap between them, if only.

The Elder but was cunning. Subtly, he had exploited the grief of the old and turned it into hate. The old were aggrieved as the kids had left them to decay. It was then easy for the Elder to play them by weaponizing their grief into a mob of hate. While the kids left them in lurch as the old were either too busy or impatient to love them back. Disillusioned, mistrustful and hurt by the family bonds, hence both had run away from each other. The Elder wickedly capitalized on it, and despite his insipid ideology, he had them by the neck. What perturbed me was Vicky's role in it. What was she up to? The girl was a kid. And she had sided with the Elder. Did she feel like an incongruity in the Lights Off?

As she prattled on and on about the humanitarian projects of the Elder, the girl could sense I found her conviction highly appalling and even ridiculous. Vicky was certain that war was imminent. She also believed that the Elder would be a crowned king. King of what? Debris? The Elder and her errand girl had sadly ignored that inevitable eventuality.

Vicky paused herself to solemnly look in my eyes. She wanted and even demanded that I take her seriously. But the utter pomposity that she was cracking at me, it had my mind swirl. Nevertheless lighting my eyes with amber, I softly implored her to continue.

"Go on. I am listening"

Vicky would get confused at my reaction. She could sense I was riled up at her blind sense of patriotic fever, yet I would plead her to continue. Safe and in cahoots with the Elder, she thought it was power and not a paltry job that was being made of her. Of being an errand girl. I could see the confusion that was wringing her. The girl was unsure who to trust. The Elder seemed to notice her, so she trusted him. But Vicky couldn't see she was being viciously hoodwinked even when her subconscious was aware of it. But the girl refused to listen to her subconscious and remained deluded to believe the appearances. Seeing her, I felt pity for the girl as there was once a time when I also used to be like her. Bereft of caution. Caution is after all what makes a girl a woman than the strategic tales of coyness, manners, virtues and other kitty of severity.

Uncertain, she then continued with her capricious belief.

"With my eyes open, I see this ordinary spectacle. With them closed I see the Future. Aa! what do I know. I have friends everywhere. And I am not a warrior. No one will hurt me. The Elder will save me!"

"Okay…"

Vicky, though thoroughly ignorant, was still aware of the danger that was pointed at their future. But what that danger was, and who posed it, she didn't know. And that was where the problem rested. Hence she lived with a consolation, 'no one will hurt me.'

In the cities where I came from, Future was not called Future anymore but Fuction. Future had become a forgotten name, and the title of 'Fuction' was accorded to it. In the past, Future had promising connotations. Even when people had misgivings about it, they still dressed it as a definite end of the world. But the Future that began to live within the cities was neither promising nor a decisive end, so it was called Fuction. When the cities began to overflow, naturally Fuction started to make its way towards the towns, then villages and then some cabins far off in the mountains. In its wake then, leaders like the Elder began to mint power, power and power. Some future indeed.

As Vicky rambled on about her insecure future, I could see her confidence in the Elder was acutely fragmented. One minute she would believe him and the next she would second guess herself. She would stutter and then exclaim. Walk then limp. And then back at it again. Like a circle. She was false to her true self as she had rejected her own instincts and believed the Elder's. It was pitiful when she spoke about the man as if he was her guardian and a lover. The Elder was none of these and one look at him, I was certain of it. But the girl, even after spending hours of nights and nights with him, was pitifully deluded.

In some minutes, we reached a structure that was erected to stand as a gate. It looked as if it was intentionally anthropomorphized to look like four humans standing in vigil of the Grey Zone.

"Grace, you are well average tall. I will help you jump this gate."

"I can manage. Is the castle beyond this gate?"

"Yes. You first."

The gate. There wasn't any peculiar advantage to have built it. There were bushes covering up the weak rivets that made it stand. It was not a sturdy piece of work. A trickle of wind could have washed it away. Besides, it was locked. On its top, iron machetes in count of four were stuck not too close and not too far. Those iron machetes were emitting an illusion as if faces were marked onto them. It was uncannily disturbing.

"Be careful, you don't cut yourself."

"You don't a have a key to it, Vicky?"

"It's with him."

I climbed the gate and jumped to the other side of it. Vicky followed. Then I saw beyond it. Beyond the sturdy gate, a shamiyana, tattered but huge, jostling in the wind and swooshing here and then there. The ground that carried it, had stones and pebbles while the surroundings had the same potpourri of trash, I had been seeing in the Zone of Greys. There wasn't any road to lead us, but beaten tracks which went treading towards the door and the backdoor of the castle. The gate had machetes, and the castle was a cloth in the wind. How was he, the Elder, making a statement?

"Is that it?" I asked without hiding any reproach.

"Well yes! The castle."

"Vicky, you see your Future in there? Seriously?" I lampooned her while hoping to rile her up.

"It's everywhere, Grace and it's ours!" But she remained solemn, as if it was beneath her to argue with the likes of me. Her non-stop monologue about the town's future and the future that would be carved by the Elder was making very difficult for my bile to stay put. I but tried to keep humouring her. Just had her talking after all.

"All the Zones have a castle?"

"No, only this one. The Elder cares much for our Future."

I really tried to stay calm despite her constant use of the buzz word 'future'. Then she stopped while deciding which path to use. The front door or the back door. I didn't want to wait so I took the lead.

"No, not this way, Grace, we will go from the front door." She interrupted me.

"Why, would he be angry if we take the back door?"

"He wouldn't want you knowing we have a back door." Vicky spoke with an official sanction.

"There are tracks to it, of course anyone can tell!" I blurted out at the inanity.

"Still…" But she avoided my reaction. So I didn't make a fuss over it.

"Fine."

We entered the flamboyant castle, and it was peopled with a raucous crowd.

"Oh! Elder is not alone. He has company…" She spoke fraught with sudden flush of unease.

"That's good, right?" I asked with concern.

"Yes…of course, of course." She spoke fretfully. The girl was in a split-second peeled-off of her authority. She was taken aback to see so many people inside as if she was not expecting them. I could hear it in her voice, she was perturbed. If the Elder was her savior, why was she then afraid?

"You will have to go in barefooted." She interrupted me again.

"It's a holy castle?" I asked with serious concern.

"No, but out of respect, so take off your shoes." She ordered while judging the quality of my footwear.

"He's a saint then?" Intrigued, I asked her.

"No, just out of decency. Everybody does it." She spoke with an obedient expression.

What kind of man, the Elder was? That he had inflicted such reverence, such supplication and such fear in his people? The more Vicky stuttered in her dignity, the more I got impatient for the events to unfold already.

"It's crowded. Should we barge in?" She shuddered in her resolve to enter, as if she needed permission.

"I don't know, Vicky, you brought me here. You think he will come to receive us?" I replied with a sharp wave of my hand.

"No he-he's about to have a session." She replied meekly, and there was a hint of alarm too.

"Session of what Vicky?" I inquired with a little force to shake-off her sudden apprehension.

"A Session!" She shouted while still looking away.

"What session? Good Halo!" I was thoroughly upset with her hesitant responses.

I heard a microphone getting adjusted for volume. There was an echo to it too. The Elder was the speaker, and session of his speech was about to get started. On the raised pedestal two men other than the Elder were sitting. Who they were didn't matter to history, so I cared not.

"Vicky, so what are we standing here for, let's go in, no?"

"It's a little crowded for us, you know." She replied as if she knew how to handle the situation.

The Elder was aware that I was coming and he had his indecent entourage around him. Some were playing dice, the ruining game. One was apparently losing while others watched with a vicarious thrill. The tent was indecently crowded for a woman, and there were two of us. While I was curious, Vicky on the other hand was apprehensive to enter. Vicky felt exposed as if it was the first time she had visited the man. Standing outside, I saw the gang leering while the Elder was most explicit in his stare.

Seeing that we had reached an ugly impasse, Vicky then asked me for my better judgment. "What shall we do?"

Impatient and even startled at her rising trepidation, I yelled at her. "What do you mean? You brought me here Vicky, so let's go in!"

"No!" She answered back.

"Then I have got no use of you." It was but natural to feel that way.

"What?" And hearing me say that, the girl was bound to break.

There we stood on a revolving stage. Vicky, a prude felt uncomfortable beyond measure to enter. Even for her I think it was unexpected. Did Elder meet her nicely before, that his lewdness was news to her? Well, she was hot in her cheeks. And I was nostalgic with a migraine reaching my eyes.

"What shall we do? We can't go in when they are watching...I mean, how can we go in Grace?" The girl fretted, and I yelled at her with disdain, "Hmm. Ridiculous, utterly ridiculous! I am going back then! You stay here in your filial zone with him... he's your type after all."

Vicky was losing it. The shame of being stared at was breaking her. And I had thought she belonged to it.

"Why should I?" She questioned me, and it really needed a blunt answer. So I yelled out again.

"You visit him on daily basis! And look at you, you are fidgeting! Do you even belong here? Call him out if you got any clout in this place or are you just an errand girl!"

"I-I have but I will have to go in to-to do that. And there..." She was panicking.

"You don't know them? Wait, is this your first time coming here?" I asked curiously.

The girl was starkly ashamed. It was not the shame of leering eyes only, but of being fooled by the Elder into such a dirty trick. He wanted to show his clout, his men and their wicked mien, which he did but in the process he had without qualms sacrificed Vicky. He had not let her in on the plan, and she couldn't stomach it.

"I-I would be in and out generally in the morn, not this hour of the dusk."

"Then you should have scheduled like that."

"My brother...I couldn't. He had to be seen off. And the Elder insisted..."

Vicky could be apprehensive, and the Elder a tad revolting, I was a fool not to see it. The Elder had without intimating his errand girl, arranged that way of meeting. He wanted to show he was in control, well of course he was. It was his Bridge after all.

At Granny's, he sure haggled about my cup size, but wasn't able to find a price of it due to the old lady's intervention. But in his Zone, he thought with his men in drunken and disorderly state, he would be able to. I didn't blame Vicky at all for this ambush, for I didn't know whether she had a hand in it or not. Even if she had, it was Granny who had to be responsible. As an elderly guardian of that careless girl, it was her duty to break the need of caution to her. But the old lady just proved useless or helpless to teach Vicky the ways of the world.

Standing at the foot of the castle, while getting gawked at, I knew we should have left. But I wanted Vicky to come up with that response. I was exposed once and had people expose themselves to me. Nothing I could learn from it, for it was done, and I was far far from return. But Vicky still had time to learn. I was there with her. So I stayed put to make her realize what in fact was happening and why.

"So, Vicky, what are you going to do? Or do you blame me again for this predicament?" I asked.

"It's no one's fault Grace." She spoke as if calculating whether she herself was at fault.

"Then what are we doing here? Standing like lampposts! Call your Elder to meet you half way," I reasoned.

"I don't know. Don't know. G, I can't go in there!" Terrified of what to do and what not to, she called me G. The last time I had heard my name nicknamed like that was a long long time ago. And Vicky's nickname-calling overwhelmed me with such memories of ancient times.

Nevertheless, I remained stern with her, for her own good.

"Then?"

"Then what?"

I wanted Vicky to be the one to take the decision to leave at once. But as she wasn't budging, I feigned to.

"I am leaving."

"No, why but he called! You can't leave!"

Vicky refused to listen. She point-blank was refusing to let reason enter her mind. In that incident it was evident. She was certainly being used by the Elder. He had brainwashed her to such a level, my words were falling on deaf ears. What was I to say, but be rude again. So I was not gentle.

"Can't leave? Really? Get a hold of yourself, or are you a prisoner here?"

"Wait!" She cried out in fright.

"What, little girl?"

"It will rain soon, very heavily, we can't leave now." She spoke while pointing at some smoky clouds dotting the sky.

"Then there will be a rainbow, which I will gaze at from my doorstep!" I was but stern.

I turned back with a determined intention to leave. I even gestured angrily to suggest what a waste of time and venture it had been. I could hear Vicky still stuck at that post, screaming my name. She didn't budge and was stuck at the notion of how the world is innocent and how she was the only cunning one – delusions of grandeur indeed. I left with a firm footing as I knew if Vicky wouldn't come, the bawdy Elder certainly would. Not very soon, had I reached the gate, the Elder came running to pacify me. He was huffing for air. The old man had run from his post at the castle to catch up to me. Vicky also had followed him. The Elder didn't have the physique to be running like that. Seeing him catch his lost breath, I wondered. Why was he planning for a marathon war despite his failing health? How was he going to run it? Then again, he had his men and women who would run for him.

"I-I called you and you are leaving. That is not kindly of you, now is it?"

The man had a cheek to turn the blame on his guests. It didn't surprise me though. The Elder clearly was delusional of his power. He thought I would pleasure him like Vicky.

Hearing his crafty words, I replied in a beguiling tone in order to disarm him. After all, soft and sensual were my lips, as they hid the pointed and poisoned tip of my tongue.

"You were occupied, and we well… we didn't want to interrupt, I hope you understand."

Vicky was positively shocked to hear me change my tunes. And she thought she was the con girl. The Elder while listening to my kind words kept running his eyes to catch a glimpse of what lay underneath my dress. He also kept racing his mouth that even his spit tried to reach after my skin.

"Oh! Well! Vicky informed me that you had come, and I rushed, look barefooted, to receive you, my guest. Ha ha! This rotten soil must have smitten me with worms in my feet. Ha Ha!!" he laughed gratingly. His voice became even more guttural, while he continued to chatter and snigger hoarsely.

"Worms yes, one or two might…" I spoke with a gentle voice while trying hard to restrain my repugnance.

"Ha! Let's go back. To the castle. I believe you enjoyed our scenic Zone?" he asked with a serious strain.

"Yes very much. Is there a place we can talk without any crowd in there?" I whispered to indicate the delicacy of the matter I wanted to discuss with him.

"Oh, you mean the business! I like it. I like it. I have sent them away. They are my henchmen you know, gotta look frightening for the security and all. Besides only few remain to hear my sessions. They make my people snore, they tell me. Ha!" He spoke just the way he stared. Lecherously.

"Sure, sure."

"Grace, you are new here, I hope you understand." As we turned back to return to the castle, the Elder spoke while dialling up the solemnity of his tone.

"I don't understand what?" I asked without being too curious.

"You are new, and it is my duty to tell you who is friendly here and where the enemy lines are. Nothing is in black and white. It's all grey. I have heard you are from the city. It must be hard. Now you are here, and you need someone to protect you. Do you have anyone?"

It had begun to drizzle sweetly. Vicky was right, it did start raining. The trash mixed with rain water began to give off an offensive stench. But the mud and water of nature worked just fine. I took in a whiff of air, and it aroused my blood with oxygen.

The Elder asked again.

"Do you?" he looked at me patronizingly as if I desperately needed his care.

"Well…."

"Well, what?"

The crowd had left us. Vicky was the only one around. We all sat facing each other. He wanted a brief chat and so did I. He wanted the real business done, while I too. Though his manner of business was different than mine.

In the brevity of time, someone had to start asking the right questions. The Elder wished to question me of my life, which I knew a lot about. And as it was his life which concerned me, I put him under the scanner.

"Elder are you on the cloud nine, that you are feared? That you are a real time Grey?"

He was not expecting a straight question as that. I was also not expecting to put him under inquisition so soon. But it had started, and the Elder gulped back his obvious shock, and replied in the proper mien of a tolerable leader. If anything, his acting looked natural even when affected.

"I am, look around, my Zone is called by that name." he spoke with pride etched in his voice.

"What's in a name?" I but rebuffed him. Catching the slight in my tone, he got a little enraged at my being sassy, and roared, "You judging me as a fake?" He was positively flustered, as his ego had been pricked, so I appeased him, "No no why would anyone need to."

"No one needs to." He was certain.

I was terse, curt and rude, and I knew the risk too. But I also knew how the Elder thought. He was under the impression, if he answered all my questions, then I would repay him by acting as a nude dancing angel. The Elder wanted me impressed, bewitched and even drooling over him. Knowing his dirty state of mind, I knew I could importune that mighty leader. As he would eagerly suppress his ego to seize me there and then. The thought of it was irresistible to him. Meanwhile Vicky kept biting her nails at the shocking turn of events and I continued my deceptively discreet exposure of the Elder.

"So what makes you grey greyish or grey like. You must have a list of things, vile things." I asked in a polite tone.

"I am not vile Grace. I am lesson to everyone, if you mix the colours, evil is wrought. White and black cannot and should not merge, otherwise I will be born. My life is an oath to preserve the life of the town. An oath, Grace." He boasted as his spit flew right and left.

But, what was most noticeable about him was his thumping use of words. He had a way with words, did he practice oratory? Even when I would corner him, he would reply as if by reflex. I wasn't asking questions, more like shaming him for his nonsensical logic. But he would spruce up logic in his illogical answers, and it was commendable though condemnable.

"So that's what made you, intercrossing?" I laced my question with ridicule, but he was dense to catch it.

"Yes." He was again certain.

"Explain to me how that messes everything up?" I raised another question.

"I am a living proof." He was just so convinced of himself. If he had been a clown with such wit, I would have liked him. The town would have liked him. But he was aspiring to be a leader on account of his laughable wit, well that made him dangerous.

Again, with hidden contempt, I probed.

"Oh-okay. So your mom and dad were different strokes, huh. And the mess has got nothing to do with your errors but with the color of your skin, or theirs?"

"Errors? What errors? I say again I am Grey in totality. I am not vile. I am lesson to everyone, if you mix the colours, evil is wrought. White and black cannot and should not merge, otherwise I will be born. I am a living proof, this zone is of how it messes up everything."

He just repeated himself. I guess the Book of Genes he had read, was the only book he had read. And that too wrongly.

"You intend to bring a change?"

He fisted his hands, and declared with hate, "Yes, even if I have to shed blood for it."

"Whose?" I asked innocently while he raised both of his arms, fisted the air, and clearing his guttural throat, pronounced. "The LO's! They will cry for mercy. I know. Those brats will even cry to their Granny for help. I have heard the word mercy some many times that my arms move deliberately against this word, as if out of disgust for it. I could blame the LO for it. They keep using their tongues to utter this syrupy word. Knowing very well that my arms can only be cut with arms, not rhetoric tongues."

The Elder and I were engrossed in our talk. While from time to time Vicky would snort her nose to make her presence felt. But the man wasn't interested to pay her the attention she wanted. The respect she had bragged Elder had of her. What defect was in the air, that the girl was unaware of the Elder's game plan? Like some weakling, she was hooting for the bad king. Believing, he would be on her side and would not harm her. Hoping to remain protected in return of the favours he unashamedly asked of her.

"If that is true, Elder we all would be armless."

"Ha, ha yes yes. But for some parts of the world, armless men would be a blessing on us all." He spoke thoughtfully as if he had come up with a new fact of wisdom. Then seeing me raise my eyebrows at him, he continued, more like threatening me for my impunity "You are a stranger. A new one. But you are on the foothills of Granny's alps! I can't touch you. Come out of her protection, and then we will see, huh!"

"You intend to make me armless?" I asked to expose his intentions.

"Oh I have others things planned, arms you can keep. I will break something you keep behind your crossed…ha ha…You need not worry." As the Elder began to slip into his original intentions, Vicky got intensely exasperated. I would look at her, when the Elder would smear me with such indecency. I looked at her to make her see what she had gotten herself into and that there was still time to get out. I wished for her to know and see how he treated girls as a mistress not a confidante or a friend. Actually, it didn't really matter to me whether she still consorted with him or not. But I still tried to do my itsy-bitsy part to narrate to her the cautionary tale. Lest she crossed the Bridge in the mist.

"Right… Tell me what is this feud in the Zones? You are so derisive of the LO." I asked.

"Yes the feud…." He paused to recollect as to why was he fighting them anyway, then remembering something, he resumed. "We had a blackout here once. And I was out of candles. I was at the gate, and waited for some time for the lights to come back, but they didn't. So groping in the dark through the broken ground, and sidestepping any dangerous stone or a glass, I looked for some light to show me direction. But I fell on my head, and barely made it to my place. I had blood all over my clothes. The next day I find, those brats had used up all the power, and there was a big fuse. HA!"

"What did you do?"

The Elder was reaching the expert level of his hate speech. He desperately wanted to be asked about what he could do to change the present and secure the future. It was fun watching him blow hot air, and watching Vicky get mesmerized by his antics.

"I complained to Granny, and if she hadn't stopped me, I would have had their heads by my machetes! But their arms, yes their arms I will cut." He was abhorrently hateful, so I asked him outright, "What if they think of doing the same to you?"

And he retorted with absolute certainty, "They can't."

"Why?" I asked again to probe what powered his mad enterprise? What acquitted him of his mad crimes? And what made him the mad Elder? And he replied with pride, "Granny is on my side."

"Granny? You like her Elder?" I asked thinking perhaps they were a power couple. But he cringed, and scoffed at what absurdity I was spewing, "Nonsense! I am not old as she is. "

The Elder was into young girls, and liking Granny was, as his face declared, gross. The man clearly valued his youngish virility. Calling Granny old, who was nearly his age or perhaps younger, proved that he was an old raunchy lecher. All this made me feel pity for the girl Vicky. But I couldn't show any concern as she wouldn't have it. Even so, the girl was intensely disturbed by our conversation. Disturbed and jealous. The Elder was an inveterate lecher, and Vicky wouldn't spot it. Was her love for him that strong, she didn't see he had none? Pitiful.

"Just checking, she could like you, you know. LO doesn't bother you, and you are allowed privileged passes to her town, why?"

"Why?"

"She might just like you."

I had hit the kernel of the Elder's war plan and what manner of ideologue he was. Though it was a reluctant exercise on my part, I enjoyed it nonetheless. Mostly people like him went on to become leaders of the world. And what brave worlds they left behind that made histories weep blood. From Future to Fuction. It certainly begged the question – was it in our ignorance they grew or in our deliberate evasion?

As I figured out what I could from the Elder, I didn't feel like analyzing him anymore. That would've only ennobled the absurdity he stood for. So, it was time to finish the tête-à-tête sooner than later. Of course, I was aware of what he expected after the session's conclusion. His quid pro quo policy that I literally open up for him.

"The Elder, if the session's over, I shall take Grace back to her cabin," Vicky was naturally aware of what was to come next. Delirious to leave at once, she reasoned to end the day with only words shared.

But the Elder had his desires restrained for far too long then. He scoffed at Vicky, and spoke with a biting scorn, "Grace can stay. You should leave. Now!" As he uttered his ultimatum, he looked at me, and began to lick his dried lips. Dried because of the temper of his mind. His wanton mind. The more he would indulge in that activity, the more Vicky would muster her courage to confront him. She knew what it implied having seen it for herself.

"It has stopped raining. It will be no trouble, I can take her back, the Elder." Undeterred, she spoke again. But the Elder got more ferocious, and barked at the girl, "What did I say? You leave, Now!" Vicky, then, lost her will to confront him. She was in fact petrified to have confronted him. It was evident in her shame. She felt betrayed that he could direct his lechery at someone other than her. Vicky indeed was distraught. In a matter of scenes, the Elder had broken the popular myth of her illusion of love. She quickly asked for forgivingness for upsetting him, and prepared to leave. But then someone entered the castle, and the Elder was furious at another interruption.

"Jon, you skunk, what are you still doing here!" The Elder barked at the boy who had interrupted us.

The boy was the Elder's page. He looked underfed even when muscular. He approached us. The Elder seeing him, blasted into a fury, which then made me realize fool or not, the man was an angry fool. It wasn't then difficult to analyze why Granny didn't fear him, for she only saw a fool in him. But the LO, who were in revolt against him, saw an angry fool.

"The microphone was still on, the lights were on, I came to switch them off." The boy spoke timidly.

"Switch them off? You think we are the LO! We will have the bloody lights on for long we like, even in sun and scorching sun! You made me dinner yet?"

"Not yet."

Though the boy was getting browbeaten, he in the full open view of the Elder kept staring at me. That stare was more of a concern than anything like the Elder's.

It was as if instinctually he could tell I was in trouble. And he wanted to block the Elder from harming me. I could see he had in a blink of an eye happened to like me.

"Bastard aren't ya. Grace, why don't you join me for dinner, and then later..." he winked at me.

"No, I am good. Vicky, would you want to join him?" I refused him point blank. And rubbed salt to Vicky's wound as the Elder didn't invite her. I wanted her to run off to the LO than allow the Elder to abuse her anymore.

"I am fine, really just fine." The girl was but grim with shame. And the Elder didn't even care to give her a shoulder. He remained starkly aloof of the pain he had put her in. And then he realized how Jon was staring at me.

"Jon, you skunk! What are you staring at our guest for? I am sorry for his behaviour, Grace. His indecency as well. He broke my eggs today, was running with his hands about them. I will beat him later."

Jon still kept staring in my direction. I felt a shudder run through my veins. It was a shudder of a different kind, one which I happened to like. I liked it so much that the Elder's impertinent remarks at the boy, made me feel every sting of it. Jon nonetheless kept staring unlike the libidinous way the Elder would. The Elder could sense I was attracted to his page, something which irked him even more than Vicky's constant gesture for attention. Disturbed to see I was more fascinated by the slave than the master, he pushed me out to the real world.

"Grace, where did you go?"

"Yes, no. I think it is late already. When will you have your next speech?"

"You wish to attend?" he asked ecstatically.

"Why not?" I replied with a fake yes.

"You can stay, I have a special speech prepared for you." He spoke while again licking his lips. It had become a nasty sight and as it began to bug me so much, I let out a brief scorn. "Huh..."

Seeing how I was not being agreeable, he asked again. A tad more repulsively.

"You will stay, I shared my part of the bargain. I need you to share your secrets."

The Elder had become so confident of his sexual prowess that he was sure I would reciprocate my part of the bargain. It was his inanity that almost made me giggle. And as I couldn't contain it inside. I giggled at him.

"Ha ha. You are serious, aren't you!"

He was shocked at being taken so lightly. But what was interesting to see was the look on Vicky's face. It was pure diamonds. Vicky was waiting for me to fumble so she could dance back into the Elder's arms. Jon, well he was concerned about me before but after my insult, he took it upon himself to distract the Elder. Even at his own peril.

He intervened without any care for his own safety. "The dinner, you will have it here, or in your house?"

The Elder was still seething in shock, and Jon repeated in tandem.

"The Dinner! You will have it here, or in your house?"

The Elder did not listen. He was enraged. I saw his red fiery face, his flared nostrils, his dumb silence, and that vein raring to burst in his head. I had opened up his wounds, and so it was upon me to nurse him a little lest Jon got hurt because of me. I had due to some peculiar reasons, begun to like the page after all.

"The Elder, how about we keep my part of the bargain for the next time? A reason to meet again."

The Elder was as I had thought pacified a little. He was furious at my crass behaviour and when I gave it up, he was no longer mad. But as I was becoming a forbidden secret, he became even more forward and vile. As if it was his right and a just right to have me or any other girl for that matter.

"You will come or else I will have to make you…" He didn't conceal his wantonness anymore.

"Yes, yes. I will visit next time. I will be prepared." I assured him.

"I see. You will come straight to my house." He spoke with authority.

"That would be nice…" I assured him again.

As Vicky and I made a move to leave, the Elder stopped Vicky at the door of the castle. He held her by her arm, and then covered the girl in an insensitive embrace. I felt awkward as he stared at me while talking to her.

"Vicky you can stay."

She was nothing to me. But my eyes goggled to see him compromise the private vicinity of the girl in my presence. It was all a show. He wanted me to regret leaving him. And wanted me to see that it could have been me in his arms. That I might've deprived him of a sweaty night, he still could have his business after all.

"I can?"

The girl was killing me. Despite the entire exposition I had made on the Elder for her benefit, she was eager to be used by him. She couldn't even see, that all that time when he had wrapped his arms around her bosoms, the old man had his eyes locked at mine. Why was she blind? Why was he dirty? Why was I caring? The Elder didn't reply to her. But gently poked his hand at her bottom, which had me look for the door and leave at once.

"Grace?"

I had almost left, when he called from behind.

"You would know the road back, right?"

He was still rubbing his hands at indecent places. While Vicky, a young and foolish girl, let him use her as a toy. She was dastardly confused it was love.

"Yes I know."

He took his other arm, and closed shut Vicky's eyes. Whispered something to her, and began cupping her bosoms as tightly as he could. She twitched a little as it must have hurt. But let it happen anyway for she thought that was the pain of love. I turned around, in shame, despair and anger while leaving the dark abyss of the Elder's castle. The Elder was filth. Age, his colour and his dress code, did not make him one, but his state of mind. And what made his outlook so bleak and dangerous? The women on the street? The men listening intently to him? The girls who trusted him? The boys who worked for him? His parents? Where was the epicentre indeed?

Jon followed them unbothered as if he was used to these events happening that way. It would have been wise to fight the Elder and drag Vicky out of the castle back into the Black and White Zone. But then again I wasn't her Granny, yet when I should have been. Besides she had seen enough and still wished to stay behind, so what more could I have said to her to change her stubborn mind. It was certain and it was exposed what kind of relationship they had. So I tried to brush it away and forget about it.

I reached the shack soon enough. It was soon for I knew the path, and knew the time and length of it to moan over its distance. I was cold when I reached the doorstep. It was a feeling then but even a feeling can hurt physically. I guess it was the dread of the cold which killed me more than the cold itself. But I was cold all the same. Tired too, I just wanted to grab the quilts and get under it. And sleep with eyes firmly shut and body drawn in the way I once was in my mother's womb. It was good of me in the womb, extending myself would have hurt her. But I still did hurt her while coming out. She had been sickly ever since my birth, so used to say my mother's mother to me. I didn't understand what she was insinuating. How could I? My mother left before she could teach me these things. Unlucky for me, and my mom, and father and everyone, I still did not deserve what happened under the Bridge…

"Grace? You in there?" It was a familiar voice.

"Yeah…I am coming!" I opened the door, and it was Halo.

"Oh! You were sleeping, I am sorry. Here Granny sends the soup. I came before, you weren't here. It's hot you should have it now."

Halo had brought Granny's soup. Did Granny send her to offer soup or spy on me? It was obvious. Granny would want to keep tabs on me, that is why she had offered me the cabin in the first place. The cabin was close to her house, she was indeed spying. There was no doubt.

"Hmm. I will thank her myself, where is she, at home?" I asked inquiringly.

"Oh don't bother, Grace. Thank me instead. You owe me…" She spoke sweetly the way she always did to win approval.

"Of course. Come in, we can share." I invited her in all earnest, but she calmly yet hurriedly refused my invitation as if she had to report back to Granny. I didn't look much into it, and asked her again just in case, "You sure?"

"How sweet, but I had the lion's share, it's all yours. I will see you later. Sleep tight." She again spoke in a hurry, which was quite unlike her gregarious and clingy nature.

Still, I didn't mind, "Thanks Halo, see you later."

She left, and I relished the hot soup. Hot soup even after going behind Granny's back. I felt a little naughty while lapping it up. Besides, it was cold and I was hungry from all the pomposity of talks and churning of egos. The soup was a fine rest to my mind. I hoped it would bring me good dreams. Good or bad, it was a dream I dreamt. A dream…

Chapter 5

To Be The Last Supper

"Burn her. This cunt! Cops will be here soon. Burn all of these cunts! No one can catch us! Burn them all!"

While crossing the Bridge, it was Rustam's warm pashmina that I had wrapped around my chest. A jacket underneath. With pants touching my feet. Knitted plaits running through my hair. The wind would toss my scarf and a little skin would show. But then I would grab it and cower underneath it. It was the peak of dawn yet cool winds of the night were still flying about. I was but warmly covered to brace myself against it. I was riding my cycle to visit a place that my father called the Tortoise Mountain. The mountain was so far and deep into nature, where even the graves weren't made. There could be places deeper than graves, I had been there. Walked there. Sat and bobbed my head casually about them. Dad and I would bond at such places. Crack jokes, hear things about school, and make tall tales out of the silly idiosyncrasies of our family. No one was spared. From aunties to uncles, and cousins to cousins, we had pet names and pet anecdotes for everyone. It was a jovial exercise that we indulged in to keep the banal and the baneful happenings of our life at bay. Our family like any other family on earth had its moments of unreasonable grief and then boundless joy, which would come and go as they pleased. But I could never have imagined that one day the grief would decide to stay and stay forever.

Things changed like the sea in a storm when mother passed away. Father relapsed into a violent man of grief and the loss of his wife stole his duties for her child. Day after day, it became uneasy for me to talk to him. Hear him. Stay around him. Mom's passing had left such a gaping hole that he started to beat me to get out of it. It was frightening when he would come home or knock at my door or leave home. He could do anything, say anything and in front of anyone. I would be fitful even without a fit. Threatened to sneak around in my own home. When the steps I took, doors I opened and the air I breathed began to annoy him, I had to become a thief in my own home.

The jugular pumps the heart and mother's death had cut his. So he died every day, to live the next and he blamed me for the livid temper of our lives. I was the reminder of his loss and I became the cause of his loss. As a naive little child I could not counsel him, so he thought I was indifferent. And for that he beat me even more. Dad was a good man who just the other day brought me toys. Then, as his growing bile began to flow in his veins, he started to whip his belt on my back. Sometimes it would be a strap of my school water bottle. Green colour it was.

Astutely then I began to hate my mom than hating him. Anyone who would look like my mom, talk like her or even had a habit that would be reminiscent of her,

I would shudder with hate. It was strange, how I began to misplace my fear of father towards strangers who bore any resemblance to my mom. Not just fear but livid hate too. When dad would cross my way, I would hatefully wrinkle mom's photographs one at a time. After he would be done with his piercing words, I would pray to my Maker to give my mom hell. Anything and everything I did to endure her helpless absence, as she was not there to protect me after boldly giving me birth.

With age, I learnt to tolerate dad's miscreant behaviour and so the hate towards mother also subsided. But when I would again get consumed by it, I would run off to the Tortoise Mountain. Sometimes father would also come along and sometimes I would go alone.

That lovely green tortoise mountain. With father, planning an expedition of this sort, would be one of the days when he would revert back to humour. The way he was when mother was alive. Cheerful. Decent. Humane. Human. On the mountain, he would revert into his natural form while allaying the constructions of fateful hate and grief. Though it should have made me happy, but I was not. It was tough to tolerate him when one minute he was kind and the other unkind. Then kind and again unkind. So even when he shifted from being distantly kind and then unkind, I maintained my emotional distance from him. It was the only way I could moor my senses than have them cast me adrift.

It was during one such trip, that father got me a cycle so I could ride in the wind. Insulting as it was, I smiled at his effort to cover up his beatings by giving me a band-aid. As I rode it, he ran by my side as we crossed the bridges, took the unbeaten routes while climbing further away from civilization. Towards the Tortoise Mountain. In hours of trifling with time, at last we reached the place. Though we had seen it a million times, it still managed to steal our breath away. Even the mist cleared itself from it, as if spotlighting the rock of beauty for us.

The tortoise mountain was a rounded rock, finely weathered by rain and dust. And had tortoise type scales on its back. It was mushroomed by a pack of wild green mountains, and stood out as a clean shaven honey-combed head. A funny looking exotic mountain, it was. A rivulet swam around its borders, and some stones immersed in it looked like stepping stones. The tortoise rock was accessible from only one side, as the other sides were blocked by the adjacent mountains.

When we reached the place, father started the climb and pulled me up. We sat on its back, and wondered if a tortoise neck would just scurry out of it. It was a serene time with a gentle cool downpour and tweets of exotic birds and beasts. Father was lost. I was lost. We were lost which was why we were there in the first place. On the mountain, I bobbed back and forth with my legs crossed close to my chest. The mist would blow whiffs of cool wind and my hair would swim in it. It made me feel like some queen with nature at its command. It was such a place where even dismal rains seemed golden. The sting of sun calming and the matters of grief mere songs.

After few moments of calm silence, father then began to talk rather mince, mumble and mutter. It was as if someone else was speaking through him. Someone he had killed by his hands.

Father confessed his guilt of giving me such an irrational childhood. I wouldn't believe his words as not only were they paltry, they were also temporary. It was his hate which was decisive as come night or day, it would certainly come. While his confessions of hate were only effervescent as the beauty of a bud. In his eloquence and composed heart, dad then went on to paint an elegy of his vitriolic life. How his crudeness towards me hurt his wet body like a flash of lightening. How it pained his heart and anon. He mourned in mournful sighs of a griever while at length confessing the virulence of his nature. I but intimidated myself to remain stoic to his charms as it was hard to suffer him otherwise. It was always the same with him. On the mountain, dad would look in the mirror and feel contrite for his madness. And when we would return, he would no longer remain a repentant miserable fool.

Tired of his satanic whimsicality, one day then I crossed the Bridge alone. Without him and his fickle temper. I had also worn the embroidered drape of my dear friend. As the breeze of the setting sun was foul, it tossed my pashmina and a little skin showed. Seeing the glint in my eyes, one to four officers then began to whistle ever so passionately. Next they tore my clothes, clawed at my skin and drank the sweat of chastity on it. Even when I had covered the vulgar parts spread across all over my body, it didn't matter. The skin of my hair and of my flesh was all in the dark, still the officers were provoked. Covered or not, it wouldn't have mattered. Night or day, it wouldn't have. If only I had flayed my skin as well.

They wanted me, I was there. They had me, I was there. It was lust. But then they were viciously violent as well. As if I was a reminder of their grief and a cause of their aggrieved life. Such hate that in comparison the salt on a wound would have tasted sweet. When they were done whistling, it was the hate in their eyes which then moved them to rip me apart. Viciously.

Minutes into it, the officers then rested themselves on the deforested grass, while peacefully absorbing the dew, the moonlight, the brooks and the cool breeze. The hate was gone in a flicker, the way it grew and subsided in my father's temper. The officers then were no different. When the sun was setting, they were brimming to hurt me. Then as the moon rose, they were serenely absorbing its light. As hours passed into hours, the Head then sat by my side while carefully straightening my ruffled hair with his long fingers. Then he took my hand and began to read my destiny. "Two kids, you will have. Husband will love you. A nice house. In the suburbs. Gentle neighbours…" He spoke while continuing to gaze at the growing night sky, and then at my palm to find a common crease of stars in both. I kept straining my eyes at the jacket, to cower myself in shame as I was naked in front of men. While I scavenged for something to hide behind, the Head kept on looking intently.

One gasp at a time, then my breathing began to wane. It was time to recite my last prayers but before I could say Amen, they buried me deep.

Days later, as I was still decently covered in mud, the officers were again provoked to chase after me and burn the evidence of my dishonour.

The officers had proudly believed I would stay in the dark for years of darkness to come and go. Not realizing I was to be their last supper as my kind Maker was going to make them pay.

"Burn her! Burn them! Burn these cunts! Burn the graves!" First officer screamed the orders.

"Head, what's the matter? No one will know. We will burn all these bitches! No evidence of what we did!" Second officer cried out to bolster the diminishing spirit of the Head.

"Head? Head? What are you muttering! Why is he acting like that! Why? Why? Why!" Third officer was losing it just like his boss.

"Our past is catching up. There is no escape. We will die thousand deaths." Fourth Officer had already lost it.

"Shame! Shame!" The Head gasped.

The Head was hysterical with shame as his dishonour was no longer his own to keep. The terror of a public revelation was wringing his mind to mutter – Shame! Shame!

First Officer: "Don't pour the oil, they will see you. No! No! No! The reporters are here too. Stash the trophies, they mustn't know about them. Burn the evidences!"

The First officer cried out as he stood before my grave. I was buried deep and still his screaming noise pestered me. I couldn't even press onto my ears to keep him out.

The Head: "Shame! Shame."

There was a ruckus outside. While the officers were trying to burn the evidence, I heard a ruckus. Cops! Reporters! The entire cavalry of law had decided to pay them a visit. Buried in the dark, I kept my eyes closed. As the matters of the living didn't matter to me anymore.

Second Officer: "The cops are here. The cops are here! Head! Where are you running? We must act normal!"

The second officer cried out as he stood before my grave. The officers had once disturbed my life. And when I was buried deep, they still couldn't keep out of my life in death.

The Head: "Shame! Shame!"

Third Officer: "Why is he afraid? He was not afraid then? He is freaking me out!"

Third officer cried out as he stood before my grave. I was unable to rest in my lasting repose. At least, I prayed, let me rest in peace.

The Head: "Shame! Shame!"

I kept my eyes closed. Let me dream sweetly in my death, I wished. But the officers kept screaming at each other.

Fourth Officer: "He has lost it. We are exposed. Dishonour upon us! Upon our families! Shame! Shame!"

Fourth officer cried out as he stood before my grave. The terror that they had shoved into my life. Like a hell hound was catching up to them.

First Officer: "These cunts will have us hanged! We shouldn't have buried them. Burnt them! I told you to burn them all! "

Second Officer: "No they will see us! They will see us! Head do not go that way. Reporters are here!"

Third Officer: "Shame! Shame!"

Fourth Officer: "Shame! Shame!"

The officers wanted to burn the nooses which were going to hang them. But they were very proudly late. Reporters had barged in. Cops had barged in. To cuff and shame the fallen angels of law. Shame shame everywhere.

The police took out the handcuffs, they had their pistols armed. While the reporters who were flashing their vivid cameras, had their recorders armed.

The officers then began to flee. The assembled reporters and the police began to chase. Meanwhile I kept myself immersed in the mellow peace of my serene burial.

First Officer: "The Head is running away! We will be hanged! Our shame! Our families! We will be hanged!"

Second Officer: "The reporters! The cops! There is nowhere to run. Mist hide us! Mist hide us! Trees hide us! Trees hide us! There are no trees here! Weeds hide us! Bushes hide us!"

Third Officer: "Shame! Shame!"

Fourth Officer: "Shame! Shame!"

Chapter 6

Tear My Pretty Dress And Hit Me

"Be mine Marcella. Mine own. The dream of who-oo-m is heaven…Be mine, my Maarcella-aa…what the duck? Who locked me out? Did I? Who is in there? It is my shack!"

I was still under the horrid dream that a musical voice woke me up. The voice was garishly pesky. The sheer prick of it was so strong that I almost had another migraine. Someone was singing and not in a good way. The singer was not too far and not too near. Its voice was shrill like nails scratching the black-board. There was a strange tune latched to it. It felt classical one minute and then all nonsense the other. It was a boy's voice but it was strangely mannish.

As I needed time to climb out of my dream, the boy, in his impatience, started hitting the door with his foot. That made even more noise, which potentially threatened any repose I wished for myself. Rushing to the window, I angrily looked outside. There was a drunken boy outside the shack. He knocked, then drank, and then blasted his voice with mannish fury.

"Open my door! I don't have the key! Open it before the Witch gets me!"

In an instant he fettered my curiosity when he joked about the witch, some witch. That magical entity which had the town in a tailspin. How could he overlook the horror and paste humour on it? It was not an entity to joke about. Granny had to tarnish her goody-goody nature in order to suppress the story of the witch, some witch. It had created a chaotic mess from which to escape was no laughing matter. One girl had fallen ill. One boy had to cross swords. Woods had become forbidden to enter. How could the drunkard then joke about it? His trivializing of the issue did not sit well with me. After all, I was seriously into the whole witchy thing. And if it was not a serious issue to begin with, I sure felt like a fool. What if the whole affair was nothing but a witch-hunt? Even the thought of it was disturbing. I had to calm myself thinking perhaps the boy was just being drunk and that it was his intoxication doing the talk for him.

Despite his outrageous belittling of the witch, some witch, the drunkard but certainly seemed handy. All drunkards talk. They spill the secrets which sober men and women of the society keep hidden in their closets. I needed someone like him who would talk, and talk garrulously. I wanted to know about so many things. Waiting for the secrets to reveal themselves would have taken ages. Certainly then, the drunken boy seemed to be a viable option. Forlornly I had believed Granny would condescend to tell me the secrets or the Elder would deign to. But no luck there. Just when I had apparently lost, a jolly young drunkard came knocking on my door while singing his lungs out. The mannish boy was frantically eager to meet who had crawled into his shack. However, all said and done, his hitting the door with his pissant foot was nonetheless pestering.

"Will you knock it off? I am coming!" I blurted out in annoyance of it.

"A lady calls! Who is in there? I don't know your voice? Hello?" Unfazed, he blatantly asked.

Unwilling to answer the door at his discourteous request, I kept reading him from the window. While he went back to singing his drunk lyric, "Fine, fine. Dance in the trance of a d-d-drink. In every pa-aa-use I find a want for another d-d-drink. I don't have all d-d-dday you know."

The boy was an odd fellow. He was not a drunk but he was drunk. It was slightly noticeable that he was acting. Though he was a little tipsy, but the depth of his drunkenness was an act. Perhaps, he wanted to be left alone and so had put on the repellent mask of a drunk.

While I read the boy's skulking shoulders and bright eyes, I was fascinated by the bluish overtones of his pants. From an angle, it looked green and then it would look sea-green which was also the colour of his eyes. He had the sleeves of his bold red shirt rolled up in half. Hair was golden black with streaks of white lines here and there. Face had drooped with scary black dents under the eyes. Though he was a young boy, his drinking had made mannish and not in a good way. As I read him from his attire to his skin, the boy seemed quite predictable and that made him insufferably dull. To top it, he mocked the witch, some witch and it broke my head in half.

The Elder had a spotless white bark of clothes on him, and by his face and gait, many poems could be composed on him. The day of the puke which was so tastelessly named, even that event shook me to dance with it. Even the Elder's page had stirred the ambers of my heart that I was infatuated to some extent.

Certainly, the town was a revelation at every corner. The antique post-mill. The witchy woods. The border made of chalk-lines. The flying castle. The humanoid machetes. The elegant stutter of Mrs. Portia. What a revelation the town was, except when it came to the drunkard. He had no pun about him. Was he a brother to Halo, as both didn't evoke any thrill in my mind? He was utterly predictable and his inebriation was a shallow act. Swinging his arms, it was predictable. Singing with a drunken strain, again expected. Sighing with a grin, too banal indeed. Undoubtedly, I felt so disappointed that I wanted to scorn him. Like a jeremiad. Pull his hair. Like a maenad. Kick in his groins. Like a horse. True, my reaction over him was too exaggerated and even uncalled for. Then again, I was disturbed in my mind due to the cunt dream I was under. And his debasing of the witch, some witch further disturbed my calm.

"The Witch is coming! The Witch is coming! Open up!" He again cackled with affected fear while turning the magic entity of the woods into a comic relief!

In a thud then I opened the door. In a thud then he swerved his head to look in my direction. I heard his neck bones crackle a bit, as he had swung his neck in quite a rush. It had to hurt. The sheer force of it. Then, while looking at me with admiring eyes, he gushed at the strange stranger standing by his door. "Wow, Who-who are you?" I didn't feel like replying. Instead I asked with redoubled force, "Who the hell are you?" But he remained persistent, and smoothly rephrased his original question, "I asked first. Who are you, my lady?"

I tried to be patient with him. I had to be patient. He seemed to know what magic danced in the woods. And that was the extent of my fascination with him. Rest, no matter how much he ingratiated to be liked, I only abhorred him for his banal dullness. Even his drunken stupor was an act. It made him look like a fool. A common fool at that. Who would want to look like a common fool?

"You drunk?" I asked brusquely.

"At your service" he bowed his head, and replied in a gallant tone. I didn't like his frivolity, no matter how courteous. So I only ranted back, "What? Are you mad?" Despite my explicit rudeness, he still spoke slickly, "You know my name."

"Drunk? Is that your name? Really?" Startled, I asked him, while he bowed down his head again, and sang it out, "My name is Drunkard!"

Amused and at the same time repulsed at his overly predictable carriage, I yawped at him, "Seriously!"

He nodded his head while thoroughly ignoring my jibes. Then he spoke while remaining persistent to befriend a creature who had his home to herself.

"And what is a fair person as you doing in this choked-up town?" he asked curiously. Snobbishly I remained quiet, and he again pursued, "You are from these parts?"

"I am from the city…" I declared but not with pride.

"You come from the city? I have been there too and made it back." He but spoke with pride in his voice knowing only the brave can survive the city. Suspicious of whether he had been to the city, I inquired somewhat impolitely, "What do you know about it? All of it?"

Though I was impolite, I was serious while posing him that question. My life had been too grim to waste it over merry lies and foolish playfulness. That is why, in every meet, I had to look for profit than entertainment. Every venture had to have a reasonable purpose, an advantage and some worthy target. If not, then I would move on even if it meant acting rude and hurting someone's dignity. Needless to say, Drunkard was wasting my time and I had to attack his mindless gibber-gabber to stop him. Even when I was fierce, he would still let me degrade him.

Not thinking too much on how I was testing him, he carelessly responded to my query. "City? Well, not much I think."

Unimpressed, I announced to his face, "Well what use then." I uttered in disgust. And that finally put him on edge. "No! I know enough." The drunkard backtracked. Perhaps he had begun to realize I didn't wish to prolong the tedious banter between us. And perhaps he had even begun to like me. But then again, he couldn't have been enamored by someone as inelegant as I was. So if that was not the case, it was certain the drunkard wanted to feel useful. He wanted to show he was capable and that he was worthy to be made a friend of. The mannish boy was needy for attention.

"So you know a lot?" I asked in all seriousness.

"No, yes…I didn't before, but do now. I mean I knew it already." And he coughed up whatever response he could. Drunkard tried hard to impress upon me that he had something useful to offer. In his desperate sweat to catch the right chord, he fell and rose. And I watched in silent giggle the mien of a drunkard. What a half-human and half-creature he was!

Though in my heart, I wanted to sit on the stairs and pass the night in mindless chatter with him, but I also needed to do my job. Find purpose. Reason. Profit. Certainly then, Drunkard's harmless flirtation made me feel guilty as I was having fun at the expense of my job. It ate me from inside. Time had always hung heavily over my head. As if by a strand of hair. And so I had to keep moving lest I got cut by it. Thus I made a hasty move to leave. Walking past him in a rush, I declared.

"Well, I gotta be somewhere?"

"I can accompany…" He was but quick to respond.

"When you are sober may be then you come along…" I sighed and then smiled to end the conversation. But right then he blurted out.

"Beauty you are!"

Beauty. I never was beautiful. Especially not my hair. Was he then mocking me for my impertinence?

During my school days, my friends had pretty long hair. Shiny. Lustrous. Ornamented with beads and bands. While I, in my youngish flush of beauty, had pygmy sized hair which were quite hardcore to touch. I was kind of tomboyish to take to conditioners and stuff or wrap my hair in essential oils for luscious growth. So they were too split ended to follow their genetic trajectory of femininity. To hide them, I would plait my hair into thousands plaits. It certainly made me look like a girly boy. In my voice I was sweet and in my appearance, I looked like a brat. Besides, there was yet another thing which felt very scandalous to me. My developing bosoms. They made me feel uneasy especially during school. I would have to avoid running or playing any game, as they would bounce so weirdly and so conspicuously.

When it came time to wear those awkwardly shameless brassieres, I felt even more provoked to hide, suppress and despise the flesh growing out of my skin. When I would talk to my friends, they would stare and even mock at how my chest looked. Like a mound. It made feel even more humiliated. Not just friends but strangers too. Earlier they would look in my eyes, and then suddenly they started to gaze at my intimate parts. Humiliated, I then began to wrap tight sheets of cloth around my chest. To make it stop looking so obvious. I continued to do so, and eventually I got left with small boobs which were just what I wanted. It was a disgusting time of my life, and when the drunkard called me a beauty, I suddenly became conscious of my private endowments

"What?" Self-conscious, I exclaimed. While he winked, "I don't know your name so I called you that."

The drunkard was being eager to make friends. And he even flirted but strangely, he didn't mean it in a vulgar way. He certainly bored me. But not even for once did he mean to harass me. Just like Lee, he was curious to talk and know me better. He was not offensive in his nature nor had a deceptive meaning behind his conversation. He was plainly honest even when drunk. How could he control himself? When the sober world acted like a mad mad alehouse, how could he?

At first, I had gotten too conscious of his comment but soon realized he was not mocking me or anything. Drunkard was not being nasty about it. He was different.

"So old a trick, you really think you are charming, huh? I winked back.

"Yep. And the trick worked, you are smiling." And I was. Drunkard was beginning to tickle my nerves. I was smiling, and that was all he wanted.

"Yep. I am. You are a funny sort." I replied while toning down my temper.

As I stepped down the stairs, we shared a lighter moment. There was no need for me to keep my guards up. And he too didn't need to re-assert his rapport. So we were at ease in each other's company. In his case, he was certainly at ease. But I still felt getting back to business as I wanted to meet Granny.

Since the time Granny had sent me the soup, I needed to thank her. Of course I didn't mean it. It was more like an excellent opportunity to converse with the old lady. To hear her side of the story. Even before the drunkard had come knocking I was planning how to interact with the old lady. It was absolutely necessary I hear what she had to say in order to see how close or far from truth the Elder was.

Seeing that I was in a rush, the drunkard asked while hoping he could tag along, "You going somewhere?" Facing him, I replied, "Hey, I am going to meet Granny, you can come along if you want. Besides we have to umm talk about the shack as well. What say?"

"Granny, now?" He had a cricket in his voice.

"Is there a problem?" I asked him, as he fretted at the notion. But he didn't disclose it and replied with an exaggerated calm. "No. Everything is good, as long as I have a bottle with me."

Underneath the appearances, it was obvious, the boy was hassled to meet Granny. Granny of all people. She, who had a soft spot for every persona non grata of the town, he was reluctant to meet her! Honestly, I also didn't want to go and say hello to the old lady. What for to get humiliated by her proud nature? What for to feel like a criminal because of her? What for indeed. But it had to be done. The boy also felt like I did. In his reluctance, I could see my own. Nevertheless I had reasons to fear Granny's suspicious looks. But why did the boy have to fear her? Sidelining our unwillingness, we walked towards Granny's house. It was a short walk, as the shack was right in the centre of the old lady's den.

We reached her place and saw people drying colourful sheets of cloth outside the garden. The drunkard purposefully walked behind me. I would slow down my steps, so he could overtake. But he would deliberately use me as cover. The old lady had inflicted such rounds of fear into us, that we feared even the sight of her. I was not family, but the drunken boy was. It was really unbecoming of him to copy my style and cower before Granny. As we approached the gate, the old lady saw both of us enter. She, without any exaggerated welcome, called out to the boy. "Drunkard!

Good of you to come. We needed an extra hand here." She called him 'Drunkard', and I turned back to face him. He didn't seem to mind it at all. I again looked at him to register my surprise. And he realizing why I was flabbergasted, whispered, "Yep. My name is Drunkard." And I had thought he was joking about it.

Granny again called him out, "Drunkard, come on over!"

I was with Drunkard, but she blatantly ignored me to address the boy. It had me wonder what was then he scared of. Granny didn't seem to hold any grudges against him. Rather by ignoring me, she certainly proved whom she had a pickle with. Not the boy but a petite stranger. Drunkard looked at me with surprise as if he also wasn't expecting a cordial welcome. But he quickly adjusted while hiding his surprise. Reaching her as nonchalantly as he could, he sparked a casual conversation with the old lady. In the way he approached her, without letting off any alarms, there didn't seem to be any tinge of bad terms between them. The boy was certainly adept in his act. Realizing how Granny had curtly ignored me, he left me with a smirk on his face.

Seeing him approach, Granny raised her brows. Before she could say anything, the boy while hiding his drunken stupor asked, "Granny, have you finished with your gardening?"

"Yes, I just did. Besides Pooh needed help with these clothes, so…" Granny also responded as if she didn't mind his drunken stench. Seeing, she was being normal, Drunkard let go of his anxiety and continued the casual tête-à-tête. "I see, and it's good that the weather is fit for it…the breeze has a sunny side up, they will dry up soon."

"Yes Drunkard indeed. But we need more hands though, just look at the pile. Grace, you can help Halo. The more the merrier. What say?"

Granny then called out to me. It was certainly unexpected and even notoriously moody. How could she in one minute act so warily and then turn affable? From day one, she had acted manipulatively nice and then gregariously pretentious. Why the town respected her, I had thought. What eccentric aspect of her did they like? It was a puzzling state of affairs. She had that endearing smile, even when lies seemed to creep out of it. No one seemed to doubt her or recognize her deceptive play of other people's weaknesses. It was like she was their godmother. Then again, I might be wrong. After all, she had snubbed me and I couldn't help but dislike her with aversion.

During the day of the puke, I had noticed how she had her white and black hair tied softly into an awry bun. Her complexion was what it had been during her birth; red and brown and delicate. The lower pants she wore were some inches above the ankles, so they didn't get soiled or come under her feet. She had tied a scarf on her wrist. It didn't seem to serve any purpose, but the old lady wore it nonetheless. The townies called her Granny but she was not old more like in her forties. Perhaps she was one of those people who didn't look their age. I could see her countenance was endearingly cherubic. She would intentionally downplay it in order to look serious. Otherwise, it would have been quite unreasonable to take her seriously. It was easy to empathize with her condition for I was cut out of the same cloth. Like her, I also had to intentionally frown, purse my lips, speak coarsely, and even flare my nostrils so that people could take me seriously. It certainly was taxing especially because it would rarely work.

While I was caught-up in the moment, Granny had to repeat herself to steal my attention.

"Grace, where are you lost?"

"Oh! Yes! I would love to!"I responded while not forgetting to show my euphoria over it.

Airing the laundry. Such a menial task and Halo seemed to be happy about it. Even Drunkard was pleased since it could serve as a bridge between Granny and him. I too shared his enthusiasm as though it was drudgery, the job could get me closer to the old lady. As I assisted Halo, one thing was peculiarly discernible. The change in Halo's moods. She was repulsed by someone. It was not me. But Drunkard. The girl did not seem to like him. She was happily assisting Granny before but when he walked in, the girl was infuriated.

Halo kept a stiff upper lip while her ire against him remained unwavering. Even when it had a loud din, Drunkard totally ignored her. He didn't pay her any attention and overlooked her anger as a minor fracas. All the while as he conversed with Granny, Halo kept eyeballing him with tenacity. I didn't feel so curious about it. As I wanted to finish the dreary task at hand. But the girl was lost and her dampened pace was also beginning to annoy.

As she kept playing with her vengeful furies, I discreetly whispered to her.

"Pssk, Halo, what is with you?"

Without breaking her vigilance of the boy, the girl spoke irately. "Will you just hear him and look at our Granny, how she is being conned by that monster!" She didn't even care to lower her voice.

Drunkard as a monster? Could it be that his behaviour was monsterish, or that he did something monsterish? I couldn't tell, but the way Halo behaved it was as if Drunkard had done some wrong to her. That is why she couldn't handle Granny carousing with him as if nothing had happened. Whatever the case might have been, I wished to extricate myself from the entire situation. It was fun watching people work, but not doing it. Just then, Granny called out to me.

"Grace, come here!" She looked at me with intent. There was no disdain in it. Then turning her gaze at the boy, she steadily walked towards him. While firmly placing her hand on his shoulder, she admonished him, "Drunkard I know you are not here for more than a day, so Grace will maintain her lodgings at your shack. You can make the store your home, unless you want to give up the booze and mend?"

As and when she said those piercing words, Drunkard whined, "The store, Granny, no..." But before he could fully express his annoyance, Granny while ignoring his tantrums, called me again. "Grace, come here. These two can take care of the drying, let's do some gardening..."

Drunkard did not whine anymore. I also promptly heeded the old lady and took my place. Yet I found it strange that Drunkard didn't protest much. Why was he being so pliable? What had he done to act so amenable? He had cringed to visit her. And then a second later, he wanted to keep her happy. It was a curious spectacle. Though it piqued my interest to pry about it, I had another matter which needed my utmost attention. Gardening with Granny. One on one. I had waited for that opportunity. Desperately. But after doing the laundry, I didn't have the stomach to do gardening. It didn't seem fair. The old lady had not chosen the right time for it. It was sunny. The nights were cold but the days were simmering hot in the town. Drunkard was sweating like a pig. I didn't want to. It would have been awkwardly unpleasant and the fear of it had me fear it.

"Grace, good here, hold this one softly. Cut down in its prime, not here not here... keep the branch straight." She began to guide me through the process of pruning the greens. Her face would lit-up with a gratuitous satisfaction as if she was doing a favour to nature. While she went on disturbing the wild growth and the pesky bugs all over it, I started to feel thirsty. It was beginning to give me a headache. Why was it so cold at night and so sulphurous in the day?

"I can't work on a neat garden. Cutting them again and again. These greens aren't nails not even hair. Hold it straight Grace." She kept on directing me what to do and what not to do. The old lady was thoroughly engrossed into her business of farming. It didn't matter to her whether sun was smirking or whether nights were shivering. She didn't seem to bother. Granny had fallen right into the rhythm of farming even when I was thoroughly parched.

It was past afternoon and the glare of the sun had begun to grate my nerves. I wanted to wring my hands bloody. Take cover underneath a shade or run away. While all the time, the old woman remained happily immersed in her tedious work.

"The garden must be bushy to really work my magic. You see this one. I put an all-nighter to let it grow. To a layman's eye it looks hairy, but I know it's pruned the way it needs. Like a child."

While gardening with Granny, I needed someone to slap me. The smell of the plants and the weed, and the wet soil was giving me a shock. I was on the verge of falling unconscious. My eyes were beginning to burst out of the balls. To flip out of range. And all that while, Granny remained busy in her plants and didn't even bother to see the foul condition she was putting me in.

"Gardening helps me think. What's your garden theory? What do you do to keep nasty stuff away?"

"Penning down this and that..." I just chattered without thinking too much on it. And she caught my attention by declaring, "A reporter?"

"Wha? How did you strike at that?" I was startled as she declared I was a reporter. She declared it without being subtle or devious about it. Even when I anxiously kept measuring her assertion, the old lady kept herself busy. She did not even care to notice my shock. She kept stroking the shoots and roots as if they bore more life than I did. In a laid-back manner, she had stunned me and then quite offhandedly ignored how staggered it had left me.

Granny again emphasized the point, without taking into account how troubled I was at her finding.

"So you report to think?" Nonchalantly she asked.

As she continued to disregard and even provoke my surprise, I couldn't contain my alarm any further and asked her outright. "Granny, are you playing me on? You knew about it or someone tipped you off?" I had flipped there for a second. Despite the urgency in my tone, the woman replied rather callously. "I have my spies. You were invited to the Greys, right? And you went as you like to note down facts perhaps for memory and then may be history. I thought hard about your intrusion in our life, and when you decided to visit the Elder, it was certain. You are a reporter. And it's not a criminal thing. Lee also does it. His pamphlets, you must read. And he also earns by it. Do you too? I mean, is reporting your livelihood?"

"Oh…" I paused as it was too much to sink in. Strangely, Granny had begun to warm up to me. Still, what raised my stature in her eyes? That I was a hard-working reporter? The cunning old woman knew about my trip to the Elder, and was not mad. The way she talked, it felt as if she orchestrated the trip in the first place. She was calm while throwing me off balance. But she was anxious as well. Underneath her pacific composure, I could see Granny was having a mixed flush of emotions. She was glad that I was a reporter as that neatly explained why I wanted to snoop around. But she was also apprehensive as to why I had chosen her town, and her people. Nevertheless, such a change in her nature was a good start for me. I had her doubt everything she believed in. It was a good start.

Noticing my pause, Granny again prodded me to speak.

"Go on, is it?" she pried again.

I had to compose myself. Anymore fretting or wringing from my side would have severely dampened the rapport between us. Besides, I still had the upper-hand as all she knew was that I was a reporter of some kind. She was in the dark about why I chose it and what purpose had driven me to their town. So finding my own calm footing, I replied, "No, no it is more like, um, a job that does not pay. Like you do gardening to think, I do this to pass time…"

The old lady put down her scissors and wiped her hands with the scarf tied to her wrist. While beckoning me with a solemn look, she asked, "So what do you report?" She would switch from being serious to being nonchalant again. It was a trick she was playing with my mind. First, letting me breathe, and then seizing it away. Noticing her ploy, I also began to stay wary of it. Nonchalantly, I responded, "People, their lives and all. That is enough for me…"

"Reconsider." She was sharp in her tone. Just when I would find my balance, she would throw me off it. The woman was interrogating me without letting me know I was under interrogation. I realized it in time but not soon enough. The box of secrets I was hiding had made me apprehensive. The more I tried to hide my gory past, the more I became dangerously anxious. And the old lady was hell-bent to find that weakness of mine.

Again, noticing my pause, she demanded, "Reconsider."

Caught off-balance, I stuttered. "Why are you stressing it so m-much?" Naturally, I got somewhat defensive. The old lady was capable of upsetting my experienced calm. It was very unprofessional of me. She was but glad. She was discreetly ecstatic to see me fumble for composure. While preening herself, she continued with her inquisition. "You can't think of any other thing. Single-minded are you, and it is scary as you have nothing else to worry about. No friends, family or someone else…" She spoke with sarcastic admonishment.

While groping to find words, I tersely replied, "Sure…" I couldn't talk glibly as I could. I even couldn't hide the gulping in my throat. Did I want her to find out about me? Why were my instincts failing me? I think deep down I had come to trust her. Her good judgment. Even when I would mock, jeer and undermine her elated stature in the town, I believed she was right. So when she had cornered me, I didn't want to ram into her. I wanted her to dissect me and reach me the way my mother used to. Though the old lady was not being a motherly figure, I wanted her to be. It was strangely very unbecoming of my instincts. I wanted to show her my wounds, and hoped she would mend them. It was unbecoming. I wrongly believed if she knew about the clots in my heart, I would be loved than banished. So, I was weak in front of her. It was very unbecoming.

As I remained stuck in my maudlin thoughts, Granny continued.

"It's not a complaint Grace. You know what you are looking for, and so you have found it. Some people just don't know, they still keep looking, and chasing their tails… Is there something you wish to tell me or ask of me?" Granny looked straight into my eye, as if I might slip up a secret or two. Suppressing the pull of my instincts, I again responded as tersely as I could. "No Granny."

Granny then took a deep breath. She scrutinized my entire face. The brows. The lips. Even the pink cheeks. She wanted me to twitch with guilt. And I thought she could be a mother to me. The woman was not letting go at all. To an outsider, it would seem like a normal conversation, even when it was an inquisition. She was that good at it.

Without pulling any punches she continued. "The day of the puke, and the ugly thing with the Zones. You know enough of our history in a matter of a day. You must be a good reporter, even if it is your pass-time." There was a discernible stain of doubt in her voice. She had to be curious as I seemed to be sort of omnipresent. What seemed to bother no one, bothered her. She was aware that something was not right about me. What it was, and what danger did I pose, that is what she was trying to probe into. Sadly, she only had earthly tools to decipher an unnatural creature that I was. Even so, she was good at making me climb down from my unnatural tower and see her as my mother. She was indeed doing a good job.

In her need to expose me, the old lady was not curious like Vicky or the Elder. She was concerned whether I should be allowed to roam freely? Or should she throw me out? It was a natural concern that had made her vindictive and even conspicuously vindictive towards me.

"So?" She interrupted my pause, and I replied without being terse any more. "Granny, I just happened to be here, when it was all happening."

With a second deep breath, she took off her gloves. Then left the pruning of her garden, and held out her hand on my shoulder. It rested heavily suggesting the solemn import of her concern. Then she smiled quite innocuously without showing any sign of distrust. I remained firm in my posture without letting her imposing contact rustle me up any further.

It was certain. The old lady had begun to reach what was Grace, by letting the stranger know who was Granny.

"You just did. Grace, I must be frank with you, as you are not being. This town is very dear to me. I have lived here all my life…" She left her gardening tools symmetrically in the box and continued. "We washed our face and sprinkled away the water from our hands. Then we dabbed them on our pants. This town had a direction to it, even when only two or three houses were standing in the midst of a jungle. If someone wanted directions to it, we said - it's in the corner of the east-west side of the north to the south. We didn't want outsiders here, so we confused them. And now when people ask where Halogen is, they know it's our town. Back then we were more addictive to territorial jargons. Even when it was only a lonely bunch of willows and a cozy bar to keep a stage for get-togethers. Well the point is we were just living for the sake we are born, and death was too painful to self-inflict. There was nothing to prove…."

While saying so, Granny would pause and then pace right and left. She would lose herself and then come back as if remembering some sullen past. Too sullen that her words and her melodramatic mien felt so overemotional. Just a while ago, she was unforgiving with her inquisition, and then minutes later I could hear her heart crying. It felt so tedious than insomnia itself. Why would she embark and then disembark? It was such an attitude of hers that made me resent her fluctuating, indecisive and half-baked intent to know me. Nevertheless, I listened intently as she continued histrionically.

"We had little interests to look forward to. Just daily morn and night eating, bathing, walking and fretting over to keep time and money for each other. And the thing is we couldn't leave this place even if we didn't like it, as there was no other friendly place. Every other town was a selfish hub of its own. And we were also no different. When a man from any other direction would come, we had him run away with our inhospitable sneers and frowns. That is why such a complicated name we had for our own town. Like all the other self-centered sods we needed nobody, divided as we were. And to move around in the puddle of our town, we had mules and dogs to carry us around. The guy with a truck however would be the rich one."

The old lady paused to salvage her breath. She looked at the spot by the side of her house. I could tell that spot once used to park a truck, someone's truck. While absorbing the memory of the spot, she treaded a little towards it. She had only walked some distance, when she hastily turned back. There was a glow of grief on her face. Even her steps were taken by it. I could hear her sighs of regret, which she also didn't wish to hide. Moving closer in my direction, she resumed. "Sometimes a famous man from the city would come here to run away from the crowd. He would build a wonderland to himself and age in leisure. He was famous, and he had money, so we didn't hound him out of the town. You know he used to romanticize our lives as a romp with nature, complimenting how tasty our lives were. But we didn't feel it that way. Romp! Kidding me, huh! Still it was strange to note how he left the city just because his mind couldn't take anymore of the paparazzi. And we wanted to go to the city as our place reeked of stagnation, dullness and narrow-mindedness. That stranger got us thinking. For a stranger our hamlet was ready to be calming on his nerves and not for us! Perhaps we hated this betrayal of our hamlet that we became derisive of outsiders. If only we could make some of that money and relish the calm of our own hamlet. Narrow yes we were. So bored yes we were. But now this town is not east or west, but a Halogen. And I, for one, am its fine supporter even in the face of the Zones."

The old lady stopped. And as sternly as she could, she frowned at me. The woman had a question on her face. To ask whether I was listening or not. Uncompromising in her gaze, she was ready to whip me if I had been mentally absent to her story. After all, she had put her heart out, and so demanded to know if I respected it. She was judging my mute silence, not realizing how she had meaninglessly droned on and on. It was a long and a theatrical speech she had dumped on me. The woman as usual had spoken in a lacklustre tone. And that too with a dry fervour that just killed whatever sense she wanted to make.

Nevertheless, I intently listened to her even when it was an act. So when she discontinued her talk, I conveyed a confused expression. I also conveyed that I wanted her to continue. That I wanted her to remember the past, and churn it with emotions. Even after reassuring her of my presence of mind, she still remained mute. Granny didn't just want me to listen. She was anxious to hear me say that her town was normal despite the scurry of scandals I had seen. She expected me to break my silence and reassure her, that her town was all right. That there was no foul play. That it was pure gold! She wanted me to say that about her town. Of course I had seen its dark realities, but she wanted me to ignore it and assert how it was a normal town with hunky-dory issues and pasts.

Even Drunkard and Halo looked on as if expecting a sagacious reply from me. They were privy to our conversation. And as Granny demanded that I rest her doubts, those two also added to it. So I had to prove to all the three that I was capable of listening well and furnishing a perceptive response. I had to prove to Granny, I was better than what she had expected. I had to prove to Halo, I was a worthy outsider. And I had to prove to Drunkard, I was capable of knowing about the witch, some witch. I had to prove. I had to say something wise. It was a deadening pressure. The sky, I wished would just bolt at me. The ground, I wished would just eat me up. Nothing, but came to distract any of us. And I was stuck to demonstrate in any which way that I was an observant reporter. Though I was listening to a sob story, I was expected to say something keenly perceptive. And I did speak, which was not incredible, but it was certainly politically correct.

"Granny if you are worried I will upset the peace of this hamlet, you should know I'll not do any such thing. I am not a third-grade reporter."

I spoke with indignation in my voice. It was a good way to let them know I was hurt by Granny's insinuating allegations and accusations. Hearing me take an honest stand, Granny quickly retracted. "Oh dear, no-no, I am not saying you will. I just want to impress upon you the love I have for this town. You know about the Zones, but you don't know what made them. The Elder will not utter a word of truth, and blames the LO for it. I wanted to be the one to tell you this. But you wouldn't have believed me, till you met the Elder."

The Zone? The truth? The horror in the woods? She didn't tell me anything to counter the Elder. She didn't disclose any facts just a play of emotions. The Elder had lies to tell, and she didn't even have them! Still, Granny expected me to call her town normal as apparently she had given all the particulars about it. Was it not then presumptuous and even nonsensical of her to have such expectations? Naturally, I was incensed. And I wished if I could attack her with it. But, I kept a lid on it. After all it was still a triumph as I had at least gotten her to talk to me and didn't want to disturb our newly-hatched rapport. So I courteously spoke, "I see. Granny I-I really appreciate that. So you did arrange that meeting?"

"Yes, I asked him to…I wouldn't have, but you had heard enough. And the doubts in your mind about who is right and wrong, I knew they had to be cleared. If you are going to stay here, then it means you must be a part of its machinery which moves forward. And doubts are a cog which halts everything. You see these plants, they look dismal when stunted and crowded. I give them space, by letting each know its place. I will have the side branches or as one can say petty affairs cut down, so the shoot can grow high and high with its roots deeper and deeper."

Again she went on talking with a melodramatic finesse. It was then certain. Granny never wanted to disclose the truth. Rather she wanted me to accept that there was none. So I would stop snooping around than go looking for it. So I calmly and even ingratiatingly nodded, "Yes Granny, I appreciate it."

At this moment, Drunkard came close as if to say something. But Granny didn't seem to be in a mood to hear him out. Not that she didn't want to, but because she knew what he had to say. And the old lady was not interested. So before he could utter a word, Granny made an attempt to disperse the gathering and call it a day.

"Halo, dear child accompany Drunkard to the store."

"What me? And what about these sheets?" Halo was derisive of the idea to work with Drunkard. It was all too obvious. Granny, but didn't heed it, and brushed it aside as sibling rivalry.

"Pooh will take them herself. Drunkard, go with her." Granny spoke casually. All the while ignoring Drunkard's vivid approach.

"I will not leave!" Drunkard then exploded as Granny was not heeding him.

"Drunkard?"

The drunken boy had finally caught Granny's attention. The old woman reacted knowing what was about to pass. Even Halo also understood it. They were taken aback, and yet they were expecting it. I thought when the dreary sheets would be done, we would all drearily leave. But interestingly Drunkard wanted to disclose something. He wanted to reveal the shiny veneer of the town and then rake the mask off of it.

"You will tell this girl of our history, and leave me behind! I lost more than you did." Drunkard called me 'this girl', and it was not respectful. But I let that slide, as it was Granny who in fact was going to face his anger.

"Drunkard, you don't have to. There is no need…" Granny tried to silence him. After neatly wrapping the story of the town, she didn't want Drunkard to spoil it. The boy was but inconsolable. Time-worn, the old lady then looked at me with curiosity. She must have wondered how events come to me than I running after them. While she mulled over it, Drunkard began to huff and puff as if he was ominously scarred by some past of the town. Some gory past that had made him hate the town than revere it like Granny.

"Granny, you will only bare the facts, this much died because this much erred. And rounding off all these, this much were guilty, and we were not. That is not how it happened!" He was ferocious in his voice. Granny while noticing the high pitch of his insolence raised her tone as well. "Speak it out the way you want, but it will not help you to rake up the past! You remember it with hate. If only you could see that Drunkard."

Some past the town had. Was it political or magical? Both Granny and Drunkard began to fist over it and I got even more attracted towards it. If the past was pretty, I wanted to know how beautiful. If it was grey, I longed to see how grayish. So many questions were buzzing in my head. Every time they quarreled over it, my mind would get dizzy. I wanted a definitive sheet of facts. But so much emotion was invested in the past that no one would give it up so plainly.

The town was borne out of that past. When the likes of Granny remembered it with forgiveness and even regret, the likes of Drunkard remembered it with odious hate. The hate was too much for him to wear in sobriety hence he would drink himself to a stupor. He would in a manner extricate himself from its claws by running away from the town and its sins. To the echoes of the past, he had his ears shut. But he could not shut the avaricious throbbing of blood ties. The bonds which tied him to the past and the town inextricably. To douse such a wild fire, he would drink himself to amnesia. Become someone he was not. What dark chapter had him create an anti-particle in his mind? The boy was inflicting self-harm by remembering his past with a gulp of poison than remembering it with a prospect of a panacea.

"Granny, I have heard all about it. I can't have this again, I will leave, I can't!" Halo interrupted Drunkard mid-way. She pushed past him, and demanded Granny to let her go than listen to what grimness she had tried to forget.

"Halo?" Granny began to tend to her.

"Granny, if all the work is done, I better be going." Halo, but was raring to leave.

"Halo, of course, my child, you don't have to…will you be all right, look at me Halo, will you be?"

"I will, I will…"

Halo was not a coward to have run away. Even when Drunkard by his scornful look suggested that she was. He scathed her for fleeing than confronting the crisis not realizing bygones were bygones. The boy was oblivious to such a truth, and rolled his eyes in contempt of the feverish girl. Granny was however perceptive and even empathetic. She understood the girl was not a coward in asking to leave.

"Halo, where will you go, will you be meeting up with Pooh?"

Granny was certainly worried for the girl. She was also tediously annoyed and even overworked because of the sudden entry of Drunkard. But she was calm, and tried to show it by putting on a brave front. Alone and frail in her age, Granny had her hands full to stay calm even when it meant to act it than really mean it. And then there was I, another species of the same motley of the world. She had to address me too. One moment I would hate the old lady and another I would admire her. Why still I couldn't empathize with her state. Perchance I happened to see my traitor and sweet mother in her. Perchance I could also be wrong…

"Granny, I am fine, I am going to see Lee. We have got some pamphlets to write. Noor will also be there."

"I will join you too. You know how much I admire it, go ahead, okay?" She responded with a vigorous assurance.

As Halo left, Drunkard saw her leave in disgust. He was sorely contemptuous of the growing chasm between present and past. He wanted to lambast at what was becoming of the town. The old lady saw Halo leave and turned to Drunkard with a proposal to listen to him knowing that I was there. But I was someone she could then trust. While treading each street of the Black and White, she and Drunkard fought each other's narration of the past. In doing so they took me back to a time when Zones weren't there. It was Granny's idea to go down the memory lanes by literally going down the streets where it all happened. I walked in tow while recording the past as narrated by the old and the new. I listened so I could in turn report the history of the tiny town lest it was forgotten.

"The town…" Drunkard began his story as he thumped his foot. "No corner was spared". Granny looked on, while I started memorizing. He continued, "The Zones, it might be a scandalous thing to you, but it is our history. Towns which neighbor us know of it. Some details of it you can find in the library. But the Elder is not the horse's mouth that you should go to, even if he has been a part of it…"

Drunkard was aware thanks to Granny that I had met the Elder. And was quite critical of it. The guy had just transformed. Where did that drunken silliness and humour go? He was still drunk, but in his stupor instead of being silly again, he was all serious and alert. Granny wasn't furious at him or attempted to stop him anymore. Let it all come out…

Drunkard continued.

"…What was upon us? I was pinned on the ground to notice anything else than a foot clubbing my face till blood began to show. I would have felt the terrible pain, guess the hocus-pocus noise everywhere charmed my nerves to sleep. Just the throb of a foot clamping the only face I had if my family intended to identify it. It stopped, after the foot had taken out its rage on me. By what miracle I got up I know it was plain curiosity and instinctual need to run away. I got up and saw only clothes, not people, just clothes red and white and purple but mostly red amok on the streets flying about. On whom were the clothes hanging? Everyone was invisible like thin air, and all that was visible of them were their attires. The foot didn't traumatize me, it was hurtless. It were the flying clothes with no heads and bodies, they gave me a heart attack! There was smoke and blood, pelting stones and blood, fire in the hole and blood and when today I close my eyes I see blood…"

Drunkard looked at Granny, with anger mixed with derision. He had become so vindictive in his diatribe. If he were given an axe, I knew he would cut a tree down! What if he had not been drunk? The measure of his wrath would be unsurpassable. Time to time he would assault the old lady with gazes of fire and brimstone. Not even once did he let go. He was burning with hate and wanted to burn all. The boy continued.

"…My Granny, our Granny was scarred in the riots. Though she doesn't have those scars anymore and her blood too seems to have clotted… I have but kept them green!" Drunkard fell into a fury and came at the old woman for having lost the scar. The scar which was an evidence of what had happened in the town. He was in rage and was brimming with it.

"Were you even there Granny?" The boy asked her contemptuously.

"Drunkard, don't start with it! Scars might have deserted us, but we remember. But you! You resurrect the past in hate. Stop this!" Tediously again, but a little more explicitly, Granny demanded Drunkard to give up his anger in looking back. It was a plea, a gentle plea even when Drunkard remained egregiously disrespectful of the old woman. Granny, as was typical of her, continued to stay pacifically considerate towards him. Even when he was being a brute.

"I am sorry, Granny. But the way you tell these tales, there is no passion! You narrate what vaguely your memory remembers about the catastrophe, but your details are always scorched of the passionate turmoil that went down here. Just details with hardly any passion of angst and anguish. I was there, we were there, and you were there! Are you still in a breakdown to be able to feel when some foot was disfiguring your face as well? I had a foot in my face, but I remember and I remember with vigour!"

Despite his obstinate incivility, Granny relentlessly tried to persuade some sense of reconciliation in the boy. She was forced to re-enact the role played by her countless times, placating the inconsolable. But at that time I was also there. Acting as a jury. So they were doubly expected to put the best foot forward and set the record straight.

"You are right. Drunkard is right. I should beat myself and even have my face disfigured again. I am old and weary. It takes a young blood to recall with passion events of this nature."

"Young Bloods! I am a young blood, and I cannot take it anymore, the silence on this matter. That is why I drink because if I don't then I will become a fanatic. Festering on the mistakes of our past and wishing everyone dead in the present! What was our past? Hue and Cry! The Hue fighting the Cry, and the Cry fighting the Hue! Hue and Cry! Bloody ruckus! The ones responsible were let go, by our elders. By you Granny, by your friend the Elder, and his Zone! The Malafide Five! They were let go! Where are they? Which asylum did you buy them? Where are you hiding them? They were let go!" The boy went on spouting pain and poison, while Granny tried to show him the real picture, "Drunkard, you know very well, they ran away. We did not hide them. Many of them died, many of them…"

"Some still are living!" Furious, Drunkard declaimed.

"Yes, some are living, but without them this town would be a graveyard?" Sullenly, Granny let it out. It was a good thought. Had all the vermin died, what would be left? But seriously, what a thought! The Zones were three and formed a small patch of the world. A tiny dot in the universe of the earth. The world where lived the ignominies, austerities and splendidness of one and many species. Sure, the town was a dot. But if one of its Zones had died, it would make for a grave, small again, but a mass graveyard nonetheless.

Even when the graves would be of countless parasites, I was provoked to ask myself, should then the vermin be excused?

"Let it be then! I see them, and my blood boils!" Drunkard, not caring for Granny's assurances, kept ranting and raving. The boy had become my questions for Granny. In a retort after retort he tried to justify his stand and impress upon me why that stand was irrevocable. He continued.

"I drink to smother the fires, but they don't go away. And I leave this town, but their faces haunt me still. People in rage – where will you hide? The crowd turning into a mob, where will you run? A simple man, a shopkeeper by trade, suddenly serves the devil, hits with his horns men's skulls into paste. Kids' hearts into deaths. Women's secrets, skulls and hearts to shock, pain and death. When one is alone, one can run for himself, die for himself, and mourn for himself. He has nothing to lose. With a family one can run too, but with a family if one is caught, he is played most treacherously. His family is butchered in front of him! In a mob, how can you save yourself and your family? Dispersed in the storm of tongues licking and hands grabbing, how will you see to it that your family remains dry? …my sister screeched at me to kill her, but father couldn't euthanize her…and she was left to the hounds to do it."

Drunkard got overwhelmed in his voice as his memory eked out a whining shrill. The old lady looked at me, as if to see if I understood the pain. One look at me and she was flabbergasted. Why the jury wasn't in tears to hear the most tragic and traumatic experience ever told. Was I cold-blooded? A cold-blooded reporter who didn't care? Was I just worried about recording? But I knew why I was not crying or reaching after a hanky. Such tales of trauma, I had seen enough and experienced them with vengeance. All tears had dried up to weep anymore. Granny didn't know it. She couldn't even guess it. No one could. Horrified at my calm composure, she was screwing her brows and puckering her lips to analyze who I was.

Grace. Such an innocent name, innocent eyes, broken body, and petite aura. How could I be dangerous? If anything I could be a trickster for prying here and there. But not a cold-blooded girl that nothing could overwhelm with tears. Just when she had thought I was all decoded, some other part of my enigma would slap her on the face. And that made her feel helpless and even more guarded to protect her township. She had to stop Drunkard from spilling all the secrets as there was more to me than what met her eye.

"Drunkard, let's go…you are turning pale, you need to rest." Granny spoke with heightened concern. But the boy was determined to squeal all the secrets of the past and shame the keepers of it. "No! No! There is no rest for the likes of me. I was alarmed, Granny, I was stabbed to see the faces of the rioters. I knew most of them. I was friends with them. They used to call me their son! But that noon I saw them pillaging through the streets and eating up everyone who came their way. They had no guilt. As they knew no one would be coming to report them. No one would be visiting their dingy corner and shame them. It alarmed me. When no one would report, the rioters wouldn't stop! In broad daylight the riots would then certainly continue. It was a circle of chaos! I wanted someone to report it. And you know what I did…"

Drunkard didn't ask Granny. He seized my attention while fixating his raised hand in my direction. He was desperate to prove himself. That he had been useful. That he was more than an aimless drunkard. He wanted to prove he had not just wailed over the loss but done something about it. In that ritualistic mess, he had a role to play other than getting his face bashed by a foot.

And I asked him.

"What?"

Prompted by my interest, he vociferated with regained confidence.

"I risked my life and called the offices of every newspaper. I called them. Gave them the address and viola the next noon the reporters found me. From my house, they captured with their cameras those insidious faces."

"Why not the police?" I asked to keep him kinetic.

"They were in on it. None of them had intervened before which was a clear sign they were not going to help." He revealed it while also expressing his shock with a swing of his hands. Drunkard had become a different man altogether. He narrated with a purpose how valiantly he had alarmed the reporters. How he had the rioters feel ashamed of themselves. He was glad rather ecstatic to sing in the air the vigil he had kept. Otherwise the riots would have gotten ignored and repeated again. He didn't even once share his nostalgic enthusiasm with Granny. It was his way of getting back at her for constantly bickering over his wasted life. Though he belittled Granny's concern, she was right about him. The boy despite his brave act, had in fact turned into a wasted drunk. He was reliving the past and carrying its burden. When he should have shed it altogether. And lived the life which he had risked his life for.

I was not in the mood to become his Granny. So I didn't try to apprise him of his current dissipation. While keeping him involved, I asked again.

"But didn't it point suspicion at you?"

"No I kept low. The reporters told me to keep low. And it was done. The next day their pictures were published in black and white." He stated with a sense of profound satisfaction. And as for me, I acted to seem interested and attentive towards him. Of course my concern was affected as I needed him to talk. So I could become a witness of his past. I acted and he unbarringly spoke to my listening ear. All the while I remained true to my act. Though it was a clever pretension, I did not mock him by it. Certainly, his tale of woe didn't move me to tears. But I still had the courtesy to listen than jeer at his theatrics. I was intent on memorizing him for the sake of memorizing him.

"So what happened? Were the rioters paralyzed with it or more anger-rent, tell me?"

Failing to see through my act, he continued. "It was quiet. Every one of those faces they were subdued. They saw their faces in the papers and they saw in them the same picture of sin. The same picture of hell. The same devil they thought they were burning alive. This morbid realization silenced them. During the riots they had this-this mask of insanity writ large and when the papers exposed it, their senses were shamed. So there was a quiet..." Drunkard paused in his tirade. And then let out a sigh. To someone like me his tears mixed with sweat didn't matter. But Granny, she was moved to tears for him. Even when he had insulted her, she was stirred and shaken. But the boy didn't realize how Granny cared for his version of the past. She did care, and he didn't notice it. I didn't care, and he trusted me.

As Drunkard paused, Granny took the opportunity to salvage what she could. She had to show her empathy towards him. Otherwise he would take my word over hers. Filled with affection, she then spoke to him. "It was him. It was Drunkard who called the reporters. The riots then stopped. Grace you are a reporter as well. Drunkard, this is who she is. She will report the Elder!

While Granny tried to reach the boy, he kept his eyes averted from her. The boy didn't wish to return her empathy with empathy. He was trapped in such extreme measures of derision, that his own seemed like enemies to him. He was drunk but he was sober enough to remember the hate. The sun could also be responsible for his foul mood as it was scorching hot out in the open. It was humid too and there was no wind in the air. If Drunkard had the weight of his past and the sun messing his senses, Granny was more burdened. The old lady also had to look out for his future. Knowing how incorrigibly lost the boy was, the task was certainly a Gordon knot. When I looked at the boy, I could feel his grief. But when I looked at Granny, I still felt nothing but aversion towards her. It could be my prejudice. Or it could be that she was able to see through me. And I didn't like being exposed. Whatever be the case, I just couldn't help but judge her with vitriol.

Granny was certain I had come to report the Elder or some other miscreant like him. As a reporter that was my job as she believed. To report the crime, so the criminal is exposed and others do not follow him. If that is what she had believed, then I could ask her about the Elder. So with a justified stance and insistence in my voice, I asked.

"Granny, you are right. I intend to report him. But I need to ask you, how did this Elder become The Elder?" I articulated my rather irking question as patiently as I could.

"There was no one to rule him." She gave a stern reply.

"Why? Where were you?" and I asked her even more sternly.

As her words began to echo in my head, I started to rationalize her statement. With what logic should have I made head and tail of her words? No one to rule him. The sheer inanity of it had me look at her differently. Was she that dense? No one to rule him! I had heard of this alibi. People, mainly idealists often said it. The game is too dirty so it is better to shrink away than be a part of it. And so they shrank pretty far off, that the game started to play them. Like long threads pulling at the marionettes. Mere puppets who didn't even know they were being played.

In the school I was sensitized to the fact of bees and birds. But it was only the anatomy of it we were told about. What about the attraction, the lust, and the lecherous minds who take out their desires on little boys and girls under some Bridge? No one taught us anything about it. They feared by telling us they would make it happen than prevent it.

When the officers were being kindly kind to me, I was confused as to why did they then tear my pretty dress and hit me with such hate. What behavior was it, I had asked myself. It was certainly violence, I had thought, as I had seen the vicious school fights. Generally, when the students who would get bullied, if they begged or attacked the bully, they would go free. That is what I did under the Bridge. I begged and attacked them, but the officers still didn't let me go. Rather they were further enraged when I pleaded them to stop hurting me. I didn't know that type of violence for I was never told. The town but knew the game and was still ignorant about it. They had deliberately decided to remain ignorant. Deliberately decided to unlearn it. Naturally, Elder had to become the Elder to remind them of it. And so they all had to watch helplessly as their future got ravished ever so dishonorably.

My father and mother cocooned me from people. They knew how some people can be so they protected me. In doing so, they but failed to let me know about it. When they asked me to leap, I learnt it, and I leapt off the Bridge. They taught me how to say sorry, and I did it when I wore Rustam's pashmina. I was taught to be courteous and so I made friends with well-dressed officers. I was taught to diminish my spirits, my instincts and the wisdom I was born with. Hence when there was danger, I just hung on to my constructed virtues as if they could help me. How could my piousness ever help me? Besides, it was not enough that I be virtuous. I also had to be honorable. Virtuous for the world and honorable for the world.

My parents and the society I lived in did not want to dishonor me with words. So they thought let the reality do it for her. When I can experience, why tell me of it. Why tell her the truth about some lowly men, when she can meet them herself and get to know about it. Why indeed stop a bad man from becoming a bad leader, as people can experience him. Why indeed dirty ourselves rather let the world find it out itself. Such an alibi. Such an absurd alibi. And Granny had the same alibi. It was infuriating.

Noticing that I was not backing off, Granny again tried to reason. She didn't seem to care whether her logic made sense or not. It could be her pride that disallowed her to admit her error. Or it could be that she didn't want to lose face in front of a stranger. Be that as it may, she again reasoned and that too insipidly.

"No one was ruling. We didn't know someone had to."

"And you let him go berserk?" I didn't ask a question, but outrightly accused her of the crime of apathy and indifference. Granny wasn't expecting that she had to be answerable to me. But she tried to justify herself, and she tried. Drunkard however wasn't going to let me do the talking. He had his own scores to settle with her. So he spoke for her.

"No one was ruling, as no one wanted any responsibility. Naturally, Elder came up with the idea to rule and ruled like a headless chicken, isn't that right Granny?"

"You can say that, Drunkard…" She spoke as if meekly agreeing. The old lady would go defensively meek before him. But her meekness didn't mean that she agreed with him. Drunkard knew this, and so he wanted her to confess and confess with all her heart. So he condemned her again, "And you don't hold yourself a little to be blamed, Granny?"

At this, Granny couldn't control her proud ire. Infuriated, she rebuked him for the tone of his voice, "Respect is what I give but not when you will misuse it, Drunkard!" He but didn't let go of his tirade, and further berated her, "Respect? You respect the same, this Elder!"

As they both began to rabble-rouse and berate each other, I felt a little entertained. Granny was no longer in control of her ire and Drunkard wasn't letting the drink douse him anymore. They were quarrelling without any qualms of what I might think of them. During the soup party, the purdah of formality was breached. Then during the gardening the same issue repeated itself. I felt amused by it. As only after a breach, false skins are shed and the exact blood of the human is revealed.

In that some parts sylvan and some parts sand town, some aspects of Granny were right and some aspects of Drunkard. To the present, the old woman had pinned her redemption. She knew by ignoring the Elder, the old lady had done an immense wrong but she was looking ahead to rectify it. While Drunkard was harping on the wrongs too much that he believed in rebutting Granny he would get his life back.

He kept rebuking her, "Anything! We could have done so much, Granny! We could have stopped the Elder."

While, she kept badgering him with the reality of the present. "We can. We could. He didn't. Enough of this! Don't live in the mistakes of the past. Look at the LO, they have built a haven. What have you!"

"What have I? You have made yes-sayers out of us! That is what we have become! The LO is a bunch of yes-sayers! And that is what will be the future!"

Stubborn to swim in the ditch of the riots, Drunkard made little of the LO Zone. He also disparaged Granny's trust in the future of the town. As he was forlornly contemptuous, the old lady was forlornly idealistic. Who was right and who was wrong? I was not in the position to judge as the town didn't need a trial by media. But it was certain. If Granny's approach was quixotic then Drunkard's was fatalistic. They needed to find a middle ground than condemn each other's idea as ridiculous.

Hearing his incessant outburst, Granny then sat down with a thud. She was exhausted. She then looked into the sky as if asking it to rain a little. Noticing how Drunkard was bent on chasing his tail, Granny while sitting down made one last attempt to shame him into life-affirmation. I admired her even when she seemed to whip a dead horse.

With a sigh on her lips and a disgruntled look, she began. "In a name, by a name, for a name you drink now, Drunkard. The past was terrifying, but the LO have found their purpose, not still mourning by a drink! Who is in a hangover here, you! Look at Halo, Lee, and all these people right here in the Black and White, and what lovely ambitions they have. They are just a glimpse of what potential the LO holds. So many times I have told you to find yourself a job in the LO, and don't rake at your wounds. Nothing good will come of it. You aren't helping anyone! Lee is, the LO are, but you are becoming nothing, nothing, and nothing at all. I lost, yes I lost…I lost my husband in the riots. My son in the riots. And, and you lost your parents. You lost your sister whom I loved like a daughter! The LO, all of them lost their families. You think I don't protest. I protest!"

"How is your silence, a protest, Granny? Tell me!"

Granny didn't requite him with an answer. It was a cycle he was riding and even I could see he wasn't reaching any conclusion. Tired, exhausted, and tanned even, Granny and I looked at each other, and then at him. He was but energetic to have a go at it again. If only he showed that much energy in rebuilding his life. Well, who was I to say anything about him?

Putting a stop to the oscillating pendulum, she patted Drunkard and spoke.

"I promised Halo, must see how the pamphlets are coming out. Grace, you should also try your hand at it. Come on! Lets meet up with Lee."

Uninterested to look at some trivial pamphlets, I courteously refused her offer. "I would love to, but Granny I think…" The old lady didn't have the time or the strength of mind to judge my negative response. She let it go. Then she tenderly held the drunken boy by his hand and nudged him to follow. It had me wonder how Granny could so easily forget and forgive his insolence and act motherly towards him. It was evocative of a mother who loves her child so much, no matter how disgraceful he turns out to be. Nevertheless, she quite adroitly clutched the boy's hand. She had that affectionate look on her face that all was going to be all right.

Though Granny was quick to change her colours, Drunkard needed a push to give up his rancor. Realizing that it was time to let go, he then gave up even if grudgingly. Granny then got up and as we all were flushed with sweat, she wiped her face with her scarf. Then she offered it to the boy, who but refused her peace offering. Without offering any of it to me, she then whispered indistinctively to the boy. Then we shared formal farewells, after which the old lady along with the boy retraced their way back to the house. I also left them in peace to return to the shack. As I walked the journey back alone, Drunkard's lyric 'Be Mine Marcella" wormed its way into my head. I knew it then that the song was going to latch onto me forever. And would continue to repeat its annoyance till I succumbed to it. While walking I sang it three to four times, and strangely enough I began to like it.

It got me thinking why Maker gave us memories. Simply so we could have roses in wintry Decembers. And so as I was bored while walking alone, my mind just hummed that song, and I felt revived again.

Chapter 7

Armour for the Dead

Though I had been in the shack for some time, I had not quite looked at it. So when I reached home, I thought to kill time by scanning its inaccessible corners and silken cobwebs. The cabin had a bed with pale sheets for a mattress. There was a chair but no table. Walls were mouldy and had time-worn wallpaper covering them. There were no pictures hanging just an illegible graffiti here and there. The ceiling fan made a humdrum noise after every fifth rotation. While the window would squeal like a witch when winds would hit it. It was a small space where one would merely get to stretch his legs. More like locked-in. Still it had so many features that despite its claustrophobic form, the place seemed boundless. I was happily engrossed in its universe when I heard a knock on the door and a familiar voice.

"Hello, come on open the door!" The voice had a peskiness I had heard before. It was drunk. The hour was hanging around midnight. Drunkard was outside the door and he was knocking with a purpose. It didn't seem he had strayed off. Yet I wished if he had not come to bore me again with his tedious diatribe. As he knocked, I half-heartedly opened the door.

"You still up, this late? Or did I wake you, huh?" He asked with a smirk.

I had seen the true face of Drunkard. A lost rebel. But there he was back in his mask of a jester. He wore it with such finesse like nothing had happened the same day. I think Granny was beginning to rub off on us. Even when it was an awkward meet, both of us overlooked it. I didn't see into his eyes and neither did he. We just surfed each other's faces without reading into the wrinkles that made them. The minute we did so, we became relaxed in our comforting pretences.

"What do you want? Didn't Granny hook you up in the store?" I sneered at him while trying to keep it normal.

"Yes yes, but tell me are you sleepy or do you want to see some things in the woods?" Hurriedly, he proposed his intention. He was quick with his gestures. Hastily stern in his voice. The boy had not come for another flippant conversation. He had purpose in his visit. The more I paused to discern his intent, he would surrender his patience to haste. He would even fist his palms so that I realize his seriousness. In his hurry, it was evident he wanted to feel useful again. Hence, without testing his patience anymore, I replied in the same buck. "I am ready as I will ever be." Seeing me acquiescent, he then tried to dress it up with danger to make me even more curious. "It wouldn't be pretty." He grinned. And I assured him. "I have been in worse…"

It was seconds after midnight. The time of less light and more shadows in the wind. When he asked me to walk with him, he was aware I might reject his offer. It is not seemly for a girl to walk the night with a boy. And Drunkard wanted me to walk with him. I should have been cautious. But caution is not an armour for the dead. So I didn't need it to fret over it. Agreeing almost hastily, Drunkard blushed at my impeccable spirits. Nevertheless he was also relieved that I was going to accompany him. He had something risky in mind, and couldn't do it alone. The boy also didn't trust anyone else with it. He needed someone like me. Without doubt, he lit-up with a smile as I settled to join him.

Isolated and slept as the town was, we took our steps close to the woods.

"The Woods? In there?" I asked with curiosity.

"Yes, in there." He was grave with a tinge of fear.

The woods were a hall of horror. It was night, and all the nightly creatures breathing inside it had come out. The woods were awake. There was no light coming from it. Just some eyes that would shimmer and then disappear. It was a frightening spectacle of mighty darkness with life right down to its atom. The more we treaded deep into the woods, the more I got curious. What were the creatures holding the trees tall? The insects keeping the ground fertile? The crystal dew, the meandering vines, and the surreal light of the moon.

When an owl would sing, I would clap with my eyes. The snakes which hissed moved me to hiss back. The ants that would crawl over my skin, I would crush them with my kiss. In the mist I seemed to float. Piles and piles of dead leaves seemed to drag me down. Any flutter in the bushes, and I would repay with the same buck. I was at home in the circus of nature. In its wanton wildness. In its perilous savagery. Woods were the only place in the world where I would feel safe. The mob of trees could have saved me once. If they had been planted underneath the Bridge. The vulgar space beneath it, if it had some trees. Such was the reason, why I would always find peace while walking in the woods. While in open spaces I would feel exposed and threatened. Woods are indeed beautiful places, and when people would fear what they foreshadowed, I felt insulted. The deserts and the wastelands are the mindless places of pain and torture. Not the woods. I would be stricken with a trauma at such deforested places as they had no cover of the trees, the animals, and the darkness. Where to hide then?

Valiantly, as I walked the night trip in the jungle, Drunkard would get a little petrified. All the while he would fret and whimper as if a raven was cawing at his neck. Drunkard didn't seem to take in the darkness as gladly as I was. From the beasts to the tiniest monsters of the woods, he didn't appear to like any of them. Owls to him seemed like monsters. The woods appeared to him as gallows of death. I guess, it was the drink that was playing tricks with his mind. If my fervour made me ravish the woods, his drink made him fear it. Still, despite the dread, he was persistent in his walk. Was he making amends for his sorry life? Could be. The boy was determined to prove he was more than what his current disposition implied. The need to reassert himself was dire in him. Though the night and its deathly shadows were terrifying, he was resolute to break out of the cocoon. Once again.

I was curious. He was afraid and still unwavering. What were we hoping to get out of our jaunt in the woods? As we walked, I made monsters out of the grasshoppers.

And ravens out of the glow worms. Frustrated at the cyclic tick-tock of the real world, I compulsively drank fear to stay riveted. The more the woods would howl and reverberate with horror, the more aroused I felt. Drunkard too felt like me, but he was not aware of it. Why go to a place which reeked of dread? He could have taken me someplace human-like. But it was the jungle he had chosen. Chosen to escape to. The boy despite his fear still wanted to walk in its den. Even when he couldn't see it, he wanted it.

In the woods, his face would twitch erratically while cold sweat would grow on the sides of his forehead. He would falter in his steps when the forest would break his spine. Yet he kept walking deep into the jungle. Why? The fear of magic was something his mind needed like medicine. He needed it to forget the banality of his past. But he was not aware of it consciously. Even when his subconscious was aware, he was not able to connect to it. Without fear I would have been a dead decaying meat lying in some grave. Because of dread I arose from where I was buried. The threat of reality had once killed me more than once. But the fear of magic caressed me to wake up! Else, I would have remained a food for the nightly creatures of the mud.

When the real had slept with my skin, magic had helped me live through it.

In the town, the magical entity of the woods, the witch, some witch, kept me going in spite of the monotonous rhetoric of the Elder and the old lady. So much I needed to escape wherever I went. Drunkard needed it as well as without it he was nothing but a wasted alcoholic. For me living with the fear of magic was like hanging by a silk thread. The threat of the real world had left me hanging by nothing. Shut-out. Buried. In the dark. It was magic which saved me from falling eternally. It was magic. The dread of it. Hence I was in the woods. And Drunkard too was with me.

We walked while talking to the silence of the woods. Since we had stepped in, none of us actually said anything to each other. We were too absorbed in the beauty of the shadows that words didn't matter. Silent. Hushed. In the dark. We were spell-bounded.

Then, without warning, Drunkard held me by my arm. It didn't hurt. He was gentle even when severe in his gesture.

"We are not alone." He spoke grimly.

"Okay." I brushed aside his concern.

"No I mean it. We are not alone!" He reiterated with force.

As I refused to heed him, he tightly held my arm and pulled me close. He didn't do it to suggest any lewdness but a grave concern. Though it began to hurt as his fingers kept pressing the nerves under my skin, I didn't mind it. I was wishing if it were the witch, some witch who had stolen his calm. After all, it was in her world of woods we were in.

What an entity she was! First she had appeared as a chanter in the woods and then no matter how hard I tried, she wouldn't show herself. When she had chanted the Maker's name, her voice sounded paradoxical. It was calming even when haunting. I had only seen her shadow during the day of the puke. She seemed to have a slender shape and wore a dark gown. I could see the flow of her hair in rhythm with the winds. She had tall, curly and golden tresses as they shone in the sunlight through the mist. She wouldn't stir from her place as if certain I wouldn't come after her. During the day of the puke, the entity had tightly clutched the bark of the tree. Rather she had her entire body clung to it. Though aiming to hide herself, she was visible. I couldn't see her eyes in the dark. If I had I would have known everything there was to know about her. Was shy coy? Strong? Criminal? Naïve? Even a look at her lips would have been a mirror into what she was besides her name. I didn't see a goat anywhere near her. There was no aura of strangeness about her. Greenery didn't seem to rot in her presence.

In my heart if I was afraid of her, it was because of her voice. She was praying to the Maker and it felt as if she was casting a spell. And she had spell-bounded me.

When Drunkard hurt me with his firm grasp, I had to look back. I had to see it before that entity of magic squirmed out of my hands. So I pushed him away, while grunting into the darkness behind us. "The witch, some witch is here! Where? Where?"

Drunkard was taken aback at the sheer force of my push. And that I knew about the entity. It had been only a day or so in that town. Still I knew about the witch, some witch. He bit his tongue in utter astonishment. Mystified, he knocked his head with his knuckles and blurted out. "No, yes, wh-! You know about her too? I'll be damned." He was certainly taken aback. Disappointed and startled at the same time. That I knew the witch, some witch before he could even tell me of it. I had robbed him of a secret he wanted to be a sole processor of. He had thought of extorting my company by dangling the prospect of meeting the magic thing. Seeing his discontent, I grinned at him. "Yeah, of course I do! That's my job."

I kept straining my eyes for the witch, some witch, but there seemed to be no presence of her. I was impatient. He saw me impatient. And as I had stunted him of his pleasure, he took his time to reveal what in fact followed us. There was nothing but darkness and no slender figure to go with it. I looked at Drunkard again. He didn't seem to be afraid. If it were the witch, some witch, he would have been frightened. But he was undaunted. His lips were dry. Eyes were not dilated. Fear had not sucked out his verve. The boy was certainly not insinuating the dark entity, but someone else. Before I could beat it out of him, he answered. "It's not the witch, some witch. It's your shadow."

I thought he was joking. But he didn't giggle while cracking it. It was dark, and I certainly didn't have a shadow. Still I looked at the ground and saw nothing but wildlife roaming about. Seeing me look in the wrong direction, he declared again. "Not down there. Behind us. Don't look!"

I had looked back before and there was nothing but the whisper of darkness. But provoked by his dangling, I again rebelled to glance at what was behind us. Right then, he caught my face by the jaws and stopped me midway. He wouldn't let me have a peek. I was perturbed and even aroused by his actions. As I struggled to budge, he preened himself that at least I didn't know about the shadow. Before he had impressed his hand-print on my face, I gave him a cheap shot. He whined in pain, and I saw what tailed us.

It was Jon, the Elder's page.

"Jon! It is Jon? That's the shadow you are talking about?" I grunted with disdain.

We were being followed by the minion of the Elder. But Drunkard didn't seem to be bothered by him. He wouldn't see Jon as a threat. What if he prattled about our night trip to the rest of the town? The Elder certainly would use such a piece of information most maliciously. Even Granny would, without doubt, use it to cement her doubts about me. But Drunkard remained impervious to my apprehension. He was more hooked on the idea of Jon being my shadow.

I tried to assail him with the truth. "I know him of course! The question is why let him follow? The Elder must have sent him to spy on us!"

Even when realizing I was serious, Drunkard overlooked my concern. Discreetly gesturing towards Jon, he urged me to understand. "That is not what should concern you. He is your shadow." He was solemn in his tone. Even when speaking in mad riddles. The occasion did not demand such levity. Yet he was stubborn to discount the gravity of the circumstances. And was more intent on persuading me to see Jon as a shadow. My shadow. Due to his vile obstruction of facts, I was beginning to lose my calm. Flustered with bile, I demanded to know.

"What the hell is a shadow? Is that a funny word for a stalker in your town?"

He but responded with calm.

"No, not at all. A shadow is not a cheap stalker. They only follow, and never talk."

Drunkard's answer was mischievous as it was nowhere an answer. Besides I was disenchanted seeing Jon. It was the witch, some witch I had hoped to see as she had cast a blinding spell on me. And Drunkard expected me to arouse my curiosity over the page. True, the Elder's page had stolen the whisper of my heart, but it was just a whisper. I wanted to see the magical fiend of the woods. Drunkard but was persistent. He beset me with the tale of the shadow. If the town had a political history of the Zones, the magical story of the witch, some witch, then it also seemed to have an unusual song of the shadow.

Irate, I asked the drunken boy again. "Drunkard, don't mince words. Be straight with me, what is this shadow business?"

Drunkard took a deep gulp of his drink. Then he gestured that we talk while continuing our trip. He was no longer epileptic with fear, and seemed very well in charge. As we walked, I could feel my eyes drooping with heaviness. Saliva began to ooze out the sides of my mouth and my heartbeat kept beeping. Beep! Beep! Beep!

The boy was tediously slow while revealing the song of the shadow. He unraveled the truth at a snail's pace. "Before you, there were no shadows. But your coming to this town has sort of reincarnated them." After saying his piece, he paused to render it a pull of gravity. The boy was pushing my buttons, and I didn't have time or the state of mind to tolerate it anymore.

I held him from his collars, the way he had held my jaw. Then I shouted right in his face that he got hit with my spit. "What are they Drunkard, tell me or we are done!"

Shaken, he whimpered while fiercely blinking his eyes. "Okay okay, relax! They are people, Grace. People, people who find pleasure in other people's sufferings. It helps them to get over their own grief."

Taking pleasure in someone else's grief. That is a sadist! Jon was a sadist? As shocking as the news was, it didn't matter to me. What mattered was that Jon somehow knew about my grief and so had decided to shadow me! The very thought of it perturbed me. It was a threat. I felt a sudden chill run down my neck. My grief was in my past. Shameless and dishonourable as it was, it was mine to shadow and no one else's. Hearing that Jon somehow had gotten a whiff of it put me in a tight corner. I almost couldn't breathe.

Arming my shock with rage, I yelled at the drunken boy.

"Nonsense! Nonsense! You mean my suffering! Where am I suffering?"

"Wh-what? I don't know, but he does." Drunkard was taken aback at my sudden change in temper.

How would Jon, a fly trapped under the Elder's foot, know of my grief? It was impossible for any human to know of my sordid past. What happened to me, happened a long time back. Under the Bridge. Ages had passed. No records, no history. How could Jon know when it was unwritten? When it was long lost? The strain of Drunkard's words was too much to bear. Jon's relentless following was too much bear. And the uncertainty of whether it was true or not was like a stone pricking my foot.

While keeping a guarded watch at Jon, I struck Drunkard again.

"What else you know about it, uh? Tell me everything! "

Drunkard was intrigued. He wouldn't get it as to why I didn't feel like a princess for having a stalker. He thought I would feel elated in having a creepy follower. He also had believed that it would be an honour for me to be associated with the town in that fashion. Naturally then my fitful backlash pricked his belief. To make me appreciate his right way of thinking, he responded.

"The shadows were long dead in this town. The last shadow was, I think of Granny's great great grandfather. It is an honour to have one." Before he assailed me with the notion of honour, I interrupted him brusquely. "What is this? A silly ritual?"

Before I could have further dishonoured the shadow, he interrupted me as well. "Ritual, yes. An honourable ritual. The town is not made aware of a shadow till a week passes. That weeds out the committed from uncommitted. Grace, you should know a shadow happens only when there is a strong cause behind it. You are the cause. You made it all happen again!"

I was made to suffer to become a cause?

I had no volition in this matter. To be made a victim. And then to be shadowed. As Drunkard went screaming honour, honour, and honour, the sharp stab of my dishonor rattled my heart into thousand songs. Beep! Beep! Beep! I could hear my guts disemboweling themselves. Too influenced by the honour of the ritual, the boy couldn't see how it irked me painfully. I was also in rage. The absurdity of the ritual was too much to bear. It felt they were mocking me for having a sad past. Consecrated rituals. Turning victims into martyrs. Beyond the pale.

Infuriated with a sudden gloominess pervading over me, I kept muttering. "Nonsense! Nonsense! Where am I suffering?"

Unable to grasp the frenzy in my voice, he responded as a matter of fact. "I don't know, he knows, and may be you too…"

Jon? How would he know? If he were a clairvoyant, a telepath, or a mind-reader, may be then. But there are no such things in the world. Magic which exists is either organic or not at all. It does not subsist as a part of a human. It does not occur in parts or attached to human. It is either whole or not at all. Not in pieces.

As I hyperventilated, Drunkard couldn't understand why was I so guilt-ridden? The questions I kept hitting him with, they certainly defined me as guilty. But what was I guilty of, he was sorely in the dark. As he tried to reason it, a doubt raged in my mind. What if it was true? What if Jon knew? What if he decided to talk about it and tell the town?

Taking control of my breathing, I restrained my attacking doubts, and asked the boy.

"Do they talk about it to anyone?"

"They never do. Your secrets are safe…" He spoke in a manner to console my misgivings. Even when unaware of what ailed me, he tried to comfort me. Though he was perturbed at what secrets I was hiding, he let it go.

Secrets. I wished I had pretty secrets to keep. A little diary with a lock and a key. A letter hidden behind a photo frame. A street cat which I would raise and tell no one about. Secrets as pretty as these I wished I had some like these. Mysterious as is life, I but had secrets of untoward kinds. With whom could I share them? But bury them deep in my heart. Let them burn for ages to come and go.

What had besmirched my life was not of my doing. But the dishonor was mine to bear. I was made a victim without honour. A dishonorable victim. After my death, I knew my friends who were jealous of me must have drawn malicious delight. Even relations near and far who despised my presence, must have shed predatory tears of joy. What to talk about my mother. She was gracefully dead to know what dishonour her daughter had dug up. And my living lost father must have judged me from wherever he was. Judged me in death. Judged me for my moral make-up. Moral dress. Moral voice. Moral skin. Moral soul. If these secrets had become public knowledge, I would have relived the Bridge all over again. Hearing my past from someone else's mouth. Reliving it when people would gaze at me with pity. It was good I was buried. Dead. Locked. Shut down. Unable to stir. Move. Cry. Scream. See. It was peace. But then, Jon apparently wanted to undig me. The thought of it had my body and mind in fits. Drunkard assured me. My secrets were safe. As long as Jon kept quiet. Was I to then pin my hope in the drunken boy's fickle guarantee? I knew if I had to take extreme measures, I would gladly hurt Jon. Silence him. Anything. To such a thought, I pinned my hope.

When we had walked some distance, Drunkard then declared ecstatically. He was ecstatic as he wanted to distract me from Jon's shadowing. Seeing how it had unnerved me, the boy asserted with rapture.

"Here we are!"

"What is this place?" I asked with patient interest.

"Grace, I will be honest." He paused and scratched his temple with his knuckle. Then he continued "I do not know what we might see, but I know it's a memento mori of some sort. I had once eavesdropped on Granny and the Elder but couldn't gather my nerve to check on it till now. "

It was a forbidden secret. Drunkard didn't know what it was. The entire town seemed to be oblivious of it expect the elders. That is why Drunkard had chosen me as his accomplice. He knew no one else would want to go behind Granny's back or dare to cross the Elder. So it had to be me. An exotic girl from abroad. Besides he needed to purge his own regression and hoped the memento mori would fast forward it.

As we reached the spot, Drunkard began to look for anything out of place. He touched the trees, its leaves and bark. He was berserk to find anything up in the sky. The boy even climbed the trees that entombed us. He checked if there was something left hanging by a silken thread. Anything suspicious that the elders had deemed to hide. He was frantic in his search. Eager to expose the dirty linens of the town. He didn't share Granny's concern that an outsider might get privy to the secrets of his home. His sole concern was to find something incriminating and prosecute the town for its rose-tinted vision.

As he kept ruffling up the leaves, I asked him.

"Drunkard, I need to ask, why are you telling me about this mori?"

"You report." He replied as succinctly as truth. Unsatisfied, I asked again, "Is that all?"

Peeved, he unholstered his bottle. Took a big gulp while spilling most of it. Then he replied with an introspective face. "I need to know my past, need to revive it and feed it coal so it can burn again. I need to…"

I was piquantly fatigued by his diatribe before. I didn't want to go at it again. I stopped him. "Really? I will not go any further if you still plan on fixating on the past and…"

Disgruntled, he almost crushed the bottle in his hand. Then striking the wind with his other hand, he questioned me with impunity. "What do you know about my past?" Taken aback by his insolence, I hit him. "I don't want to compare our pasts, but who has a shadow you or I?"

He was stumped. If Jon was shadowing me, it meant that my past was more grisly than his. Drunkard was certainly stumped while imagining what manner of misfortune had I seen. The boy but did not importune me about it. After a stroke of silence, he spoke with a tear in his voice.

"What will you have me do? For a day or a week even if I will mend myself, I will revert. I am done Grace, I am done for. Revenge is all I have, and without it I am just a corpse living…"

A corpse living? When Drunkard uttered the word 'corpse' my hair stood on its end. I was made a corpse one fine daynight. Did I like it? No. But when someone would take this word in vain, I wished to flog them. I hated what I was, but couldn't have anyone running their mouth foul about it.

"It's funny you should say a corpse. It's funny and fair, and so very fair…"I whispered while fidgeting with fury.

The boy seeing me lose it again frowned at my prickly nerves. "Why, what do you mean? Grace?" Before I had further debased myself with frailty, I changed the subject.

"You want to forget it all?"

"No! I do not want to forget. I want it to fester!" He grunted with passion.

Drunkard wanted his wounds to fester. I wanted mine to end. Walking since the time under the Bridge, I wanted to stop walking. It was mockery enough when as a human I was humiliated by gentlemen. It was added salt when as a creature I was forced to walk in the world of gentlemen. It was a grotesque way of living after death.

Drunkard wanted to replay his tragic past over and over again. He was bound to it. Chained with blood. He should have swapped places with me. When I wanted to forget, he yearned to memorize with hate. It had me wonder. Were the criminals who butchered his past, let go that he was inconsolable? Was that the reason he had not found any closure and was precariously devastated?

Burning with pain, he continued.

"I will have my wounds again. I am afraid to be a walking corpse."

I didn't want to take his harangue personally. But the boy was tenacious to malign my kind. Not all dead bodies are evil. Why did he then hold all of us accountable for his grief? He wouldn't leave us alone. I couldn't have it. So I attacked him while smacking my fist in his chest.

"You afraid to be a corpse?"

"Yes! I am afraid. I will kill myself I know this. These wounds are my only purpose, and without them I am dead. The peace, Granny talks of, it reminds me of a graveyard! On debris, they all are building a home. On corpses! What can be more morbidly sick than this!"

He didn't get the hint. Drunkard would lose himself to curse his life. Then he would curse the corpses. If he did not want to live or die, then what did he want? Did he want to become someone like me? Life in death? Seeing him vomit his angst at the carcasses like me, I was beyond offended. Taking a step back, while viciously kicking the dirt beneath my foot, I lunged at him.

"Corpses can also be, be…be harbingers of life, damn ye! Damn your life!"

"You are a fool to believe this! You are a fool!" He was but resilient in his act.

If I were a fool, then what was to be said about my Maker. He who hired me to do a job even when I had conveniently died. I was dead, and buried underground. Yet he gave me a job. Does that not make Him a fool?

I felt vulnerable as Drunkard would not stop. He had exposed my wounds green. I had after much toil calmed them into a clot. Decades after decades, they would get infected again. I would again nurse them into death. Why does the world of living brood over cadavers? The past was a corpse. Drunkard while cringing over it still wanted it back. If only he could make peace. Let it rest in peace. But he raked it to ooze pus out of it! He should have buried it with a gravestone that revealed everything about it. But he wanted to desecrate the grave, fling it out in the open and let the world see the naked figure of shame and dishonour.

I felt vulnerable. As if he was doing it to me.

In my vulnerable state, I lashed out at him.

"You hate corpses? You think building on them is morbid? Then help build homes on your living precious body, huh! You are alive, why not pitch in! Do your part to rid the town of its grotesque fetishes for corpses! And if you can't so just shut up!" I raved and ranted gibberish. Drunkard was befuddled to make any sense of it. Harassed by my seething temper, he walked towards me. If my words were not making any sense, he wanted to look into my eyes. To understand my pain. But he was lost.

"I am…What are we talking about? Corpses?"

As he kept reading the controlled anguish vivid in my eyes, I looked away. I glanced at the night sky. At the nothingness of the darkness. At the vague shadow of Jon behind us. As Drunkard groped for something to say, I stomped my feet on the ground, and strained my eyes away from him.

Then he spoke.

"I will try."

"What?"

"I will try again, get a job, something to do somewhere, and drop the booze…"

As he said it, I sighed and kicked the ground again. It struck against something. It felt tilled, soft and green. It ominously felt like home.

Apprehensive, I asked him.

"Something was dug here."

He was but clueless. "What?"

I asked again while faintly losing my hold on the ground.

"The soil. I can see the difference. What is it? Is this the place?"

He made a frenetic recce of the ground beneath us. We had been looking at the stars, when all answers were down below. In a split-second, he effused with fear and a sense of euphoria.

"We have reached!"

We had reached the place. It was encircled by invictus trees which didn't dare to grow on it. Even mob of bushes refused to grow on it. The place with its nude space felt like home.

Something was buried where we stood. It was the place. We had reached. It felt like a burial. Home. The thought of excavating a buried secret did not sit well with my stomach. I wanted to puke. What was buried didn't matter. It was buried. The thought of it was torturous.

Drunkard kept picking the lay of the land. Then he proclaimed. "Something was dug here. You are right, Grace. Finally! Something! Help me Grace! We need to use our hands as claws! Grace!"

"B-Buried here you m-mean? We, we shouldn't. We mustn't" I stuttered with shame. Seeing me dizzy with sweat, he gently held me close. "Grace, you are getting paler than before. Are you all right?"

Drunkard's voice drew into a smoke. I couldn't hear my own voice. I felt a certain weakness in my heart. A lost rage. Beep! Beep! Beep! I clutched at it with all my strength. But blood seemed to drain from it. I could see my eye balls receding behind my lids. Even my gob had opened up in an awry shape. Drunkard held me from falling as my feet had almost lost their moorings. It felt nastily deathlike.

"Grace don't be afraid! Look at me!" The boy grasped me close to his bosom. He was strong but his strength was halved by his drink. He nevertheless tried to keep me from falling. He was, without doubt, alarmed. But then as much as he tried, he had to let me fall. His arms couldn't bear the heavy weight of my fitful delirium. As I fell most humorously by the edge of the small wasted patch, Drunkard kissed my cheeks. My hands. The forehead. I was shivering with cold and stuttering with frenzy. Even when he pressed his body against mine, I couldn't stop. The boy then covered me with his full-sleeved shirt as warmly as he could.

In a while I was somewhat calmed. Tearing away from his grasp, I anxiously reassured him.

"I am fine. Drunkard! I am fine. Why don't you go exhume what's buried. I will stay right here, catch my breath, okay?"

"Wh-what! Are you sure?" He was flabbergasted.

Despite the pain of keeping up appearances, I tried to reason with him. "Yes! Yes. It was just the curiosity killing me. Huh! Go ahead. The sooner we get it done, the sooner we can go back, right?"

He was but restlessly concerned. The boy didn't care about the memento mori any longer. I had to divert his attention from me. I had to. But he would still crowd me with his distress.

"No, we can go now!" Drunkard was inflexibly adamant.

I then stood up to make him see that my condition had improved. But he still remained apprehensive even when I was standing like a normal girl. The boy was testing my patience. I then had to strike him in his chest so he would leave me alone. I struck him. "Drunkard! Will you just get it done with! It's the cold that had caught me off guard. That is all. Go on, do what you gotta do. I will stay here."

Noticing I was stubborn to remain in the ditch of my pain, the boy reluctantly left me. While unearthing the site, he nevertheless kept a stringent watch. He was torn between his concern for me and the need to dig out the memento mori. As seconds turned into minutes his eyes began to busy themselves with what was buried. It was then I could let go of any restraint and simply relapse into my delirium. The more he sunk into the underground world, the more I kept rising and falling in my feverish shock from the past.

I never told myself as I hated to believe it. The Head was kind to me. Of all the officers he was kind. I remember how I was struggling to reach the waters, to wash myself and he helped me reach the pond. He even ordered one of the officers to return my pashmina so I could dab myself dry. When it got soiled in blood, he also washed it in the pond. Seeing how I loved green green nature, the Head was kind to bury me close to it. He could see my affections for nature, for the brooks, and the green green grass. He was kind to bury me in it.

When the officers had begun to dig me a grave, the Head had kept a kind watch. All the while the cold gathered with mist and the night garnered by the rising moon. Then, picking what was left of my body, the Head made me see the empty grave drawn with flowers, weeds and worms.

After that, he caressed my plaits and whispered romantically. "A night to remember. In it you will become fertile."

I didn't tremble with fear. I was too broken. He didn't seem to like it. It certainly pricked his ego. Irked, he still maintained his chivalrous calm. When the grave was dug, the Head didn't throw me into it. Gently, he himself stepped inside and laid me comfortably with hands on my chest. Then he also removed any pointed pebbles that could prick me in the back. He ensured the ditch was empty but for the flowers, weeds, and worms decorating my wedding bed. A night to remember, and become fertile.

Drunkard: "A s-skull. A broken jaw s-skull. Halo! Grace look at this! It's a mass grave! My Halo, there are more corpses! Unmarked graves! Skulls and bones. It's an unnatural graveyard!"

Grace: "But mine was empty…empty when I was put there. The Head ensured."

Drunkard: "Grace! Grace! Are you all right? Hold fast Grace, I am here. We will dig it up. Fleeing from it wouldn't make the corpses disappear. Nothing is unnatural ever. The bedrock of this soil, I want to go and see how deep it is. Open her up. Claw in with me now! Grace! I need you. Grace? Grace?"

Grace: "I didn't know, there were so many! So many of us, so many of us…"

Drunkard: "Grace, are you going to get sick and spoil my excavation? Count with me…There are five of them. Didn't you hear the legend of five? The sorry tale of the five. The Malafide Five. They were never found. It is said so in the books. The civil war. In this town, and the ones responsible- the multiparty of five leaders! They disappeared before they could be proven guilty. And, and here they rested all this long! More like rot in an unmarked grave. It never bodes peace for the dead."

Grace: "Both good and bad, rot the same. This sneering skull and I. We look the same. With or without skin. Who was good or who was bad? Who dragged me and who was being dragged? We all look alike. Bones and carcass? I was them, and they were me."

As the Head cleaned my bed of any pricking stones, he laid the crushing weight of his body on top of me. Then he…

Drunkard: "Grace! Grace! What's wrong? No! Hold my hand. Lie still, lie still, Lie still! It will be all right. Grace can you hear me! It's a paroxysm, the ones Noor has, Grace! Wake up! Don't die on me! I am here! Clutch my Hand! Jon! Jon! I am here! Find me in this halodamn mist!"

… softly brushed the dirty hair off my face. I looked in his eyes, he was cruel. Why was he then acting so surreally kindhearted and patient with his hands? I was too weak to assemble the words coming from his lips. They nevertheless caressed me like a lullaby. The Head was unafraid. Unafraid if a passerby had seen him. Unafraid of playing with time. Unafraid of playing with my body which was soon turning into a corpse. Unafraid of whether I might scream. Unafraid of the curses I spoke through my eyes. Unafraid of my blood that could convict him. Unafraid of his blood inside of me. The Head was calm and unafraid, and it made me sleep...

Drunkard: "Jon! Jon! We are here! It's another one!"

Grace: "S-skulls, and mine, bones and theirs, all the s-same..."

Drunkard: "What are you muttering Grace? What is happening?"

The Head's last words to me were, 'Do you want it quick?" I wanted it before when the pain was overflowing. And when it was done, he had the cheek to make such a callous offer. He asked again, and I saw in him agitation building up. He was frantic lest without answering him like a servile thing, I died. What if I died on my own accord and left him unrequited? I refused him the pleasure of answering to his will. That made him violent. He then started to strike me down with his weight. Defied by a lost girl! He then spit in my face with anger slobbering from his sweat. I was weak to fend him off, but I was still living to heed him not. What more hurts he could have inflicted, I was done for. My eyes started to die. The lids began to close. And the Head was realizing he was not in power after all.

In death, I defied him.

The Head kept pushing his face into mine. But he was to lose. Soon a cold touch of death began to envelop me as if to protect me in my dying. From fingers to arms and the tip of my nose, then all was cold and wet...

Grace: "I had groveled before the officers. I begged for mercy, of mercy, but they didn't listen! Banished from Honour!"

Drunkard: "What! What are you muttering! Jon! Jon! Here we are!"

Under the Bridge as death kindly took me, the Head still kept hammering his interlocked hands at my head, my breasts and everywhere he could. Then, he turned away in shame. He was hurt as I had the cheek to defy him. While the Head dunked his head in defeat, the officers buried me in an unmarked grave. Where no one comes to mourn. Where no one is a good man or a bad woman...

Drunkard: Jon! Find us in this halodamn mist!"

Grace; "I defied him! In death I defied him!

In the woods, the moment I saw the unmarked burial, my mind had lost it. Body then had to break. Drunkard kept yelling at every direction to force Jon out of his ritualistic hiding. The mist was overpowering. He couldn't see where Jon was perched. The boy beat me with his hands while I convulsed in anxious rhythms. But his warm body didn't make a difference. His voice soothing and drunk didn't seem to work. I was gone somewhere. Lost while reliving my past. Drunkard also wanted it. To relive the past. If he knew what ailed me, he would have never asked for it again. Never again.

The drunken boy was agonized in his helplessness to save me. The boy kept calling out for the page, knowing it was against tradition. While he punctured my skin, caressed and kissed it, the mist began to grow more. Just then, I heard strides of steps running towards us. It had to be Jon. I could hear anger in his inhalation. He was vexed as he had to shun his shadowing and heed the vulnerable thing he thought he knew. The page appeared before us in a matter of minutes. While grasping me into his arms, he began chanting some strange music in the wind.

"Watch over us the night spirits of the dead. Watch over us the night spirits of the dead. Ravens make them refuse our eyes. Tigers can wrong not the delicate treat of our skin. Spirits cannot take our flesh. Watch over us the night spirits of the dead. Skulls will be born to be skulls again. It never stops…"

The music was erotic while its verses almost maddening. Drunkard was certainly disturbed by Jon's absurd incantations. "What are you doing Jon? What are you doing to her? You a shaman?"

"I am right now." Jon was but stern.

Jon had an uncanny shiver in his fingers, as he grasped my body. He began to notice something strange about my creature. I was cold, he could discern. But why a living thing would still be cold. The scientific thought of it pestered him.

"She is cold, Drunkard. Why is her body cold?" Skeptic, he put across his doubts.

"I am cold too. So are you! It is past midnight in the woods! Jon can you take care of her or not?" Drunkard was but aloof. Pestered, Jon still continued with his magical music. The boy kept singing strange rhymes into the air which I found consoling.

"Build a fire, we need to build a fire…fire fire glow in the dark, burn the darkness, and keep your spark, in air why breathes death, fire fire to ashes turn its wreath."

The more Jon touched my skin and breathed its lifeless odour, he got suspicious. I was cold. I was cold as in devoid of life. Dead! Drunkard couldn't but understand it. While brushing aside Jon's gifted assumption, he gave out an agonizing shriek.

"Grace! Wake up! Wake up! I will not have you die! No! No!"

Jon had to balance his suspicions and his concern for me. It was certain that I was in pain. Even dead, the pain with which my body convulsed was enough to subdue him. He had to take charge of the situation as Drunkard was utterly helpless.

"We need to warm her, Drunkard!"

"I will not let you die! Wake up Grace!" Drunkard was in tears. Before he had gone more hysterical than I was, Jon slapped him hard on his face. Drunkard was shocked but silent. Then Jon tried what he could to keep me warm.

"Hold her hands. Rub her, and her feet. I will build a fire!"

But I was perpetually cold and it frightened Jon. His assumptions were right. In my state of vulnerability, I was not able to hide it. Even when I was touched by the flames of fire, I wouldn't accept warmth. Despite being touched by the cold of death, I was still alive. He saw it and it made him sick to his stomach.

"Jon, what's wrong? You are losing it too, we must save her! Hear me! What's wrong?"

"Can't be…can't be…no…" Jon cringed to even touch me anymore. Still he kept at it to warm my exotic form of life. Both remained by my side. It consoled me in my heart that they had not abandoned me. If I were evil, they would have left in a matter of seconds. Even buried me after playing with my skin. They but didn't desert. For as long as my fit lasted, I was consoled that they stayed for an undeserving creature that I was. I was not evil. I was being saved. It was not magic. It was real. Though my body did not find warmth in it. Even my mind mocked me. It was but my heart that was at peace. It was my heart that then coursed the blood of life in my veins. Flushed with it, I woke up and morose with unintelligible grief, I spoke softly.

"Drunkard?"

"Grace! Grace! You are alive!" Drunkard was in raptures. I could see it in his genuine expression. Jon was also relieved. But his relief was half-baked. He wanted to impress upon Drunkard the gravity of his concerns. But the drunken boy was beside himself with joy. Even if a dagger had struck me down, Drunkard would have been happy if I rose from the dead. In a matter of a day, he wanted me as a friend that he was ready to overlook the blot of shame that I was.

Seeing Jon still sullen with doubt, he tried to assail him.

"Jon, cheer up. Grace is fine!"

But the page was haunted by my creature. An exotic girl who was not living to be dead. In a town, where they just knew about life, illness and death, how could anyone of them pay attention to the wirings behind the workings of time?

Jon wanted to assault me to know the truth. It was only because of Drunkard, he held back. He had such a curious lust in his eyes to expose what I was. I knew what it meant as I also used to have it.

Hence, remaining discreet, he spoke nimbly. "Yes, yes…It will be dawn soon, secrets will be known." He was subtle.

We sat by the bonfire the boys had lit. We were all liars brought together by choices we had made. I tried to put on a brave front. Drunkard tried to suppress his despair of the past. And Jon tried to be patient though wanting to hunt me down. Liars indeed. There was a sense of gloominess pervading over us. After all we were in a midst of unmarked graves. A memento mori of harsh times. Memento mori. I kept asking myself, who had the intent to dig the graves? If Granny and the Elder knew about mori, it was possible they were complicit. That is why they bore each other's tantrums. The sins of the elders due to which lost were the young. But I didn't think too much on it. The woods had mesmerized me to think on such inane things.

We sat quietly by the fire while forsaking the fright of the woods. What fright? It was the reality of the past that had perturbed us, not the deep dark woods. As we seeped in the warmth of the burning fire, no more did the skeletons around us claw at our senses. I could hear a goat bleat somewhere. I could see the leaves levitating above the ground. I could sense the presence of a magical thing hiding in the trees. The music of her spells. It was a magical night.

As we sat around the fire, we three remained tranquil. Serene. Sad. Curious. Yet calm.

I looked at our shadows and it seemed as if we were dancing around some cauldron. I could smell snakes and frogs boiling alive in it. It was a magical moment in the mist.

While the fire lit the sacred ground, we stared into it to remember and forget to forget and remember.

Chapter 8

I Know You Want My Love

The day was breaking. It was hours after dawn but in the woods it still seemed night was long. The fire had doused itself. I was still half-asleep when Drunkard along with Jon began to cover up the exhumed skulls and skeletons. They would stomp on the ground to level the field and dispel any hint of intrusion. I woke up at Drunkard's calm whisper. He was still concerned for my well-being. He held me to my feet which though nice made me feel even more vulnerable. I didn't resist however. Our concern was to get out of the woods before we were seen at a place which was not supposed to exist. While brushing off the tell-tale mud of the unmarked graves, we began the walk.

Jon but did not speak a word. He didn't even walk with us. The boy had resumed the ritual by following us from a distance apart. I didn't mind. Though I could hear his presence, it was better than having to see the suspicion on his face. While we walked silently, the sun would intermittently break loose through the dense foliage. We would pause a little under it. Under its fury the air was warm. But when we would have to move, without it our bodies would shiver with cold dew and sweat. There were no owls or glow worms just ants of every colour crawling on the ground, the trees and the dead animal cadavers. It was a misty dawn brimming with bright creatures of light.

While the journey towards the memento mori was unwinding, the return didn't seem that long. Brief and dryly terse as the return was, we didn't talk about anything. About how I went spastic. The graves of murdered corpses. The elders' complicity in it. Words were not needed. It was evident in the eyes. The doubt was blinding. Is that what we expected to find? I certainly didn't. I had entered the woods with a juvenile wish for mystery but after seeing the wasted patch, I was vulnerably exposed. It was a deathlike reminder. Still, I tried to forget and even belittle what had happened to me. What fit, what terror? It was only a dance of nerves. I tried to forget lest I started to believe I was mad.

From the brim of the woods, we looked around and saw empty streets with light falling on deserted lanes. Discreetly and altered, Drunkard and the page walked me to the shack. When we reached the door, I could tell how the drunken boy wanted to stroke my face. How many times had I hit him? Touched him on his chest. How many times he had seized my face, jaw and even lapped up my body. I didn't mind then as it was the heat of the moment. But he still wanted to even when there was no need. Nevertheless, he remained hesitant which almost overwhelmed me to let him in.

It was a cold dawn, and the boy with alcohol in his body was warm. Besides, I could sense the tenderness billowing from his flavoured etiquettes and concern for me. The shack was an empty house even with me in it. Drunkard could have infused life into it. I could have asked him, but I had violent issues mumbling inside my head, and anytime spent with the boy would have been half-baked. Even insincere.

The night in the woods had left us vexed, purged and awry. Our faces had become a guilt-ridden mirror of fatigue and exasperation. Drunkard was ashamed of the chequered past of his town. Jon was ashamed of having to follow me. I was ashamed for being exposed to a bunch of boys. When I had puked, soiled and stripped myself, I couldn't then open up to Drunkard. I needed time alone. Besides, I needed to admonish my mind for breaking my body in twain. The hand which shook. Then the body which broke. It all began in the ivory-towered head of mine. Its convoluted stairs of dark memories and chambers of dirty secrets. I needed to be alone with it. So did they. We needed to stay away from each other to get to grips with the situation. To trust what we had seen. To have faith on those who had hidden it. To continue living unbothered of the criminal tale of the town. The unmarked graves.

Drunkard left. He had to even when dejected. Jon left too. He had to as I had banged the door in his face. I watched Jon from the window as he stood calmly while piercing through my clothes to hurt me. He prowled for few minutes whilst fully aware I had him under watch as well. Then he left with a warning to return again. He wanted to strip me naked. He was then the Elder's page. A slave to his baser senses. As he left I looked down in dismay and scanned my feet for no particular reason. Then I slumped on the bed with sheets for a mattress. First the mind was empty. Then it began to hit me like brick bats.

"Some skulls. Some tribulations. Some better men, and mud everywhere. During the night of the land fields, I saw… "

I stopped. I held out my hand to scrutinize it. It was beginning to shake. I could feel the spasm taking over it. It was certain. The hand would infect the rest if not cut. Holding it tightly with the other, my mind memorized again.

"Jon, Drunkard and the bonfire, skull was swerved, evidence, and mist everywhere…"

Sweat was worming into my eyes. I could see the purple veins bursting out of the skin. I got up from the bed and placed my stuttering hand under my bum. Then I crunched my legs close to my chest to put all of my weight on it. I was petite but my chest was a little too heavy. It too began to rattle up and down as my hand would writhe and wriggle. I could feel the spasm taking over my body in whispers of a silent storm. It was too much work that to stop it I had to grunt while exerting all my strength. As the hand shook wildly, my intelligent mind kept hitting me with the memories of the night.

"Unmarked bones. Secrets will be known. Black and white graves."

The more my mind flashbacked, the more the fits became untamed. I had to become violent as my pissant hand wouldn't stop struggling. I smashed it against the wall. Again. It made a crackling noise in the knuckles. I smashed it again. It bruised with a red splatter. It still wouldn't succumb to me. So I struck the wind with it and went out the door.

I hoped to meet and chat with anyone to distract myself. I knew the cruel intentions of my mind and desperately needed to sidetrack it from its original sin. If only I had let Drunkard in before. He wouldn't have let me break into a thousand songs. The boy would have held me strongly in his caring embrace. He would have talked to me, even asked if it hurt. He would have been gentle no matter how sickly erotic the emotions would have become. Loving me while smiling if I would err. I loving him back and smiling if he would err. It would have been a sonata that would be ours to share and replay. I wished if I could meet him again. To undress with pleasure than force. Although I regretted throwing him out, I also knew why I did it. There was no room for us to be more than friendly acquaintances. I was just way too crowded. Even when I needed a nice guy like him, I had become too crowded.

Morosely, I stepped out the door. The dewy dawn had turned into a sunny morning. The air was breezy. It was cool under the shade but hot as coal in the open. I could hear the sounds of Granny washing utensils. She was the only human who appeared to be awake. Though I had been entreating an audience with her, I did not want to meet her then. In my condition which was reprehensible to say the least, I didn't want her shadowing me with her stern intentions. As I hastily walked away from her house, some distance ahead I saw Halo. Halo was dull and did not pique my interest either. But at the time the girl was certainly in a compromising position. She was up on a tree and was comfortably veiled in its flora. There was a marked drop in the mist as the day grew and anyone could have seen her. But she had improvised by mixing the green of her dress with the green of the tree. Seeing her felt like a serendipitous moment as in one look I forgot my own miserable hand. I didn't approach her. It would have sidetracked her unnecessarily. Besides, I was curious like anyone would be to see a girl up in the tree. The girl was perched on a tree by a house with nothing but her hand to keep her company. But she was not casually lounging about. Halo was amused in an anticipation of an amusement. If I was curiously delighted to see her from my hideout, so was she. But who was she spying on?

The tree on which she had perched, it had smoothly carved grooves and cups. As if she had been climbing on it often. It was astutely weathered that even a layman could climb on it with ease. At first, I pictured Halo like an owl. Perchance I had seen one in the woods, so she looked like one. Then as seconds passed, I imagined her to be a black panther. In her stance, keen stare and absolute silence, she looked predatory. When minutes passed, then it became clear. The girl was nothing but a wasted vulture. She was feeding her baser senses by sitting in the tree. The girl was eyeing at someone with the full intent to see them undress and undress more. Her eyes were fixed. Smile was fixed. She didn't budge. The girl though dull and even innocuous was in fact malicious like a hornet's nest in the tree. And she was named after a deity, how blasphemous!

Halo was peeping at someone inside the window, and was not flinching even for a second. There has always been a certain degree of pleasure at seeing a girl, but what pleasure does a girl get out of it? Halo as it became obvious was stealing unexplained gratification by spying on some oblivious prey. The girl was a voyeur by the looks of her polished tricks and staunch poise.

Earlier, when I used to find her dull, I had a quaint sense of dislike towards her. But at that time, seeing her shamelessly perched on a tree, I found her ghastly. Such tense notes of aversion began to grow inside of me that it even shocked me. Perhaps, the night in the woods had left me appallingly insecure. That I wished to take my frustrations out on the girl. Besides she was guilty.

"Halo? You a sentinel?" I grinned at her while approaching as a wolf.

"What the duck! G-Grace? W-what are, are you doing here?" Rent with angst, she gasped. Hearing a stranger call out to her, she almost slipped from her perch. The girl in her comfortable lair didn't expect anyone to apprehend her. Since the time she had been up to no good, Halo had grown complacent of her skills. The Zone of Black and White had few houses. She knew all of them to scent anyone's meddling with her game. The sound of their steps. The voices of their chatter. Even the whisper of their breaths. Besides, all of them had grown overly accustomed to each other's appearances. Naturally then, expecting anything out of the ordinary was inexplicable. Even if someone had happened to see her in the tree, no one would have suspected anything diabolical. And as I had, the girl was in utter disbelief that she slipped but did not fall.

It was fun seeing her squirm and stumble with red shame. I didn't have to expose her. The girl was herself stripping her guilt.

"Halo, your deity, gave you hands, so you could work. And He gave you eyes too. And Halo, you voyeur with it! Nah Nah! It is in all likelihoods a sin, you know." I was filled with a rancorous need to see her writhe especially when she tried to put on an innocent face. She was shocked at my criminal tone of voice. Something she thought I was not capable of. Be that as it may, I had turned her into a cornered rat. And even when cornered, she was in denial. The girl thought she could get away with it.

While climbing down the tree with practiced footing, the girl had the cheek to threaten me instead.

"You dare Grace accuse me! It is not good of you. I am a bird watcher, and I am watching birds, that's all." She yelled at the top of her voice. I thought someone might hear her, but all were asleep. Strange as it was, I didn't look much into it. I was more pestered by her rebellious nature and the impertinence that went with it. Besides, her reaction was overly melodramatic. I was only soliciting obedience from her, and she should have caved in. But she didn't and that naturally disturbed my calm. If she had just agreed to open up, I wouldn't have to play rough with her. Instead the criminal girl wouldn't confess her guilt rather raised her voice at me. When I would have only caressed her, I was then forced to give her a harsh beating.

Building up my sadistic humour, I jeered at her.

"Ah, birds. Through the window. A yapping bird caught in the window. I see none."

Halo could see I was not indulging her in a funny banter. The girl was terribly intrigued at the coherence of my vile against her. She kept rewinding her actions to check where she had wronged me. The girl even questioned if I despised her from the beginning. As she began to pick one explanation to another, I only wished if she would stop and give in. She eventually would have to, so why not do it already. But like some stupid girl, she struggled to fight back looking for the eye in the storm.

Although it bothered me, I was also anxious as to how far I would take it. Despicable as I had become, I had let go of the four hounds of my anger – derision, prejudice, inferiority complex and pleasure. I hated Halo. I didn't like girls like her. I was certain she looked down upon me. And I just liked to hate her. Naturally I was ready to take my time into breaking the girl into a sorry tale of woe. I would have done it even if she had not fought back. But at least I would have been gentle and kind. So when Halo turned belligerent and went ballistic, I had to up the ante.

"Halo? Where is the yapping bird? Is it undressing?"

"You're crossing a line here, Grace! Watch what you say, or I will have Granny evict you for lying." She had the nerve to threaten me again. It only provoked me further. I had her in my fist. She was no snake to squirm out of it. But a bird that I was watching. So as she kept flaunting her badge of honour, I heckled her again. "I am just asking about the bird, and look at you red with anger, or is it shame?"

Despite my gentle efforts to chase and play with her, she still remained hard to get. Even insolent.

"That is it, one more word and the amity I bear you, you will lose it! Granny, trust me, will have you outlawed!"

Halo went high-pitched in her voice. She yelled at the top of her lungs, that it even hurt my ears. Still, it was strange, no one heard her. I had not gagged her with a cloth. She was allowed to scream through the declining mist. The sun was up. The windows were open. It was time for people to wake up. To crown it, a girl was screaming as loudly as she could. Still, no one heard her! If no bystander cared, I also didn't feel deterred.

So I played with her again.

"Oh! So there is no bird, my bad, and I apologize. Then what were you looking at?"

Halo wanted me to stop. And I wanted to have some fun at her expense. Halo thought I would stop after having it. She didn't know I couldn't.

"None of your business, Grace!" She was afraid but adamant to defend herself. Why was she staying to defend herself? I was wretchedly bent to hurt her. And she wouldn't leave but pander to my twisted ego.

Run! I demanded from my eyes. Flee! I pleaded from my sweat. But she stayed. The girl couldn't see I wanted her gone!

I was mad with a fury to mock her. I was mad and wanted to take it out at anyone who came first. It was Halo, the innocent dullard, who happened to cross my path. I wanted to ravish her with my scorn. Why still she wouldn't just run away? The girl instead held her ground and kept yelling meek anger at me. How was I expected to be threatened! When the town was deaf to her agitation, how was I expected to?

"It is not any of my business. I know, it is not. But Granny would like to know. Maybe I will have Drunkard spill it for me." I had her cornered.

"Why you dare threaten me like this?!" She meekly begged as if to reach for my pity.

"Fine, you are stubborn. I think I just saw Drunkard leave. You are not on good terms with him. I know that for sure. It would be nice to see what he does with you. When I tell him everything. The aftermath will be succulent!" I terrorized her again.

Halo was pale in her cheeks. Lips were dried. But she wouldn't moisten them as otherwise she would look guilty. Belligerent and perturbed at the same time, she gave out a shriek. The thought of becoming a blot of stigma was weighing heavily on her.

"What, wh---why, what do you want? I am a good person. Grace, I do not hurt anyone. My eyes don't burn skin and bones. I am named after the Halo. You can't bind me to some slurs of dishonesty!" Halo begged me to give up. To leave her alone. But I was inscrutably hurt, and I wanted her to feel that pain. She pleaded with her eyes downcast as if a horrible crime she had committed. I had made her feel like a horrible person.

"Don't worry, I don't like too honest a person. Honesty's too overrated. Like you. " I was but coolly malicious.

"What? Why?" She was brimming with tears. Her tears burnt her skin. The girl was honest even when rotten with one or two flagrant flaws. If she had been rotten to the core, then she could have fought me back. But she was only weighed down by one or two minor errors and so she couldn't.

Hearing me denigrate the oyster of her honesty, Halo pitifully tried to reason.

"Honesty? No it is not overrated. Honest people at least say sorry."

The second she said it, Halo knew I took it as a slap. Her insipid way of thinking was certainly a slap on my face. More like a bitter potion. Acidic. So I threw the acid on her face.

"Really! Then it should fix your problem. But I don't see you saying sorry. Are you not honest then? Little Lady!" I asked while placing my hand on her shoulder. It was the same hand which had been quivering with countless insecurities. As I placed it on her, even her body began to shudder. She mistook it as her own body quivering with fear. What was astonishing that the girl didn't push it away either. She let it hold her down as if she believed that she deserved it. Even if I had torn her clothes, unbraided her plaits, and soiled her pashmina, Halo wouldn't have protested. So I also didn't object. As my hand heavily perched on her shoulder, her skin felt soft to touch. It was also sweaty with dread.

"I am! I do not hurt anyone. It's a need, I don't know, can't control it! But I can't!" The girl was panicking with remorse. Even then, I was obstinately heartless as I liked the desired effect.

"You enjoy it though, don't you? Will you have me believe, you are a liar too. You know besides being a voyeur!" I bullied her. Like a bully who badgers the weakling when life has bullied him. The more she cowered, the more I felt instigated to pin her. It was squarely her fault. I had not chained her to a pole. She was free to go. But she didn't. I was the victim there. A victim of her enchanting attributes. Even when she was decently hidden in the tree, the girl provoked me to rip the purdah off her face. I was helpless. The town was helpless. No one could hear her even when she screamed bloody hell into the wind.

"What do you want? I will do anything! Don't please, don't say anything to anyone!" Halo was broken because I couldn't help myself. I was helpless and so I couldn't stop. What had I become? Who had I become? What climax was I after? It was all too cloudy.

She was already broken. But I didn't stop to break her more. She pleaded and I got more ferocious and battered her more. Halo was not on her knees yet. Was that the climax I wanted? What did I want, it was all too cloudy.

"I don't hurt anyone, Grace! I have told you so many times! If you tell Drunkard, I am done for! Please for the love of Halo, don't ruin me!"

The shame had started to burn her eyes red. The lineature of her cheeks was also burnt out. But that was not enough. I wanted to asphyxiate the living stench of life out of her.

"I am lost! I am lost! You tell me, and I am yours! Ask of me anything!"

I was lynching Halo. What had gotten into me? Was it the same fever that had once infected the fine five gentlemen? Was I the germ? Had I become their disciple?

I saw the terror in her eyes. But I didn't stop. I saw my psychotic face in her eyes. I still couldn't fetter my ire. In my heart I wished if hell could suck me down. If someone from the window would look out and beat me down. Before I dishonour the girl, if a mob could bury me down. What hollowness was wallowing inside of me? Did it want Halo's blood to fill itself with? It was certain I was becoming what I had run from once.

No one can stop, isn't it? When the fever of sickness flushes our blood with saliva and piss.

"Are you a cub lost from his mother?" First officer had asked me then.

"I know where I am going". I had answered softly.

"No you know not. You are lost in the dark. I have you right near my den". Second officer was sure.

"Stay away I will scream". A meekly threat I had thrown at them. So they continued to play with me.

"Scream for what, I am not going to bleed you." Third officer was anxious to pin me down.

"Help! Help!" I screamed but no one could hear me. It was strange.

"You have fondled enough with words, she runs, and look this one runs." Fourth officer couldn't bear the delay.

"Help! Help!" I screamed at the top of my lungs. They had not gagged me. But still no one could hear.

"Hold her. Is this your waist or a stem of rose? These lips how red and beckoning. You're soft in your bosoms. Has no one ever roughed them up?" First officer spoke. They didn't care while I was half-fainted with tears.

"I am sorry. Sorry. Please! Help! Help!" I begged and screamed. No one cared to hear.

"Just a touch little lady, stay still, the more you squirm the more I am provoked! Stay still I said! You want me to tear you from inside. She is not bleeding. Have you yet? She is young. Stay still little girl." I couldn't speak anymore as I was overwhelmed with fear and despair.

I had been subservient towards them while lying flat on the ground. Obeisant while stretching my hands out towards them. Penitent. I had leaked blood for forgiveness. But none of it worked. I couldn't even hear anymore. Only the rattle of the night insects got in.

"Shut up with your coyness, I know you want my love." My skin still felt it all. If only it had also shut down.

"Slowly slowly untighten yourself." They hit me with strong punches. It was a familiar pain which I had felt before when father would beat me with the green bottle strap.

"She is so protected, Head isn't she? But I always find my way. Where are you hiding. Open your eyes to me. Still you shrink them. Open your beady eyes! Thou art sick, little woman!" They did. The Head watched. He was the last one to destroy me.

Halo, went down on her knees. She was finally down on her knees. She was in tears. She was also afraid of me. I had terrified her. What had I become?

"Grace? Grace? I am begging you, tell me what do you want?" The girl was begging mercy, mercy and mercy.

"Wh-what?" I felt disgusted with myself. What was I doing to that sweet, friendly and most honest girl ever?

"What do you want? Don't tell Drunkard!" She kept begging while turning half-fainted with tears.

"You are a sentinel. You are...I need to go." I couldn't face myself. Let alone stand there for her to face me. I yearned to leave. Had I trapped her or had she trapped me?

"Where are you going? Don't do this to me!" I didn't hear her. No one could hear her. She was screaming and no one could listen to her.

I had become disastrous, and she was right in the middle of it. Unwittingly.

"I will! No, no! I will not. Halo! Get out of my sight! I need to go!" I grunted with shame and awe. But the girl was pitifully frozen in fright. So I had to run away.

As I made a sudden move to leave, Halo shrieked fiercely and then held me by my clothes. She was afraid I was leaving to tell on her. The girl was petrified as it was the issue of her honour. Not life.

In the crooked trash of the sea, she was expected to keep herself afloat. Clean. Decent. Protected. Hidden. Covered. By some magic. It is a magic-starved world. But she was expected to magically keep her linen clean even when the streets and the houses were awashed with dirt. Why not clean the dirt than asking her to stay unsoiled? Come what may! Ridiculous!

While the girl bleated to earn my grace, I violently pushed her away. Otherwise she would have torn my clothes. I knew what she was going through. But I knew not. Smothered by violence, I pushed her to the point of being violent myself.

As I left in a panicky haste, I wanted to but I couldn't reassure her. I wanted to tell her that my bark was worse than my bite, but I couldn't. As I ran away, Halo fell back in a resounding thud. I didn't care to lift her up. Wipe the sweat from her brows. I was not kind to her. As I didn't want to be kind to her. I was not the Head to be kind. Tied to the lacerations of shame I couldn't even look at the girl. So as she stayed crouched on the ground, I ran. I had to flee from her innocent eyes. I ran as damningly as I could.

Not towards the shack. To the woods. Near the graves. I ran straight to that horrid place. The unmarked graves were the cause of my breakdown. I ran to that small wasted patch to confront it. Accept it.

What if Jon had followed? I did not bother. What if the witch, some witch flew in my way, I didn't care. Aloof from the charms of the woods, I ran towards that buried place. The graves were bedded firmly underground. I took my claws as a shovel and began digging a sixth grave by the five. I was maniacal. While the palms began to bleed and skin began to sweat, I kept digging till it was six feet under.

Then I stepped inside and covered myself against the cold with mud.

Where joys last for minutes and dishonour forever, I slept in one of those graves. Like a baby. The motherly caress of the mud, the worms and the night insects began to sooth the spasms breaking my body. It was my home. Had always been. I cuddled within the four walls while shrinking into an owl's cough ball.

Resting in the peace of a corpse. I rested in my home to forget who was to be blamed for my condition. Who was to be blamed, who was to be blamed – the world was a hound, who could be blamed?

As the warmth of the ground began to leech inside of me, I cowered deeper and deeper into the mud. To remember a memory I had repressed which then had to haunt me. I calmly let my mind break and unbreak the circuits of grief and joy. Of my past. It would become sullen. Then erratic. Then hours later calm again. I needed time to cure what had ailed me.

But. Something happened outside.

Someone crushed the dying leaves of autumn which were lying in a heap near the graves. I heard footsteps. I was afraid what if it was the witch, some witch who had come calling. It was not the right time even for her. I was still unfit.

Chapter 9

The Witch Is A Dirty Wound

It was a humid afternoon. The sun was blistering hot. Mud under the dry ground had hardened into cakes. There was no flush of winds through the trees. During the dewy dawn, the grave was cool as the waters of ice land. But later it had turned into ambers of burning heat. Staying in a place for too long, it can get homely to hostile in a matter of seconds. And the mud underneath the ground had begun to singe the hair on my flesh.

Though it was hostile, I was still at peace. I needed to be at peace to pacify the growing fatigue in my mind. I was not in control of my words, actions and intentions and felt strangely overpowered. Such manner of exhaustion had taken over, that I was shocked at my maddening despair. It was only by sleeping in a grave, I could have slept over the losses dotting my life. Even if it meant to outstay its welcome.

The sixth grave was like a shoal in the stormy sea. When the tides were turning and twisting, it was like a little of calm here and a little calm of there. How could then I depart from it? As time passed, it seemed the tides were stubborn to land me on the shore. When I wanted to stay adrift, it sought to find me a land.

It had only been few hours that I heard an indistinct chatter outside. Something was afoot. I heard noises which had no words to speak. Discreetly, someone was meddling with the pile of mud which I had disturbed. Hearing the noise, I first took it to be a wayward animal. Perhaps a porcupine or a weasel. But when the rustle became articulate, it was certain the thing was no beast. I had covered myself with mud to hide and cower away. But the wasted patch was like a siren luring even the celibate. I was, thus, easily discovered. As the noise screamed and started to reach after me, I kept motionless while steadily burrowing deep into the mud. I wished if that someone was not the witch, some witch. Since the time I had been in the town, the illusive thing of magic had been provoking my senses to stalk and find her. Sweat, hearts and sweat I had broken to seize her from the dark. And when it seemed she was lurking and dancing nearby, I wished her to be gone. In my state, I was not prepared to jump out of the grave and take her by the throat. Even if the Maker had come to meet me, I would not have risen from the dead. The slumber and the peace of the grave was too precious to give away.

As I cowered deeper and deeper, a boy's voice called out to me. It was severely agitated.

"Wh-What are you doing here? Noor? Is that you, wh-what is this? "Halo! MY Halo! What manner of explanation is this! Why has she buried herself? Bring her out, Danny, help me bring her out. Help me pull her up!"

The voice was familiar. It was but hard to place him. Perhaps we didn't have a long exchange of words. Nevertheless it irked me when the boy mistook me for Noor. He could have mistaken me for Vicky, but Noor! The girl who had a bloody fit and then a bloody tiff over it. The thought of it hurt my ego. Besides I was also disgruntled for trusting Drunkard. The drunken boy had sworn that no one knew about the place except the elders. Yet I was not alone and I had relied on him at my peril. Whosoever I had begun to fawn about, be it Noor, Drunkard or the Elder's page, they would twist my faith in them.

As the boy almost tenaciously kept uncovering the mud, I buried my face in my hands. I was fraught with mortification while the boy persisted.

"Its deep, hold my hand and I will pull her up...Is she hopeless, that she has decided to kill herself?"

Still thinking I was Noor, he cursed me for being weak. It was disappointment I discerned in his voice. Though he was distressed that Noor had taken her life, he was also paternally disappointed. Pained to see how Noor had finally broken her silence. It was considerate of him to disdain her action. That she had finally decided to take one.

As I remained adamantly crouched in my burial, he tried hard to extricate me.

"Hold my hand tight! I will pull her up! It's not Noor! Bloody Hell! It's Grace! Run before she sees you! Go now! I will handle her, go! "

The boy went ballistic and was positively disconcerted with alarm. He hurriedly sent away whosoever was with him, in case I caught him hand in the cookie jar. It was a strange turn of events. I was vexed for getting caught and so was he. We both had issues to wince about. Seeing me, he was certainly aggravated. Even then, he firmly held me by my arm to pluck me out.

As he touched my skin, I could see the same look of horror plastered on his face which Jon also had. My skin. It was deathly cold. The way the page was shaken by it, he too couldn't hold his vomit. While his blood pulsated on my pale flesh, the boy almost lost the heat in his own. Still, he kept his hold fixed even when I protested most unforgivably.

"Back off you!"

The boy but remained impertinent in his grasp. He wanted me out of the grave as he believed it to be the reason of my madness. I again yelled, "Back off, I said!"

As I wouldn't subside, he then forced his hands on me. While I pelted him with mine. But he was obstinate to rescue me. "Grace, please let me help you!" Though he wanted to help, it felt like he was pulling me out of the muddy womb. Affronted and disturbed by his intervention, I again screeched at him.

"No! No! Leave me alone!"

Then, with evil glowing in my eyes, I roared, "I will ask one last time, why did you disturb my sleep?"

Undeterred, he roundly scolded me for what I had done.

"Are you mad? You find this normal? Wake up! Girl!"

I did not scream again as it was futile. He wouldn't have listened to me, so I did not screech. Unflustered and placid, I looked at my hand. It no longer shook with a fit. It was calm even when I could feel a rage rising in my hollow existence. The rage had taken over the fit in my hand as I didn't have time to destroy it. Filled with brash insecurities, I lividly asked him again.

"Why did you disturb my sleep?"

While he again scolded me in disgust.

"Don't you find this morbid? It made me shiver seeing you. Curled up in mud, in a grave! What were you thinking?"

It was Christian. I had seen him before. At the day of the puke, he had carried Noor on his heavy shoulders. I had also seen him during the soup party where he made an appearance with the likes of Vicky. The same Christian was standing before me while preaching me about what was morbid and how I almost made him vomit. The boy had the gall to gasp for breath when he pulled me out of the grave. As if he had seen a grotesque rise of the dead.

One minute he was concerned and next, he would be ashamed of me. I felt insulted by his insufferable mood swings. It was hard to digest the boy's double standards and it further enraged me. Rather the more he tried to suppress his discomfort. I wished to bury him in the grave I came from.

Unhinged and cornered, I grunted at again.

"Why did you disturb my sleep?"

He did not scold me again. He was afraid at what I had become. Throat half-filled with vomit, he spoke shakily. "Grace, you are different, what has happened to you?"

Frigidly vile, I demanded with terror in my voice.

"Why, boy, why you disturb my sleep!"

Pitifully, the boy tried to reason with me.

"Grace! What is wrong? You sound foul! What is wrong?"

Foul. I was not being foul. I was embarrassed of being exposed of my vulnerabilities. I was also feeling disgusted as the boy had after all compared me to Noor which was pitiful. Despite the hate spitting out of my mouth, Christian remained obstinate. He wanted me gone from the grave, which he believed was the horror that had changed me.

The boy could have forcefully restrained me. He had the strength and the anxiety to overpower me. Yet he was gentle. I was hurt and some strange quality in him disallowed him to hurt me anymore. What was it that made him leash his demons when I couldn't leash mine?

Believing that I could be saved, he continued to assail me with calm persuasion.

"You are not well, Grace! Who brought you here? This place can possess people. They get mad, you must come with me. Now! Grace!"

Christian was consoling the rage in my jittery nerves. He was bent to shield me from the wicked vibes of the place. Unyielding in his want to care for me, he spoke many a words of reassurance. Still I felt perturbed at his overbearing voice. Even when I provoked fear in him, the boy continued to be a man to protect me from madness.

"I am asking you a simple question. Why in the world would you meddle with me? You want something, huh, you want something?" I groaned and grunted while the boy became certain I was taken.

"Grace, stop this! Don't! What has gotten into you? You are not like this, this place has stricken you. Hold my hand! Come here! You are lost…" Christian didn't care out of any desire for me. Strangely he seemed to genuinely worry for the likes of me. It was sadly surprising.

It was with a purpose I had visited the unmarked graves for the second time. When mother had died, father had disappeared somewhere, who was then left to mourn over me? To grieve over my death, no one. From friends to relatives, whosoever visited me, they didn't matter. No matter how many tears and cries they shed at my perch. They were fly by night to begin with. So when my parents also became one of them, fly by night, I was mourned by none. Only I could lament, weep, and pass my condolences to what I had become. Decades of time had transpired and I still couldn't bring myself to weep over myself. Not even once did I do it. Not even once did I confront what had come to pass in my passing. It was then certain that I would lose my nerves over a piece of wasted patch. The burial ground.

I had visited the place to confront the blighted shadow of my life. But when Christian interrupted me, I was still not done with it. The boy had most insidiously stomped on my grave as I lay in it aggrieved. When he kept lending his hand to me, I couldn't hence be thankful for his humanity. Even when all he was trying to do was pick me up from a grievous spread of loss, loss and loss. But I misunderstood the boy's good intentions. As I was barely cured of the furies rummaging wild in my mind.

Pathetic and self-destructive as I was, Christian still wouldn't give up on me. The more he held me tightly, the more I felt the mixed emotions of affection and hate for him. His grasp would give off a warm sensation of sweat and love. Though I hated it, I still loved it. Why in my heart was I craving for such a feeling? It began to grow so intensely that I left the grave and we stood face to face.

Gyrating with pain and pleasure, I held him in my arms. Then without a moment's delay I began to ululate as if Noor's memory had begun to play in my body. I then vocalized what strange emotion had caught my tongue. "I want you to take me, Christian. I will not tell. Here hold me down. I want you to!"

The boy shrunk from me. Confused whether to help or leave, he then raised his voice to hammer sense. "Stop this, Grace! You are not yourself! Are you on drugs?" I was but insatiable, and continued to assail him with my ravenous wants. "No-no-no. Take me. Take me now…"

I wanted to be hunted again. Someone after me. After my blood, my skin, a liquorice that my body was. Someone to feel me up. A complete stranger, I wanted Christian to seize me like he had been waiting for that moment. In his eyes I wanted pure lust to shiver my misplaced virginity. He must run to grab me with no shame or duress in his way. His hands must hold me down hard. And again and again must he without end and no pause touch me through. I wanted to gasp. Contort and writhe to show him what criminal a passion is. What criminal my body was. I wanted him to push and shove me to get my love.

"I need you Christian. I am so alone. Depressed. Tragic. Make me happy. Come close." I quivered while wanting his love.

"No, no, Grace don't! You are not yourself!" He flinched to either run or stay.

I wanted him to eel into me and caress my face and my neck while aggressively stroking my blooms. I wanted extreme intensities of his irresistible and uncontrollable and outright vengeful love. I wanted him to force inside me a dishonouring passion. Even if I quivered, succumbed and stretched open. I wanted to be hunted.

"Why are you shy? No one is watching. The dead do not talk!" Wilting my body to fit into his arms, I kept reaching after his heart.

"Grace, w-we shouldn't. It is not right. Get a hold of yourself, Grace!" He shuddered whether to make love or flee.

I wanted his hands to clutch me as cuffs. Even if I curled up my legs and tried to hide, I wanted him to trample all of him down on me. When I would scream, I wanted him to do it more. Even if I begged him to stop, I wanted him to hang my face down the edge of the grave, and force his passion again and again. I wanted his lips to thrash and slash me to seek countless pleasures. Wild and gentle pleasures. Fitful and constant. Precipitous and slow. Dark, demanding, and forced but it should be his passion by all means.

How much I wanted to be pained in love, as that was all I had known.

"I know you want me. Right here, in the abyss, and you are not alone. Where is your friend you were talking to? Who were you talking you? I want more…" As he staggered away, I panted after him to have him bring more.

"No, no…" He was breathless with mounting unease.

"Call them too. I want more." I was famished.

"I am alone, and enough of this charade! Come to your senses! I am taking you home!" Christian was not alone when he had found me. Yet he lied about it. I didn't want him to lie to me. Not to me.

"I am home, and you are a liar. I heard you speak to someone else. Was it the witch, some witch? No that is impossible. Was it Danny? No that is impossible. Why did you ask them to leave?" I smothered him for his wicked lie. As I wanted to share, and he was being selfish.

Christian but remained impervious to my heaves and again lied straight to my face, "It was not Danny, it was no one! Grace! You need to come with me away from this ghastly place."

He lied relentlessly which again irked me. So I went brazen to oppress him in any which way I could. "You are lying, you are, why I do not know. But if you will not tell, I will make the dead talk of how you put your hand inside of me!"

"What! I didn't touch you! You forced me! I didn't want to!" He shivered with shame, even when innocent.

"And you didn't run away, just stayed." I again badgered him while he picked up his honesty and yelped out his resentment. "You lying cunt!"

"Cunt, I am a cunt! Who were you talking to? Tell me or I will tell everyone how you molested me!" Without heeding the din of his fear, I chortled at the boy. Christian was not good at lying, and I needed to exhort the truth by blackmailing him. It was a dirty game I was playing, but I had no patience to deal nicely with the lot. I wanted secrets unclasped. Truth ravished. Scandals afoot. I wanted him so badly, but when he kept deceiving me with a lie. It aroused my ire than my desire for him.

He had to be punished and I was vindictive about it. So I punished him, "You are good at groveling, is that how you keep Vicky for yourself? I bet she would want to hear what you did." Swamped in shame, and utter confusion, he bawled in dismay, "Don't Grace, why are you doing this? I didn't touch you, you know that!"

"I know, but no one else does. You are dead, you know that." I declared with a wicked snicker. The boy had seen the worst in me and believed I would frame him most viciously. Even when I was bluffing or maybe not, he didn't dare to call my bluff. Afraid of what dishonour I might wreck on him, he caved in. "No! No! I was talking to Danny! Okay! You happy now?" It but again felt as a lie. As Danny was in the city either alive or dead and I had seen him depart.

"He is in the city!" I refuted him while he dramatically reiterated, "What, no! I was talking to him. He is back! He is back!" It again felt like a lie.

"If he is, why ask him to leave, you did want me for yourself!" As I oscillated between one accusation to another, the boy was intently caught between the devil and the deep blue sea.

"No and-no! I didn't! It was his condition. He isn't normal, I do not know. He is sick, very sick, I don't know why. What ails him, I don't know. He is not himself. He is growing sicker by the second. He is sick! The whole world seems to be sick!" Christian had gone frenzied with fright. He was broken into a thousand songs. From one scream of indignation to another scream of shock, he was hopelessly cornered. I didn't feel even a tinge of pity for him. He was an inveterate liar. Besides, I was curious as to what malady Danny had caught in the city. It got me so fascinated that I neglected Christian's breakdown. "Calm your hysteria, take me to him, I will see how sick he is."

"No! I cannot. I must not." He stuttered while mustering his will to protest. But he had lost for certain. And I reminded him again, "You want to die in shame? You know what I can do, tell me boy where is he now?"

Frightened, as I was itching to assassinate the very honour of his life, he finally pleaded guilty. "The-the Witch has him."

Christian knew about her. He didn't know the witch, some witch. But the Witch! A heated flush of blood poked my cheeks like pins and needles. Brows raised in shock. Lips puckered in doubt. Nostrils flared in anger. Christian's testimony was too good to be true. Exhausted because of his unrepentant penchant for lies, I didn't believe him at the outset. Coming at him with my hand in the air, I butchered him with sheer disdain.

"You dirty mouth of trash!"

Taken aback at my surrender of decency, he retaliated.

"The-the Witch has him!"

Moved by his resilience, I questioned him most untiringly.

"Where is she?"

He lost his calm at my irritating need to pester him. The boy almost evinced a shriek as he didn't want to betray the town by exposing the magic trick. It would be dishonorable.

"Grace, please do not ask me of this. If I tell you, Granny will have me outlawed!"

Granny! Granny! Granny! That creature had been a principal impediment wherever I scavenged for dirty lies. It was certain. The town had respect for her. But it was bordering on excessive adoration that I found repulsive than acceptable. The Elder was a threat. But I didn't hear his name spoken with such fear and compliance. The town had turned the old lady into an absolute entity which deserved an unwarranted reverence.

Disgusted, I exhorted the boy for his sickening subservience. "Granny is the least of your worries. You got no say anymore. It's either this or the fact you molested me."

He broke into a fit again. Then composing himself, the boy pleaded to my humanity.

"I thought, we were told you could be trusted. And now everything you are saying is downright criminal! Have you no heart! What will you get out of this?"

I could be trusted? It must have been the old lady convincing everyone to trust me. I patted myself for having fooled her. Then lacing my words with deliberate violence, I grinned at him.

"Pleasure. That is what I want."

"Is that it?" Shocked, he questioned with derision.

"Pleasure, yes!" I paused at his nerve to downplay my need for pleasure. Why is pleasure not for the likes of me? Then badgered him again, "I have worked for a work, while other people took pleasure in working me. Why now should I feel guilty if I want some for myself? Shh- you don't have to answer, I don't have time to hear you whining. So where is it, the Witch, or is it a wizard?"

Befuddled at the strain of my logic, he cried out.

"Please Grace, don't! Granny will have me outlawed! Don't you care?" he cried out.

Everything was comfortable about Granny, or was it? They didn't know the truth but I did. They had made her into a grand epitome of justice, discipline, mores, truth and other flamboyant attributes of a civilized society. But there was something amiss about her. Gardening with her by the colorful sheets, I had the chance to closely inspect the rosary hanging from her wrist. During the soup party, the rosary had broken her and the Elder into a blot of shame. It didn't make any sense at that time. But when I had seen the unmarked graves, it all came back to me. The rosary was not made of beads but old and worn teeth. Mostly canines. Ordinary pebbles of round and rough shapes also adorned her rosary to hide the teeth. In a town where Granny was respected for her honest discipline, such a creepy habit of hers was a sheer incongruity. Keeping teeth tied to her wrist. That too in a sacred rosary. I certainly knew Granny better than the boy or the rest of the town. She was not a white sheet of cloth but a shroud hiding enchanting secrets. So naturally, Christian was worried he might get outlawed by the most honest elder of the town.

As such a prospect frightened him, it gave me a chance to string him up like a pig.

"Good! She should have you outlawed. You lie in cohorts with Danny, and you both should be outlawed." I was venomous.

"She will not let you stay too." He retorted with a hope to string me as well.

"Like I care, it's not my home."As I established my indifference towards his town, he attacked me to avow his patriotism, "It is mine! And if I leave, Halo saves this place from the Elder! You cold-hearted bitch!"

"That I am. So be careful how you speak to me." I said it loud and clear.

"You have no heart!" He choked at my apathy.

Since the day of puke, the existence of the Witch had become a legion in my head. Is she real? Magic? Am I delusional? Desperate? The town a wonderland? The depravity of such unanswered questions was maddening. To crown it, Christian's impertinent silence was tipping me over. In a while as we went on flinging words at each other, the trees began to pitter-patter with heavy rains. Even the forest was moved to drown us. Drown the din of our noise. We quarreled, extorted, shamed, humiliated and blackmailed each other. While all the while rains kept falling in buckets.

Then before I knew it, I slipped on the wet mud. But it was not an accident. Two hands out of thin air struck me on my head. It was a menacing attack but it didn't stop with one hit. While hurling itself all over me, someone hit me with another fisted bludgeon right in my face. I could hear my nose crack, tooth pull out and eyes break under the sheer force of the blow. The speed and the raw thrill of it was eerily maniacal. Bloodied in my eyes to see who it was, I thought could it be the witch, some witch. Had she come to kill what was already killed?

But it was not her. It was Danny. While ramming his fists at my face front and back, he kept screeching into the wind.

"I will kill her! She is bad, bad, bad!" Danny was back. But hideously different. He had a cut lip. A gaping look in his eyes. Hair smelling of fresh putrefaction. One or two nails had grown awfully long while his attire had gone bleakly fragrant. To add more, he was also not right in the mind. He had become a mad man. Vicky had said he was a sensitive boy, then what could have changed him so soon? I didn't care to look into it as I was rather occupied while the boy kept swinging his arms at me. He would miss some punches here and there which again was proof he was not right in the mind. There was no detectable sign of any physical damage. It had to be a result of a mental trauma.

The boy kept hitting me and though he missed most of the time, the ferocity of his blows leaked blood from my mouth, nostrils and my eyes. As the mud had begun to enmesh with the rains falling, the pool of my blood also got mixed in it. All three mixed then gave a malodorous odour that turned the heavy downpour into a bloodbath.

Even when Danny would get haggard and breathless, he still kept battering and thumping at my face. Before he had exhausted himself to death, Christian seized him from behind.

"Danny, enough! The world's sick! For Halo's sake stop this madness!"

Danny but did not stop. He growled and gasped as saliva dropped from his mouth into mine. Then he stopped and turned towards Christian. It was not a brotherly look he shined on him. But a long stare of hapless madness. Before we knew it, Danny began beating him up even more outrageously. Christian was rent apart seeing his own cousin breaking his bones. The boy was incapacitated to retaliate as he couldn't believe Danny could betray him mad or not. The sight of Danny's catatonic psychosis numbed Christian to hit back. So he held out his hand towards me while wheezing pitifully. "Wh-what the devil! Danny, what has gotten into you! Grace, help me out! Help me!"

Roused ever so passionately by the interesting turn of events, I didn't wish to stop Danny. He had after all become a delectable tool of entertainment especially when everything else was beginning to bore. But Christian had to interrupt again and he made such incessant pleas that I had to intervene. So I picked up an oddly-pointed stone from the ground and hit Danny on the head. Christian didn't object as his own life was on the stake. Besides, what could he object to? He was at a loss to make sense of me, his friend and the mad mad world. I struck Danny with a restrained force and the boy fell into a sweet calm sleep. As he slept into a tranquil repose, Christian did not get up because he couldn't. The shock had sucked the sanity of calm from his mind. He meekly kept lying on the ground, silent and blanched in fear. The boy was lost as his friend was lost in dreams.

While it continued to rain like the end of the world, I too gave up on action. And rested myself parallel to the locked-in bodies of the two boys. Hence, under the fawning shade of a fawning tree, we rested, while one of us slept.

"What madness…" Christian muttered into the rain.

"Shut up, Christian." I silenced him as I didn't want him to disturb the music of the rain.

It was a rain-drop melody everywhere. The crescendo of it would grow as second after second turned into hour and hour long.

"Cold cold madness…"

"I know, I know…"

There was no purpose in our minds. No rush to be somewhere. No guilt of the blood spilt in the rain. It was a strange mood of time. Though there was rainfall, I heard no thundering cloud or saw any darkness in the sky. From the trunks to the top of the trees, all I read was a sad melancholy of beauty and its passing.

An hour into it had elapsed and I heard an autumn leaf break somewhere close. I got alerted. Someone had stepped on it without thinking to tread softly. I remained motionless for I did not want to give a chase anymore. Like an absurd painting out of a still life, the three of us remained soil to soil. Calm even when broken in despair.

Then, haggardly, she pierced through the picture of rain while coming in my direction. She was only a voice for me, but that night she appeared to be walking towards me. Without raising any alarms, I watched her come to us. Even if it were a snake, I wouldn't have risen. Even if it were a school of ants, I wouldn't have run. Even if it were a flood of flash, I wouldn't have left. And even if it were a bunch of officers in pursuit, I wouldn't have fled. I wanted to stay still and wait. When I was so near, I didn't wish to desert. She came close while forgetting there was a treaty she had apparently signed – not to show herself to the town let alone strangers. She wore slugs around her neck. Smelt of herbs which covered her eyes, ears, lips, nose, and skin. She was also barefooted. Wore a dark scarlet gown tattered and muddy yet enchanting. Tattered like her and engaging. Lips were full with moistened dew of the woods. Hands showed cracks of handling firewood. And face glistened under the night sky. As the woods had strong winds that could break even the sturdy bark of the trees, so she had stones and bones tied to her waist and wrists to stay anchored to the ground.

She was calm in her face, yet steady in her tread. Serenely she came out of the hallowed thickness of the woods. The more nearer she came, I could vividly read her visage. She had long tresses. Though it was dark to note their colour, they nevertheless shone with a golden hue. What was ominous about her? It made me wonder. Perhaps her ominous silence, her eerie entrance or those eyes which looked at us as if she was normal. She was a thing of horror, and yet she looked so vulnerable that I wanted to shield her from the rains, the deep dark woods, and the sight of the town. Was that the reason she was hiding that she was vulnerable? She was frail, hence hidden. Or she knew she was frail, hence had hidden herself.

In her vulnerability I could discern there was fear which was not because of any lack of strength in her character. It seemed some incident had constructed fear in her gait. How is a child to know fear? A man to fear violence? A woman to fear loss? Until it is borne or seen, how is anyone to know? Such was her case. She could have been once a cheerful thing of nature, but then things must have happened. Things which must have then turned and twisted every vein of her power into fear. She feared people and not the horror of the mortal woods. Unafraid of the woods, and afraid of people. Such had become her life.

She kept pacing towards us as calmly as she could. Though crouched in anticipation of some dread, she was calm in her side of the woods. Seeing her approach, I didn't move a muscle lest she flew away. The scene was yielding a paradoxical effect in my heart. It was curiously racing and yet vividly calm. Could she be a thing of horror? Or magic? Or someone like me? I wished that she were. I needed her to be one freak of magic. For my pleasure. My adventure. My salvation.

Why did she appear as a wretched human of human tragedies? It disturbed me. Could she really be the Witch?

I asked Christian.

"Who is she?"

"Wh-what where?" Alarmed, he looked at me.

"There you fool!" I was vehement.

"I can't see! Where?" Clueless, or being deliberately so, he wouldn't see the creature right before him. Tormented, I shoved my hands onto his face, and directed it to see what I was seeing. "The Witch! That is her! Look at her you liar of the first water! Tell me it is true!"

He but audaciously remained in the dark. Then he saw for himself and burst out with eyes goggled in awe. "Good Halo, why did you, no Witch! Return! They are not supposed t-to…Bloody Halo…"

At first Christian thought I was being pestilent as usual and then a second later he got red in the face. Undoubtedly I cherished his emotion running wild from despair to shock to anger. The Witch was before us. He couldn't hide her or let me think I was being delusional like Noor. While letting out a heavy sigh, he covered his face in surrender.

The Witch was before us. That illusive thing of magic. She was close without any hangar of mist between us. She was near. While, she kept moving close I realized she was not approaching me but the boy, Danny. Reaching out to him, she placed her hand on his heartbeat and asked me.

"Is it curable?"

She spoke without directly looking at me. As if her eyes would reveal every secret about her. Her voice had a low key pitch which defied her genuinely sleek curvature. Living in the woods had taken a toll on her skin which displayed the ash, the mud, and the thorned tendrils sticking out of her body. But she didn't look like a forced exile or a refugee rather supremely at home in the woods. Composed most eerily, the woman was magically at ease than in a fit to run back to civilization.

The Witch kept raising and dropping her hand on the sleeping boy. She did not chant those sermons of divine intervention to cure him. It almost broke me. That bewildering sight of the chanter in the woods, was it all an illusion then? It certainly broke me. As Christian had his face buried in his hands, so the Witch had to ask me again.

"Is it?"

Why was her voice earthly? It irked me through and through. Though I could sense the weight of misfortunes clutching on her voice, it was but earthly. I frowned my brows to gaze at her. At her face, chest, hands, waist, feet, and the incomparably blazing gown. She evoked countless interpretations in my mind to pin point what she was. I wanted her to be fiery like some mighty deity. I wanted her to be evil like a sinful siren. I wanted her to titillate me, incite fear, mystery and alarm. An embellished fantasy. A fabricated creator. A magical malevolence. Curious to know what she was, I asked outrightly.

"Are- are you the Witch?…"

"Grace?" Christian interrupted me, which I didn't appreciate. I had exhausted my sanguine nature to tolerate his irreverent interruptions. So I gave him a deadly stare to just shut him up. Yet still, he had the impudence to interrupt again. "She can't hear you. The Witch is deaf."

Deaf? She was deaf! How could she be deaf? Is a ghost supposed to be deaf? No, that is preposterous.

But she was deaf.

The Witch was conveniently deaf to worry over the strange noises. The screams. The thunder underground. She was deaf to hear the terror. To wince at the pain of others. At her own pain. The Witch was deaf to fear the supernatural woods. The woods seem frightening more because of the rumbling echo of dark sounds and the Witch was deaf. Hence unafraid. The tone of horror could not threaten her. The tone of people's harangues and insecurities could not threaten her. She would not shudder as she could not listen. She was conveniently deaf to let any pandemonium disrupt her nerves into dread. But then what about the screams and cries of Noor? Noor who heard the Witch's chanting and even saw her shadow was made to distrust herself. The girl was most treacherously branded as insane for believing there was a witch, some witch in the woods. The Witch might have been hiding in peace but the freakish fabrications over her had leaked false magic into the real. And Noor was a tragic victim of such a propagandist terror.

To hide the unmarked graves. To hide her own self. To hide the dirty secrets of the town. The Witch was constructed. It was deafening.

"Deaf? Really? Wh-What's her name?" I asked with impatience as a name can tell the history of the person. And I needed her history. Not just the hoax she had been fabricated into. Christian, however, didn't appreciate my concern.

"She is the Witch, what's in her name!" The boy violently disregarded my anxiety as he didn't need to hide anything anymore. So he felt free to torment me. And I was tormented, "What nonsense!"

"It is the truth." He spoke callously.

"Fine, why call her the Witch, what made her a witch? Who is she?" Anxiously, I asked while letting go of the extortionist hold I had on him. I was begging for any detail and in my anxious plea for any information, I lost my power over him. Christian could sense it and began to strong arm me in return.

"The Witch is a dirty wound..." He declared with a grin. As I stood stumped, Christian then prodded the woman, and called her the Witch again. It would have been offending but the Witch wouldn't have heard it.

While I watched in disbelief the human eccentricity of the Witch, Christian gestured to her in some weird sign language. Then leaving me out of the conversation, both of them picked up Danny in the most fragile way they could.

"What are you doing?" I asked irritably.

"We will carry him home." He replied having lost his recent dread. He knew I could not blackmail him again. Christian had the upper hand.

"What about her? Aren't you worried, someone might see your Witch?" Pestered at his new-found liberty, I irked him.

"She will only help half way..." He spoke rather nonchalantly. I was but inconsolable, and attacked him, "And the other half, I will, is that it?"

Pestered by my nagging, he yelled back, "Yes, of course! You wanted to see the Witch, and you have. What more should I shimmer on the platter to make you listen to me once!"

I almost chuckled at his angry remonstrance. I was certainly a stone in his shoe that would prick him even when he would flip it out. Not caring to take it easy on him, I grunted at him with the pepper of red and black sting.

"The Witch didn't come from your bidding, and if you want help, you gotta tell me everything. Tell me else you know what charges I can ruin you with."

"You still could be so MALICIOUS!"

Christian was beyond calm as I was beyond the pale. I could even hear him breathe the incense of wrath. But then seeing how malicious I was, he inhaled deeply and politely asked me.

"What do you want to know?" He didn't address me with his eyes as he naturally hated to even look at me. I didn't mind his insult as it was the least I could do.

While we dragged Danny through the woods, I asked with an inquisitive strain.

"Why does she stay here? By choice or is she forced to?" He looked at the Witch and ignored me yet again. Then he answered with a pause, "She likes to be here, after what happened. It is her only haven left."

As he didn't care to elaborate his half-baked answer, I rolled my eyes in disdain and asked again.

"What did happen?"

He sensed my overflowing curiosity and grinned at my anxiety to get to the heart of the matter. While gazing at me with a smirk, he then dangled the prospect of truth. "You of all people wouldn't like the story."

"Why?" I demanded a straight answer. But he brashly refused me, "You will be crushed."

"Why? Tell me now boy!" I grunted at him.

He told me the story. I was expecting something else, and he narrated something else. In few shredded minutes, the story was over. In meager minutes he did it, and left me breathing for air. Not because I was shocked but the contrary. He told me. The Witch was not an anointed witch. She didn't have a goat that talked or a pot of witch's brew. Knowing my angst, he beamed with delight as he crushed me with his tedious revelation. The boy skewered me with his eyes while relishing the look of disappointment taking over me. He liked it as I simmered and seethed while his tale blew on my face. Christian wasn't just narrating but taking liberties to mock me while at it. And I listened what cruel joke of a story he bawled at me. I listened without breaking my heart. It was an ordinary story, an ordinary tale, and an ordinary extravagance of mediocrity. And she was called the Witch for being in an ordinary story. It was utter nonsense.

Boorishly, Christian killed the very jewel of my sinful expectations. I was inhumanely disappointed as if I had lost a limb. I wanted her to be magical to find a confidante or even an alter-ego in her. I was a thing of magic, dead and yet alive. I had hoped for her to be like me. So we could freely talk about it over a drink. But the truth was earthly. The Witch was a deaf woman, challenged by the high tides of the riots and crippled by its violence to spend the rest of her life in protection of the forest. Just by a name and her natural residence, she was attired in the portentous markings of necromancy. When the town was scared of her, it was she who was scared of them.

Be that as it may, there was also the issue of the unmarked graves. The Witch could have hidden in the woods like an ordinary woman. Why adopt the horror of a witch? It was certainly imposed on her so that no one could snoop around the graves. I asked the boy to know it definitely.

"What about the graves? The Witch roams around to keep people away, right? Am I right or not? Huh?" I was too anxious that he intentionally hit at my ego.

"You know nothing. Ask the Elder. You are his type." He was impudently blunt.

Provoked by his subtle rancour, I couldn't let his remark go unheard. So I blasted my fury at him.

"You run your mouth like that and I..." Before I could have finished the threat, he interrupted with vengeance.

"You will what? Listen, what I knew I have told you. Rest, ask the Elder."

Christian was certain that I had lost to him. So he carelessly rebuked me and even hurt my pride. I could no longer threaten him as I had lost my hold on the boy. Unnerved and even shaken at his newfound courage, I let it go. I had to. In my shameful anxiety, I was not doing a good job either. Besides, Christian had realized I was all bark than bite to be considered a threat. So playing him again would have been utterly disastrous. As it certainly was turning out to be.

Seeing how fanatically I was tied to my misery, the boy tried to teach me perspective.

"Grace. You know about the graves. Who told you, I will not ask. But whosoever told you, damn him or her! I will not tell Granny about you and your insolent intrusion. In return, I expect you to give up your obsession with our town. I mean it."

I inhaled deeply. Was I ashamed that a boy had outwitted me? It certainly pestered me that I ignored him with my snobbish silence. But it didn't bother him as he wanted me to know his state of mind and he had done it. Whether I replied or not, didn't matter to him. It was a deafening defeat for me and to hide it I averted the look in my eyes from him. That was all I could do to register my annoyance while dragging the sleeping boy. I was outsmarted. Shown my place. And made to feel like a loser.

The day when I would meet the Witch. If only I had known it would turn out to be such a disappointment. If only I knew.

We reached half-way. It was time for the Witch to disappear again. But I didn't raise my brows to see where she would flit off to as the entity didn't evoke any interest in me anymore. As a human she was like every other human, disappointing. All through the walk, I felt a knife of grief dagger my heart. A knife of woe dagger my throat. A knife of misery dagger my stomach. Certainly, then I didn't even want to face the Witch. It was not derision, but disillusionment. When did she leave, I didn't care. I was too deep in the pit of self-reproach that I couldn't bid her goodbye.

Thoroughly pained by dismay, I walked as Christian walked by my side, as if nothing had happened. The Witch was gone from a secret to a secret. While we kept walking, the Witch who didn't matter when human sunk back into her home.

Dismayed and fatigued, we reached the shack. It was prudent to hide the boy in the cabin as in any other place there was a risk of being found out. As we sat on the floor, Christian began to cook up conjectural stories to explain Danny's return. He got too involved to notice we all were bleeding due to the beating Danny boy had given us. We immediately needed to tend to our dirty wounds. Though Danny was hard hit, it was I who looked more ghastly than him.

"Christian we gotta clean our bruises before they get infected. Danny needs some patching and so do you." I spoke with concern. Realizing the emergency of the situation, he quickly responded. "We will have to do it ourselves. And for that we need a first-aid kit. Nothing is here. You get it from somewhere."

"Where?"

None of us were willing to face the town after getting smeared by the dark tar of magic. I had good reasons as I was an outsider, but Christian was just being a coward.

"Pooh has a first-aid kit. Grace, you go get it," he entreated even when not showing it. Angered, I snapped, "Seriously, why don't you go? I will wait here!"

He but remained unyielding. "No, no-no. I don't want to, look at me, I am shaken and guilty. My tongue under this duress will spill everything. And what if I see Pooh? She is a tough person to lie to. Besides you owe me. Go!"

Tired of his vacillation, I agreed. "Fine, I'll go. Besides I have to meet Noor anyway. She has not returned my jacket yet."

"Jacket, your jacket…" He spoke while remembering the first time he had seen me.

"Yes." I replied while also remembering the first time of it all.

I washed my face to clear the spots of blood. Waited for a while to dry my clothes. All the while, Christian kept mending Danny, as if by caressing him, Danny was going to be all better. Then I left and as I was leaving, Christian shouted from behind. "Grace, I hope I don't have to tell you, come alone." I didn't reply, and let his diktat go unheard. That boy and his gall, he was pestilent.

Chapter 10

Damning Her And Damning Me

I reached Portia's house. It was close to Granny's. The house was locked from the inside. I knocked it thrice with decent pauses, but no one answered. Even waited for someone to hear my clarion call but still no response. Only a deep echo of the knock reverberated through the air which led me to believe perchance it was empty. So I took the liberty to break and enter through the back door. Besides, I was in a rush as the sleeping Danny boy would have become a bleeding Danny boy and my patience was also wearing thin.

Portia had neatly labelled her house and its sundry entrances. Door to drying room. To bedroom. Kitchen. To garage. Even the entry to the backdoor was overtly mentioned. The door of the house led directly to a hall which was dressed as a threshold. The fragrant aroma issuing from it bit my nose that I almost sneezed. Every room in the house seemed to be scented with a potpourri of fragrances from lime to rose and honey dew. Each scent had mixed to become a new fragrance and as it tickled my olfactory senses, I almost had sneezed. When I was exerting to block it, I saw Noor. But she didn't seem to notice my unwarranted presence. The girl was pale and red, coloured yet greyish and she was pacing the floor back and forth. Too engrossed into it, she couldn't discern that I was judging her mysterious comings and goings. The girl would make discreet thuds in her gait and was walking the floor with tiny mute steps. She had subdued her weight by slouching herself. Why the girl acted as an intruder in her own home was beyond me.

Where I stood was a room painted with nefarious colours of purple patches, black spots and rainbow curtains. The assortment of contrasting colours helped me camouflage into them by keeping still and not stirring. There was a path ahead of me, anti-parallel to where I was perched. It was there right ahead of me where Noor paced front and back. She was unable to see from the tail-end of her eye, that I was standing stunned and silent a few feet away. The girl was deliriously lost but not fitful. Then after a moment's delay she walked up the stairs and I followed her in neat steps of a rat. Next, she picked up a pink pillow made from the mellow silk of the town and hugged it close to her bosom. Then she held it even more tightly while pacing slowly towards the bedroom where her mother lay asleep from the day's long work. Portia was on a futon, happily tired and musingly asleep to cherish recuperation for the day. Noor didn't wish to disturb her so in a slow flight, she flew down towards her mother's sleeping head.

How far would Noor take it, I wished to know. Besides what was her intention to begin with, I was intriguingly curious. The girl stood fast by her mother's side while her nails pierced into the pillow. She bent her knees to come at the same height as her sleeping mother's head. While caressing the pillow, she laid it by the edge of the bed. While still sitting by her side, Noor began to whisper indistinct words of sweet melancholy. Not tears, but sweat came running down her cheeks and almost tarred her pink plum face. She had no intention to caress her mother or sing her a lullaby. Noor was anxiously calm while muttering sugary cadences of muffled love. She remained in that posture and was certain Portia wouldn't wake up. All the while I looked at them with pity.

I pitied Noor. The spastic girl who had every right to blame the town for its dreadful creation of the Witch. I pitied Portia too. The aloof mother who trusted the town over her own child. Certainly then, Noor had become an anathema in the eyes of her mother. While Portia had become a reminder that her daughter needed an asylum than a tidy home. I didn't know for how long the horror in the woods had carried on. For how long was Noor prone it and for how long Portia was forced to cringe in shame because of it. But going by the looks of the things, I could guess, it must have been awfully long. Only a great length of time would have broken the two apart from each other. Such antipathy had grown between the mother and daughter, that even the sight of the other created disquiet. Betrayed by the town was all I could think as Noor continued to talk to her mother in a whisper. As seconds crossed into minutes, I thought to leave them alone. Just when I had turned to leave, Noor did something unspeakable.

She lifted her arm up in the air. Her nails glittered with a rusty sepia polish. It had chipped at some places, but still looked poignant. As she lifted her arm, I didn't know what she planned to do with it, but it certainly grew a grin on my face. I was curiously interested even when the moment called for a grim response. After holding it high, she ceremoniously touched her heart with her other hand and had almost done it. She had almost slapped her mother that I intervened, swift as I could be.

As the daynight was gathering, I gagged the girl, dragged her downstairs and out the back door. Then flung her right down on the ground. Shocked and derisive of my intrusion, Noor wouldn't stop damning herself and damning me.

"Let me do it! Let me hit her! Let me hit her! Who are you to stop this! Halo damn you! I will break you too!" She screeched in horror.

She wanted to slap her mother and also break me somehow. That was damning both ways. Luckily I had come at an opportune time and stopped her before she could have damned us all. As I didn't let her finish what she wanted, Noor then began to throw fiendish fits at me. Epileptic with grief, she was beyond calm to come to her senses. I then had to appease the girl and numb her volcanic hate rising towards me. She wouldn't stop cursing whosoever came to her troubled mind. The town. Her mother. The Witch. Even me. I needed to appease her forthwith. In any which way. So I held her head in a tight grasp. Shoved my face into hers. Hugged her in a firm embrace. And kissed her parched lips. Noor didn't protest even when doubly shaken. She kept quiet at my act and didn't scream into the wind or hurl mud into my face. But stood silent and in a clutching embrace, Noor hugged me back.

Why her mother, she wished to hit I didn't ask as it was not a mystery why she would want to settle that score. So silently we remained in a tight embrace. While wet tears began to flow down her cheeks, I remained taciturnly poker-faced. How long would she take to compose herself, I wondered. Seconds passed and even then she wasn't letting go. I couldn't push her away as that would have been uncouth. But I had people waiting on me. Danny needed me. But Noor also needed me. I needed to take care of both. As I couldn't leave Noor behind, so against my better judgment I took her along with me. I took her with me to the shack. I had to as I had saved her from damnation and she had become my responsibility. Besides, I was afraid she might relapse into a murdering spree if I had left her behind. Burdened by the impetuous speed of time, I couldn't debate over it, and so took Noor to the shack.

I entered the cabin. Christian who was rapt in his impatience saw me and blurted out his exasperation. "Grace, about time you came, huh!"

I didn't make a face or throw a pinch of violence at him. I entered and then Noor followed me. Christian was then ferociously berserk.

"Wh-why, Grace? What is Noor? Are you joking with me right now!"

Christian certainly gave up his calm. Noor too lost it after seeing a familiar face on the floor of the shack, bloodied. I could hear the cabin's floor creak under their maddening distress. I had to calm them both before it broke.

We all were together. There was nothing accidental about it. It was not an accident as to why Noor was there. Not an accident when she tried to hit her mom, and when I had timely intervened. Not an accident to go get the first-aid kit myself either. If it was meant to happen that way, I needed Christian to see that. But the boy was inconsolable.

"W-why did you bring her here? You have put us all at risk!" Christian was livid with fright at seeing Noor see them all.

He got up in a panic and lamely stood in front of Danny to cover him up. As he began to disturb the already disturbed mood of the shack, Noor began to hyperventilate. She had just been through much and having to go at it again, was certainly breaking her. As Christian wouldn't care to silence his temper, I grabbed the poor girl and caressed her. Seeing me ignore him point bank, he then grunted at me.

"Are you listening? You have put us all at risk! Why did you bring her?"

While still calming Noor so she could find her composure, I grunted back at Christian.

"She needs to see this!" I had to make him understand. But I didn't wish to tell him the reason why. We all were in a coma and there was a long story behind it to tell it. Hence, I left it to Noor to be the speaker for her life. Left it to her to decide the time and day when she would want to confront her actions and what drove them. Also, there was no time to reprimand her when Danny, the ticking bomb, was in our midst. In the clash of one event to another, I had to prioritize even when Christian wouldn't let go.

"No, I don't think so. Grace, she is weak! You don't realize what you have done…" He blurted out much to Noor's chagrin. It hurt her when Christian unabashedly kept shaming her for her stigmatic weakness. Even when he kept berating, she but wouldn't fight back. So I had to intervene on her behalf. Again.

"She is ready." I but assured him rather imposed on him to believe me. True, Christian was right that Noor was too sensitive to be of any good to anyone. But she was required in the way events had unfolded before us. I needed her.

Seeing how I was fixed in my stance, the boy didn't protest anymore. Christian wanted to trust me, but then I would throw a new mask at him, and back to square one. It worried him as to what I would need Noor for. He knew I was downright manipulative and that was a threat. Silencing himself, he sat down on the floor while watching me with guarded scrutiny. Both of them, Noor and Christian, then looked on in pensive silence, as I started to wash Danny's wound with water. The first-aid kit had somehow skipped my attention as I was distracted by Noor's excessive outburst. Nonetheless, we had water and it was enough to wash our sundry complexes.

Noor yearned if I would just tell her the meaning of that scene, but I avoided her disturbing questions. If I was not going to relay Noor's story, I wasn't going to represent Danny either. That was Christian's obligation and not my burden to bear. At least that much respite I needed than to indulge the doubts of one and all.

As I began treating Danny with water, its sting struck him and he rose from his sleep. Perchance I deliberately was a little too harsh while applying it. Nonetheless, Danny rose frightened like a cornered cub, and surveyed the room with maddening eyes. I could hear him breathe like a wild beast cornered into a crook. Startled and crestfallen, Christian didn't notice it. But I did. Danny was readying himself to attack the boy yet again.

"Watch out!" I cried out but it was too late. In his revitalized rage, Danny then attacked his friend. Yet again. The boy had certainly become a pin-less grenade. There was no saving him. I had tried telling Christian but he had not listened. Under the influence of human devilry, Danny started to bang the boy's head up and down on the ground. He clasped in his hands, Christian's grown hair, and forced down his knee into his stomach. Danny even spit in his eyes, ears and as Christian struggled to escape, Danny began to chant mad sounds of a twisted tongue. That further frightened Christian to cry out for help.

"Get him off me! Grace! Get him off! He will kill me!" Christian shuddered and flung his arms about.

In a flash, Danny then slid his hands towards the neck of the boy. What madness it was! He was trying to strangle his one true friend!

"Grace! Make him stop! Stop it Danny! It's me!" Christian began to bleed in his head. I was numb to it, but Noor wasn't. She tried to push him away but Danny had clung himself to his buddy. She even grasped him from behind by twirling her arms around him. But no use. Christian was weak to fight his own. Noor was weak to fight anyone. So Danny was free to dance. He danced and rocked the two into a symphony of a delirium.

In a while, Christian was near his last gasp. Noor was frightened and exhausted to hold him back anymore. Danny but didn't seem to wane. His madness wouldn't abate. It rather grew more vengeful with every precious second passing. I had to intervene as Christian was close to dying in the hands of a mad man. I needed to take a serious step to stop him. It was peremptory that I took a serious action. I had to. The boy would have died otherwise. So I did. I did it. In an accident, I did it. I took out the shrapnel from under the bed sheets which had pricked me in the back. It was a cracked bottom of a whiskey bottle. I took it out and then bludgeoned it on the maddened head of Danny. I aimed it right to leash his madness forever. And as the cracked bottle cracked Danny's skull open, the gathering saw what crime I had done in defense of the town.

"Is he? Is he? What did you do, Grace?" Christian gasped in shock. Noor fell back in a traumatic shock. They were the very picture of hell freeze over. They didn't seem to realize that it was the only way. The only way of keeping Danny from killing Christian or Noor or me for that matter. But they were still grappling with what I had done. Right or wrong. They had the nerve especially Christian whose life I had just saved. Both of them crept into their fickle corner and began to judge me for something I did to save them.

"Murder! Murder! Murder!" Christian sung in unison with his righteousness.

"Murder! Murder! Murder!" Noor screamed in unison with her innocence.

Stunned at their reaction, I urged the two to see the truth. "I-I saved your life! He was b-badgering your skull! In-insanity must be quashed!"

Christian but did not listen. All he saw was his friend murdered in cold-blood! Murdered most treacherously by a heinous outsider. He wouldn't see how a while ago, his self-same friend was trying to murder him madly. The boy instead of embracing me in gratitude, yelled at the top of his lungs, and then came at me with vengeance. But Noor stopped him in the middle. I knew she would prove indispensable.

Noor pushed herself in Christian's way, and yelled back at him. "She saved you, she didn't mean it! Why can't you see it?"

Christian was swept off his balance. He was taken aback that Noor sided with me. He took her by the arm, gave her a jolt, and intimidated her, "You side with her! Oh Halo, what is to come out of it!" Rendered speechless by his ranting, Noor backed off in panic.

It was his life or Danny's, and I tried to impress upon him that I was not wrong to save him. But he was too grief-stricken to read my lips. "I had to. Don't you see it! He would have killed you!" I cried into his eyes, but he wouldn't listen to me even once.

"A man is dead here. You killed him, what have you done?" He was inconsolable.

Going by his repudiation, I then had to be more dramatic to assail him with the truth. So I beat my chest, wrung my hands, and went down on my knees so he could see all I did was to save him. Moved, he too sat by my side. But the boy was still disturbed as I had saved a life by killing one. Were we to celebrate or mourn?

Noor also joined us by sitting down on her knees that we made a solemn triangle.

Then Christian spoke and took an oath.

"No one will speak. We all must take an oath not to speak of this day. Was it right or wrong, no one will judge. Nothing happened, that is how we will play it. And Danny, let it be that he never returned from the city. We all are culpable, so we have to watch out for each other."

"No one will speak, I agree." Noor also chimed in.

"I agree too. No one will speak." I consented as well.

We took an oath to lie. To never speak of Danny again. It was decided we would lie.

The only thing left to do then was make it clean. We had to clean the bloody clutter on the floor and the wall while repressing the guilt shining on our faces.

As for the tell-tale dead body, Christian was certain he could take care of it.

"Bury it. I know where." He declared.

"Is that a good idea?" I was doubtful as I knew which place he was talking about.

"Where?" Noor was in the dark.

Christian was not suggesting, he had already decided. He was firm. What came as a surprise that he didn't even ask for my help. He rather approached Noor which meant he was ready to disclose the dark terrains of the woods to her. Christian was ready to take responsibility for her. It certainly gladdened me. At least then she would stop beating her heart over a shadow that never existed. Though it was a relief, I but lost something in the bargain. The two of them began to ignore me. For saving his life, Christian was mad. For saving her from damnation, Noor was mad.

Together they cleaned the walls, while I, alone and shunned, cleaned the floors. Together they lifted the dead Danny while I, alone and cast out, opened the door. And together they walked into the woods while I, alone and frail, closed the door on them.

Then again, it was expected even when unkind. It had to happen sooner or later. Besides, the grief of losing a mad boy took precedence over losing a person like me. I then didn't mind.

Chapter 11

We all will see a Miracle Tonight

As hours passed into a dust storm, I kept my eyes peeled at the woods. Anxiously I waited to see Noor run to her mother after Christian would have told her the truth. She would certainly throw a fit while Christian would chase after her to calm her down. If I was sorely disappointed to see the dark entity of the woods Noor, on the contrary, would want revenge. Betrayed by the sweet Granny, I could imagine Noor wielding a sepia-toned knife at her. To end the lies than slap them. The girl was certainly a pitiful case that even her traumatic spasms were not enough to persuade the lot of them to tell her the truth. Noor would want to brandish her knife at the liars, deceivers and murderers of her town with a rancorous rage. I anxiously waited for Noor to return from the woods. I waited and waited while my teeth nibbled away at the skin of my fingers and my body began to itch everywhere with unease. What if, I imagined, Noor began her murderous spree with Christian as he knew everything and yet muted himself in front of her. I restlessly waited to see her emerge from the woods with a bloody head in one hand while the butchering knife in the other. After this, who would then care whether I killed Danny in self-defence or in cold-blood.

Then it struck me. Christian was a deviously smart boy. If I could measure such ramifications, then so could he. He could too foresee what would happen if Noor was told the truth. The knife? The blood on her hands? His decapitated head? He could when I could. Then would he risk it? Even more wishfully then I waited for any one of them to manifest out of the woods.

Hours passed. No one came. I didn't hear a shriek of pain. A scream of revenge. A call of nature. But I did hear something. As the dusk began to fall, I heard Noor mourn. And she mourned with cacophonous tears of contrition right near the post-mill.

Noor mourned with folded hands. She had ripped out her plaits and had crouched herself. The girl heaved for someone to ask her outrightly the secrets salivating in her mouth. Someone, anyone. In the daynight of the same day, she was wailing into the wind while conveniently perched near Granny's house.

On hearing the lamentations of the sickly child, it was not Granny but Portia who rushed towards her. Before I could beat the answers out of her, Portia enveloped the girl and acted maternal.

"Noor, wh-what's the m-matter?"

Seeing her mother close to her heart, Noor began to cry as guilelessly as she could. She stood up from her supplication while gazing into her eyes and kept welling up with mixed emotions. Love? Shame? Love and shame? Noor had filial love for her mother but was also ashamed as she had, a few hours before, tried to slap her too. Awkwardly, she changed the colours of her cheek from love to shame and back again. Then, clearing her throat, she asked her mother to remember a memory of her childhood. Out of the blue.

"Mother, you remember?"

Portia had seen such a performance many a times, that she couldn't shed a tear for it. Still, she craftily played along.

"What, wh-what is it?"

"In my kitchen I had this tub of water."

"And?"

It was vexing as the dialogue between mother and child was slowly building up. Yet I held my own to wait for a few more seconds.

"There was this rat in it. It was this particular night when I was drowsy asleep to notice it."

"And?"

Portia, quite strangely, was patient to hear what incantation her daughter was cooking up. She even held her daughter's hands with overflowing love.

"This rat was drowning and trying every meat of his muscle to get out of this tub. But this rat couldn't, even with his peanut-charged nerves as the tub was slippery."

"And?"

The memory seemed interesting. I couldn't keep my distance, so I walked step by step towards the ensnaring actress and her audience. I wanted to hear from the horse's mouth how the rat got drowned.

"I couldn't save it as I abhor rats."

"And?"

Portia wasn't stuttering in the monosyllabic answer she was returning her daughter with. It was strange. The young woman was too involved that even when she saw me approach, she didn't let my entrance distract her. Portia didn't want her daughter's expulsion stopped midway. Let it be over with come what may.

"But this rat was squirming, reeking, shitting, and rabble-rousing with its rat-claws and I cringed to look at it let alone save its rat's ass."

"And?"

I was close enough and Portia could see me, Noor was but oblivious.

"So I kept this mile like distance from it while pressing hard my ears shut."

"And?"

Inch by inch as her memory began to reach a crescendo, I felt my heart gripped. Gripped out of sheer excitement.

"I couldn't but shut my pangs so I ran to you. Banged your door down and you swore your way to the kitchen."

"And?" Without pausing for any dramatic crescendo, Noor continued.

"You lifted the tub of rat. Threw it out on the street. I called you 'brave' out loud from behind as you left without a word." Noor paused, albeit grimly. Her mother was befuddled to make any sense of it, so she gushed with maternal fear, "W-what am I to make of d-this, Noor?"

Noor noticed how her mother was in fact listening to her story. That encouraged her to dig at the bottom of her anxiety. After taking a deep breath, she revealed the pain in her heart. "Danny is dead! Danny is dead! She did it! She did it! I couldn't help! She then had to. Mom, I must come to you again, as I cannot empty the tub again. Why didn't you make me do it than do it yourself?"

Danny is dead. I did it. The tub of rat. Was that all? Then as I had believed, Christian did not tell her the truth. That reprobate boy cared more about the magic trick than the people messed up by it. I looked at her and Noor was still the same as she had been. Pitiful, fitful and doleful. Besides even if she had seen the unmarked graves, she would have thought they were a racoon's burrow. And if she had seen the Witch, the girl still would have danced fitfully as she was utterly naive too. Then again, I was too harsh on her as Noor had shamelessly ratted me out and breached the oath. I was disheartened at her betrayal. Few hours ago, we had taken a solemn oath, and there she was raring to breach it. I had saved her soul from some eternal damnation, and the girl wanted to redeem me by unburdening herself of the oath. I had swallowed her unspeakable secret and she couldn't pay me back in the same buck. Didn't she care I could rat her out as well or was she genuinely distressed? It was nevertheless pitiful that I was a fool to trust her. I was a fool.

It disturbed me seeing the traitorous nerves in her. But it upset me even more as the girl was genuinely distraught. How more fickle could she be? She was not afraid because she had seen the witch, some witch but that she had seen a shadow of it. The girl did not fear the entity but the threat of it. Even when the magical entity had not boiled her alive, she was afraid of it. Paranoid Hypochondriac. Frightened of things that had not happened. The girl was distraught as she was too guileless. Fickle indeed.

Noor then had to break the oath as she was too afraid to live with a lie. She had no intention to intentionally malign me or draw pleasure out of it. The blood on the walls, the floors and on the skin was too much for her to look over. The excruciating yoke of it had to be vomited as hiding it was a task equal to another murder. Noor couldn't have lived with such a germ eating away at her. It was akin a gangrenous growth and it pushed her to cut off the ties she had with me. Oath or no oath. The girl was naively innocent to even live another day for the sake of a murderer. Though pitiful, it was the way she was. Too guileless.

The instant, Noor threw such a revelation, Portia stomped her feet. Shocked and mistrustful, she then chastised her daughter while wagging her finger at her. "Danny is dead? What nonsense is this? You have lost it haven't ya!"

Portia thought her daughter was lying again. The same redness of humiliation began to take over the young mother. I could see how she longed to manhandle some sense into her daughter. But in my presence she could not manifest her wrath. What a shame, Portia must have brooded that her only daughter had lost it. Lost it yet again like a broken record.

Noor, nonetheless, continued.

131

"I saw him get murdered in front of my eyes. Danny did it! I couldn't handle him and Grace had to. If only I could have, then Danny would have been alive."

Portia was beyond any faith in her daughter. She point blank refused to believe the juggernaut truth the girl was burdening her with. I then had to take a drastic step. To once again help Noor vindicate herself in front of her contemptuous mother. I had to intervene so the mother could be reconciled with her daughter. I had to make Portia see her daughter was not a lunatic. That the town was inimically wrong about her. I had to put myself in the middle of their pathetic affair as Noor was too innocently fickle. She was too weak that a mere voice in the woods possessed her. That she wanted to slap her mom. That she couldn't help but rat out a friend. That she was unsure what was right and what was wrong. It was peremptory I interceded.

So I howled like the devil's hound was inside me.

"You Bitch! I will kill you too!"

It was horror that I uttered through my guttural voice. I even growled at Noor and petrified the spirits out of her. It was important that I behaved like a beast. Like a villainous criminal. Portia had to be convinced that her daughter was telling the truth. It was the only way to remove the blot of madness dripping on Noor.

Imitating a mad man's passion, hence I devoured towards the frightened girl.

Alarmed, she cried out, "What! Grace, I had to! Grace! Why are you so different? It is not you! Mom! She is a murderer!"

Again, I threatened her. "You are dead, girl. You are dead!"

Noor was horrified at my inexplicably wicked demeanour. She wouldn't believe it was me. Even after committing a murder, she believed I was incapable of it. Even when I acted to break her neck, she was furious to trust me. Certainly then, the naïve girl was every loser's wet dream. It was the same with Portia. She too was at a loss to believe I was a threat. It was perhaps due to my ridiculously adorable countenance that no matter how hard I tried to act evil, it would still look sweet. Portia, dismayed and taken aback at my words, called out my name with a growing sigh. "G-Grace, it can't be. You?"

The mother wouldn't realize that though my name was innocent, my character was not. She wouldn't see that sometimes history in a name can also be a lie. As she oscillated between dread and doubt, I brandished my fist at her daughter. Even swore to murder them both. But, the young mother like her daughter wouldn't believe me. A murder in the town. It was hilariously a joke to her. So no matter how much I swore like a buffoon, she would not raise an alarm.

So, I had to add more venom to my act. And I snarled like the Devil himself.

"How dare you rat me out, bitch of first water! You think I will let you live after what you have just done! You are done for, girl! You are done for. Even your mother here cannot protect you. You are done! Hear me!"

Fear, then bulged out in Portia's eyes as I wouldn't stop harassing her faith. She was aghast that a pretty face like me was capable of murder. I could discern that my recurrent threats were beginning to wear her down. Even the pretty can murder, she was beginning to believe it.

At the 11th hour of my patience running out, Portia then finally broke through her silence.

"Murder! Murder! Murder!"

Dumbfounded with fright, she held her daughter close to her and away from me. It was then I knew I was no longer needed. It was done. I had scoured them with fear and Portia was certainly sucked out of her faith in me. She even began to protect her daughter. The more Noor would asphyxiate into a shock, the more Portia would hold her close to her heart. She mustered her strength to protect her daughter. And she meant it.

At that instant Granny glanced outside the window of her house. She was perturbed to see which salesman was screaming through the streets selling murder. Seeing me intimidate the people of her town, fear began to contaminate her notions about me. Had she trusted me too soon?

Skeptical, she called out. "What is this ruckus? Grace! What-what has happened?"

Granny didn't wait to hear my answer. I could hear her running down the stairs to face me and grab the truth. She was a cunning old lady and unlike Portia, she would have easily seen through my act. So I couldn't stay to sway her with my terror. As her footsteps began to draw near, I ran away from the place. In my eyes, she would always look. To read me. My true intentions. At that time, I didn't want her to know what I intended.

Aghast aghast, as she came out of her house, I fled. Aghast aghast, as her voice caught up to me, I fled. Aghast aghast as she bled her faith in me, I fled as fast as I could out of their sight.

As they disappeared from my sight, I did not run to the shack. It was too obvious to hide there. I made my way through the woods, the only place where I could be unseen. It was certain, Portia would have revealed everything. Noor would be listened to and her guileless drama would be listened to. Then the news of a murderer hiding in the town would soon spread like wildfire. People whom I had not met would want to find me. Hunt me. Kill me. Arrest me. The town had been through a civil war, they were hence bitten. Certainly then they would ensure that such a malediction did not happen again. I could also be lynched. It was a certainty too.

While running through the woods, I wondered, what corporeal punishment would befit me? A murderer? Then again, one who was dead, what more could have killed it? I should have been petrified for my life but what more could have killed me. As such and more musky thoughts began to storm my mind, I noticed someone chasing me leap by leap. The hunt had begun and that too very soon. But who was it? Christian? Drunkard? No, they were not chasing me, it was my shadow. It was Jon.

Since the time of the bonfire in the woods, Jon had temporarily stopped to stalk me. He needed time to brood whether I was fit to be his solemnized idol or not. He must have regretted his decision as only in his absence, I could have killed Danny. Hence, in vengeful anger leaping out of his eyeballs, he closed in on me. But what he couldn't see that I was deforesting my way towards him. It was a maniacal chase. He was pursuing me while I was pursuing him. In our chase, he ran as if he was hunting a poltergeist, and I ran as if I wanted to be hunted. He trampled on some fallen eggs, and broke the yolk before it could flower. And I trampled on the birds that would have grown out of it. As the distance between us drew closer, I saw him incensed with hate.

Within minutes, we were face to face. I growled at him.

"What! You want to die, boy!"

Jon was frightened at my twisted face but he held his ground. While his teeth shuddered against one another, he began to read from a note in his hand. In verbatim. As if under an order.

"I know what you have done. If you want a haven, come to my castle."

Jon had brought the Elder's note. The Elder wanted to see me. I had been to his castle, and knew the directions. But Jon showed me some other way to it. Vicky hadn't said anything about that different route. Was she then unaware of his secrets even when he knew and played with hers? Jon insisted the new route was a shortcut. Though he tried to hide it, I could sense irate mischievousness in his calculated words. Even the Elder's invitation was downright impish as a murderer would never harbor another murderer. He would want to be the only one. Jon could see I was perturbed, so he shrewdly kept a composed face to wear me down.

Then he gestured that I follow him. Sickened by his blatant cunningness, I challenged him.

"You have something to say, Jon? Why does the Elder want me?"

While exhaling a deep breath, he declared with composed disgust.

"He knows what you have done. The Elder wants to protect you." Jon was odious. It was discernible in his cold expression. I asked him again, "Who told him?"

"Word travels fast." He was again cold.

"But not my word." I retorted. While still bitter in his tone, he shot back. "It's your word against them, the town." He paused as if to retract, and then spoke deceivingly calm. "But the Elder believes you."

"I will ask again, who told him?" I demanded at which he spoke with a stutter. As if ashamed to rat on his friends. "Vicky, I th-think, I heard her meet him, and when she left, he sent me to bring you."

Vicky. Then it was certainly Christian who must have told her. He too ratted me out. If someone as stiff as Christian could, then Noor certainly stood no chance. Nevertheless, he had such a need to cleanse himself, that he snorted his phlegm at Vicky's feet! He was, undoubtedly, aware that Vicky would talk to the Elder about it. He must have known it. Was Christian so threatened by me, that he indirectly sought Elder's help to handle me? He knew what the Elder was capable of. And he wanted to put me right in his den. Still, I had not given him any reasons to go easy on me. Christian didn't have to look out for me or anything. There was no need for him to keep the oath, no matter how honorable it was. No matter that it was his idea to begin with.

In such a state of affairs, what did Jon want out of it? That I confess? Do penance? Or suffer for my crime? Jon wanted to clear his conscience as he after all had chosen to shadow a criminal.

I prodded him, more so to kill time while we walked in the direction he took me. "You still work for him?" I asked satirically.

"He gives me food." He admitted without shame.

"And you work like a donkey?" I did not intend to offend the boy. But wanted him to see how his life had borne him pints of shame because of the Elder.

"A horse!" He declared with pride.

"Is that what you want?" I questioned his ill-placed smugness. Knowing somewhat, that he was wrong. He then heckled me with shame. "Don't! Don't try to be sane, Grace. How can you not be sickly with regret?"

His exhortation made me laugh at him and I eagerly retorted. "Ha ha! Look at your tone! Have you talked back to the Elder too, or you pick your fights with the likes of me."

"You are evil, and you will say whatever you can to blame others." He was humiliated but hid it all the same.

The first time I had looked at Jon, I had thought to myself. If I had a body like him, I would have defeated any number of officers running my way. It would have been a thrill to turn the tables on them. Thrill like justice. Jon had skills and a brawny body to go with it. For as long as I had watched him, it was his brute force that made me like him. Want him. Be one like him. But later he turned out to be such a disappointment. The boy had weak spirits that anyone could easily manipulate him. It was because of his eager gullibility that the boy got pimped by the Elder. The old man had turned him into a mob that he was eager to burn a house even if it was his own. When he indicted me for the crime I had committed, I wished if the boy could realize his own situation and confront it. He just wouldn't see it. Jon fervently kept his faith in the old man even when beleaguered by him.

"Your master, Jon, he is a good man?" I tried reasoning with him like some last ditch effort. But he was obdurate in his belief that the Elder was an honourable man. With a solemn justification on his lips, he enunciated. "He didn't kill a man!"

Infuriated, I shouted at him. "No, he didn't. For he is pitching for a mass grave! Right?"

Though he realized my words carried the sting of truth, he still wouldn't steer himself to see it. As it was I who spoke it. Jon had become too disenchanted in me to believe the truth in front of him. Even when he knew the Elder was in fact a criminal, he was determined to only see me as one. I had broken his heart and the Elder never had it to break it. Thwarted in his dream to shadow me, Jon then revealed the wound in his heart.

"You have travelled towns, and Halo knows how many you kill in each one of them! You are evil! Admit it! Confess it! I believed in you, shadowed you, and thought to free myself, but now the Elder, he mocks me even more for tailing a murderer!" He affirmed his shame. Jon was humiliated for trusting me. He was treated as a laughing stock, and I was responsible for it. Certainly he was indignant. The boy had pride and for once in his life he was going to protect it by rebelliously shadowing me. In his eyes, back then, I was someone. Someone like him. Beaten but standing straight. And when I had breached his lofty delusion, his pride was hurt. The Elder was, definitely, quick to rub salt on it. No matter then what I said to him, he would not listen. Jon found even my sight repugnant.

Even so, I tried to assail him with the hope of reconciliation. Even perspective.

"Mock him back for being a murderer too, that is your best shot."

"You mock me!" But he shut me out.

It was certain. The Elder in his own ingenious way had re-constructed the boy. Jon, if he could attack me for being a criminal, then why could he not confront the Elder and be free? I was a criminal and he attacked me. The Elder, he was a criminal too. But towards him, Jon's brain would turn into a machine. Naturally then he was unable to see if there was a villain, it was not only me. But the master as well.

Before we could chastise each other's foibles any further, I heard a disturbance.

"Shhh! Someone is there…"

It was sudden. There was no warning of it. Some signs were there perhaps, but I had not noticed. I had thought it was a dust storm in the woods, but I was wrong. Then I saw them come. It was the Elder, and he had come with his entourage. His four henchmen. In their right hands were sticks, while left arms were held aloft with silver blades. As they appeared from a hole in the woods, it was lit in a circle. The silver blades were reflecting the light of the moon, and they had lit up the woods with a cold aura. I had seen the henchmen before, but still couldn't place them. Then I realized who they were. Had I been under an illusion that I had mistaken the Elder's henchmen as machetes on the castle's gate? The machetes certainly looked human-like, but I somehow failed to see they were humans! They were not knives and axes as I had believed but men and women who worked for the Elder. The machetes on the gate were the same henchmen who then trudged behind the Elder with their sticks and silver blades held high in the sky. Two by the left and two by the right, they flanked the Elder while he stood in the front. In pomp and show of his potbelly.

One of the henchmen had a wound in his eye. To hide it he had used a tape to shut it. The other standing next to him had his ear cut out of its socket, which he had attached with some tape as well. There was also a henchwoman, flanking the left side of the Elder, and she had a horrid hickey on her cheeks that had disfigured her face. Again with a tape she had hidden it. The last one was the most inhuman in her countenance, as without a nose she looked like a pig. In their age, his henchmen, looked younger than the Elder. But in their wounds of battle they seemed more perverse and unkind than him. Each carried a can of kerosene which gave off a fragrant aroma. They had also brought a rope along with them thicker than the puny size of my neck. Oil or rope, they were not certain what they would need to bury me.

Flanked by his mighty army, the Elder grunted with a thunder.

"I wasn't sitting in the wildlife that the rat stung me. If I had, I wouldn't have trampled on it. But in my home of mortar, you dared sting me on my hip! In my town! In my home! To my own people. So hear me girl, we all will see a miracle tonight."

The kerosene would burn. The rope would hang. The sticks would spear. The blades would lacerate. It would be an immaculate suffering. Had I bit such venomous fangs into them that they didn't even have room for grace? I was an outsider, undoubtedly, but we all came from a garden once. Still no grace? True I had murdered a hapless boy, and I needed to be punished. But the disturbing thing was the misplaced hate in their eyes, as it did not reflect any grief over Danny's death. It seemed as if Danny's murder did not concern them. The blood on my hands didn't matter to them. They needed a reason whether I had blood on my hands or water. It certainly terrified me. The Elder's flavour for mayhem and how it sizzled over the flame of his absolute hate. It was vindictive, self-righteous and he thought it was patriotic too.

While the Four dragged me through the woods, my hands and mouth sucked in worms and seeds. I was poetry in motion as my blood began to draw dew on the grass and my skin drew dirt into dirt. They say poetry needs a tragic push, so I let them drag me without restraint. They were taking me to the site of the unmarked graves. I could sense it as the direction to it was etched in my eyes.

"You brought little men if you wish to burn these woods, the Elder." I mocked the old man even when I could barely speak. Flustered and even more livid, he countered. "These woods, oh no, they have done us no harm, you have. I was so busy in guarding ourselves against the LO, that I oversaw what vermin you were. And I have paid, my friend has paid. You killed my friend's brother!" He declared. The Elder kept wagging and pointing his index finger to show how he was the Elder.

"So I am a criminal then?" I asked with a grin.

"Yes a vile one. You have no compunction for what you have done..." he proclaimed while continuing to fling his dancing finger at us all. Though his fingering stunt did not scare me, but the mob that followed him cowered at its thunder. It again terrified me. The Elder could sway people with the ding-dong of his dancing finger, it was a disturbing reality. Alone he was a fly but with a mob, the old man was metal. He could trap men. Women. Young boys and girls. At his beck and call. I was overwhelmed to be born in such a gullible, pliable and lost world. Whosoever would try to save it, would have to fear the finger. The finger which controlled the mob. The mob which then would guide the winds of hate. And hate which then would welcome the lovely wars of ants and ant hills.

Though it was futile, I still tried to shame the Elder.

"Do you have qualms? Burning a criminal in the darkness of the woods? If you think it is right, then why not do it in the open?"

The Elder laughed a hearty laugh. He couldn't believe I still had the guts to talk back to him. He laughed and then preened himself for being brave. "I will not hide it. Once I am done here, the town will hear of my bravery."

"Bravery?" I asked with contempt.

"You killed a boy!" He grunted. Then, after pausing for an instant, he continued. "I will execute you, yes that is bravery. Yes, it would be a start."

The Elder had conviction in his plan as he knew I was not blood or water to evoke sympathy from the town. No one would want to weep over me. The Elder surfeited on this thought pleasurably and it invariably fired his gall. If he was ridiculed by the town, it was because he hunted his own. So, I was the only sin by which he could wash his own. At last, a chance to prove he was a brave patriot.

Too eager to gain the epithet of brave, the Elder commanded his men and women to finish me already.

"Take her you gawking fools! Burn her!"

As they struck me with what they could, I didn't struggle. My flesh squelched with agony but I still didn't scream. Even when they stretched my body across the dark firmament of the woods, I was silent. The Four would stutter and stagger as I would evince no pain at the ordeal. It bothered them. They expected I would scream to reach the Pandemonium itself, but I didn't. I was locked-in in my own world to scream, speak, feel or even blink at what was happening to me. I was helpless to even express pain. The shouting rains frightened them. The Elder's dancing finger frightened them. Some magical entity in the woods frightened them. The wood's aura of horror frightened them. But I was not afraid. It terrified them that they shrunk back to digest the impossibility of my composure.

Noticing the ridiculous halt, the Elder yelled fire and brimstone at them.

"Fools!! Tie Her! Burn Her! Tonight she burns, tomorrow the LO, and then I will rule! Jon, my sweet boy, build a fire. It is time for you to prove yourself."

Jon disappointed me again. On hearing the Elder's diktat, he wagged his servile tail, and without a moment's delay obeyed his order. He had a chance to scurry out of there, but he still ingratiated himself to the foolish despot. What was he thinking? The Elder would make him his son? Jon must have known it was odious to heed a tyrant, nevertheless he did it. He did it as he didn't recognize how wretchedly he was being used for the old man's ulterior motives. He didn't realize it. He then could never be free. Jon was a hero. He had the makings of it in his blood, but he was not conscious of it. The Elder had made him conscious but to his own purpose than the boy's. Such was the malady of Jon, that he knew not what ailed him.

The Four then tied me with the ropes they had brought. And when they had used it all, they then tied me with twigs, branches, and thorns. Being hard, prickly and wet, they strangled and pierced my body through and through. Some thorns went deep while some remained on the surface. But I bled all the same.

"She is bleeding too much! And so much rain, fire wouldn't start. Her clothes are wet, the Elder," Timidly, they gasped.

"What! Nonsense! Then take her clothes off! Strip this vermin! Clean her wounds! Burn her you fools!" Vehemently, he ordered.

"We need an umbrella too, the Elder." Again, timidly, they gasped

"Look around you! The trees are the bloody umbrellas here! Fools!" He got more vehement in his fury.

As they tried to burn me, the fire wouldn't start because of the rain. The matchsticks wouldn't work at all. They were wet to burn me. Seeing how futile it was to think of fire in the rain, the Elder then gave another commandment.

"Throw her in this grave then. It is dug already. Just bury her alive! Hit her on the head, so she does not struggle. Hit her hard!" he roared in excited exasperation.

And they buried me in the grave that I had dug. It strangely felt like an insult. The Four then began to cover me with wet soil. When the soil would touch the skin of my naked flesh, it would feel like a demon dancing on my belly. It was cold and nothing like home.

"That is enough mud. We don't want to bury her too deep. Now stomp on it, level the ground. She will die of the lack of air. Do it! Now!"

As he barked the orders, the Four buried me six feet under. It was then I began to change. When it was one feet, I changed my legs into one tail. Two feet under, my hands were no more. Three feet under, the contours of my bosoms and humanlike sensuality vanished. Four feet under, my size greatly reduced. Five feet under, I became a worm. While six feet under, I first skewered the soil, and then creating a little gaping hole, I crawled out of my burial. While standing at its edge, I looked at my human body going deeper and deeper into the grave. Finally returning to its true home. To mourn the misfortunes. To rest the demons. To remember a memory. Then as a pink worm, I slithered away. My soul. My worm.

The men and women saw a worm come out of the burial. The Elder shrieked with revulsion at its sight. The Four didn't care but Jon was discomforted by its rupture. Seeing it as a sign of ill-omen, he was rent apart at its ominous surfacing. While the Four poignantly wrapped me in the bed of mud, Jon kept staring at the worm. While the Elder kept singing, "Evil has been conquered!" Jon but kept staring at it.

The ill-omen worm had taken his heart out. When I was being speared and buried, he didn't mind it. But a tiny worm of nature disturbed him to lament the lynching. Even when he didn't regret his actions, he was afraid he would be punished because of them. The fear of some reckoning, some judgment and some hellfire, pulled at his calm even when the pain of my leaking blood didn't.

Jon dreaded the afterlife of sin than the sin itself. It certainly terrified me.

Anxiously, I then crawled away from the wasted patch. As distance began to grow between us, I could faintly hear the noises of the Elder and his racquet of lunatics. The woods then began to whisper behind my back. The raven eyed my flesh to eat it. The snakes hid in ambush. Owls, insects and ants waited to pounce. I was no longer a human but a worm that nature wouldn't be kind to.

Strangely as I crawled away, I began to lose my sight. It was a worm I had become but I still had eyes to see. If I could hear, then why couldn't I see? The anxiety of it had my heart race. Beep! Beep! Beep! The anxiety of it had my heart pound. Beep! Beep! Beep! It was distressed as in an instant I had gone blind. I was not blind, never blind, and could not be blind. The men and women I had met. I had talked to them and read their countenance. I could hear. Speak. See. Feel. Still I couldn't, it broke me.

It was on the ground I was crawling, but then I couldn't even feel it. True, I had become a worm to run away but a worm can feel. Had I then run away too far that I could not go back. I couldn't even go back to who I was!

I began to feel locked, stuffy and claustrophobic as I crawled over the ground. Unfeeling. Suffocated. Deloused of life. The inanity of such a torture was too much that my heartbeat became tumultuous. I could hear the beep of it as if I was plucked to a machine! It was maniacal in its thrill. Beep! Beep ! Beep! It seemed as if my heart wanted to scream out of my chest. Beep! Beep ! Beep! The more it beeped, beeped and beeped, I could hear human noises crowding and growing around me. It was painful to hear the noises as there was no one in the woods. I was alone and still I could hear strangers touching me. Feeling me up. Washing the sweat on my forehead. Injecting something into my veins. I could hear hands and lips consoling me. Curing and pacifying.

Then it happened I couldn't even crawl anymore. I pushed my skin against the ground but I couldn't. I couldn't even crawl. As I manically beat myself to the inch of my life, the woods began to fall over. I could hear them entomb me. Cover me. Ominously. With odious intentions. I could hear them rustle in the dark. As my eyes had left me, I then had to listen and see from my ears. I heard the woods envelop me. To suffocate. To smother. To choke. Nature was not kind to a worm. It seemed to hate it with derision. Such hate. It tore me from inside. The patience with which my body was enduring the situation began to rupture from inside.

It started from the tip then metastasized to all over the body. The fit. It began to take over me again. I jumped. Swiftly. Jumped again. I danced. Danced to the harp of some demon. Another jump. Jumped again. Then I convulsed that the bed I was on began to rattle under the fit. It had a soft mattress. But it pricked nonetheless as if a shard of some whiskey bottle had been hiding there. No one knew about it as I could not tell it to anyone. I could hear. But not speak. Not see. Locked-in.

As the bed ululated under the music of my convulsions, many strangers began to grab me. Hard. Remorselessly hard.

The heart rate kept beeping. Beep! Beep ! Beep! The injections kept creeping in. Creep! Creep! Creep! The shard kept pricking. Prick! Prick ! Prick! The hands touched. Bodies fell on me. The bed rattled. It went on for some minutes. I was in the woods, dark and hollow. But then there were no woods. Not anymore. It was just darkness with occasional shoots of twinkling light. As silver beams of light hit my blind eyes, the tolling of the beep, the distress, the sweat jumped and fell and jumped again.

Then someone removed the tape off my eyes. One at a time. Gently with savvy hands. What was intentionally kept dark, became white. Had I come to the Zone of Black and White? The Lights Off may be? When did I cross the Zone of Grey?

As the tapes were removed, I could see then as my eyes adjusted to the bright light of black and white room. There were people around me dressed in white aprons, black ties and grey hair. It hurt, my eyes hurt. Did they really hurt, it felt more like a memory of a pain. But cruelly as it was, I couldn't blink my eyes. I couldn't see left or right. What was standing in the line of my sight, I could see, but the corners, the angles, and the right and left of where I was, I couldn't see. From head to toe, I was stuck. Locked-in. I was not a worm. I was not even a human.

I screamed without a voice. Vomited with my mouth shut. Convulsed with my nerves dead. No one could hear me but we all could hear the hoofbeats of my heart. On a machine of an intelligent mind. Beep! Beep! Beep!

Then, someone touched my heart with a cold metal while someone else put a needle in my arm. After few seconds, a crowd of black and white aprons checked my pulse, changed my dress, combed my hair, sponged my skin, and then tied my eyes shut again.

As the top of my eye-lid touched the brink of my eye, I was back in the deep dark woods. It was a breezy night of the winters. There were grey clouds in the night sky and dark mist in the air. The fever in the wind was twisting the houses, the trees and the dogs into a fitful scream. A rumble of emptiness could be heard...